MY ROCK STAR NEIGHBOR

KATHY STROBOS

Cover Design: Cover Ever After

ISBN: 9781958894217 (Paperback)

ISBN: 9781958894200 (EBook)

www.kathystrobos.com

www.kathystrobosbooks.com

Published by Strawbundle Publishing
New York, New York

To my rock star readers.

Also By Kathy Strobos

New York Friendship Series
A Scavenger Hunt for Hearts
Partner Pursuit
Is This for Real?
Caper Crush

New York Spark Series
My Book Boyfriend
Love Is an Art
My Secret Snowflake
My Rock Star Neighbor

For giveaways, updates on new releases, behind-the-scene news and
what's going on in my life,
please subscribe to my mailing list at
https://kathystrobos.com/sign-up-for-my-newsletter/
For translations, please also visit my website.

Chapter One

Nick

Our fans are still clapping as we, the four members of our pop band Orchard Folly, exit from our second encore.

"Nick! Nick Devlin!" Fans are screaming.

We absolutely killed it. I gulp down the water from the bottle that Amira, our band manager, hands me. I towel off. The lights are hot, and we were jamming out there.

This is it. This is the year.

We hurry single file down the darkened hallway to the small dressing room at the back. Inside, I grab another bottle of water. The musical strains of "New York, New York" fill the bar—the perfect song to end this first day of January.

"Nick! The way you sang that last note..." Amira high-fives me, her gold bangles cold against my arm. "You almost made me cry. Way to go! The MusEn guy was definitely jibing along to the music." She's practically jumping up and down in her brightly colored tunic top, and then she hugs Kyla, our bass player, as if she can't keep it inside.

My feeling of joy mirrors the expressions on my bandmates' faces. We were in the zone. I hug José, our drummer, and as we separate, he pats me on the back. I look over at Sayo, our keyboard player, and she grins back at me.

The stage crew is breaking down the set and bringing our gear to the green room.

Amira suggests a photo of us together against the wall. José, Kyla, and I stand in the back, arms around each other as the taller members of the band (José and I are both 6'2", while Kyla is 5'9"), while Amira and Sayo stand in front of us in the center. The photo could be a jeans ad, if it were selling worn, ripped jeans that are as comfortable as possible. The light flashes. The mirrors on the other side reflect our glowing faces. My ride-or-dies. It's taken me a few years, but this group—the sound we have, the way we play off each other... This is it.

This is my family for life. If I can bring it home for us. So much is on me as the lead singer and songwriter.

We're running out of time. Our latest single is climbing the charts on Spotify and YouTube—it's so close after all these years, I can taste success. But José said earlier he has to take on another job for income. Sayo had nodded. But giving up our ambition to be musicians full-time will destroy a part of all of us—the part that believes that hard work, persistence, and talent can make dreams come true. And for me, I'm determined to prove to my mom that I can make a living as a musician and don't need to be in a white-walled cubicle tied to the clock, watching my soul wither away like the sand in an hourglass. Sure, I got my accounting degree, along with my music degree, to appease my mom and I still do accounting side work for money as we wait to hit it big, but it is *not* my passion.

Our security guy enters and whispers to Amira.

"It's mobbed outside, but that's good since the MusEn guy is here," Amira says to us and then asks Mr. Muscle if he has any friends in the neighborhood. "I don't think you can handle this crowd alone."

Our fans started calling him Mr. Muscle, and now we do too. He's 6'5" and built like a bulldozer but with the softest heart.

"I called my friend, but he's working at a bar tonight," Mr. Muscle says.

"It's okay," I say. Many fans are familiar faces at this point. It's not like we're that big, and their loyalty is everything. "Make sure you cover Sayo." She's tiny, and I worry they can knock her down. Mr. Muscle and I exchange a look, and he nods.

Sayo huffs. "I'm not the one they're mobbing."

We pack up the rest of our things and pull on our coats.

We exit through the back door of the club, but it doesn't make a difference. A crowd awaits, bigger than ever before. The screams that erupt are deafening, and women surround me.

I stop to sign autographs. A fan hands me a hand-drawn illustration of me. I thank her, even as I tell her it's way too flattering of an image, with wavy brown hair, chiseled cheekbones, deep-green eyes, and a perfect smile. I actually have a slight chip in my front tooth from when I stupidly used my teeth to open a package of guitar picks in a crunch. I hand out more signed postcards of our latest single.

But as the packed throng presses forward, Mr. Muscle steps in. "We have to move on. Thank you. Thank you." He shields me from the hordes as we squeeze through.

They're pushing too close.

"Get Sayo," I say to Mr. Muscle.

Mr. Muscle moves to protect her.

Lights flash. I'm blinded. *Where's the van?*

Someone grabs me and hugs me tight. "Babe. You were fabulous." The heavy perfume scent is overwhelming.

I stare into the eyes of a woman I've never seen before—who has locked me in a crazy vise grip. I freeze. Way too close! My instinct is to break free—I *must* resist the urge to push her away.

"I'm sorry, but you need to release me," I say firmly.

She leans in. *No way.* I move, but she gets way too close with that open mouth. But her focus on trying to kiss me gives me the chance to push her arms away, gently—or at least try to make it look as if it's done gently in any video captured. *I'm free.* I turn away from her. There's the van.

Mr. Muscle is back, sticking his body between us and trying to block her. "Get in the van."

I make a break for it. I hop into the front passenger seat and check to see if everyone else is inside. Sayo is seated next to Kyla, who has her bass case on her lap, José crowded next to them.

I can't see if that woman is still outside. The crowd seems to be dispersing. It's cold and dark inside. I stick my hands into my coat pockets. Mr. Muscle jumps into the driver's seat.

"That was crazy," I say. "I remembered just in time to not push her away, because that wouldn't look good on video if I were to push her or hurt her."

"Are you okay?" Sayo asks. "I wouldn't like being grabbed like that."

"I can't say I liked it either." I shudder. "We may need more security. I'll talk to Luca tomorrow." Luca is one of my best friends and runs his own security company. "But it isn't a bad thing that the crowd was huge. It means we're getting more popular."

The van pulls quickly away from the curb, or as quickly as it can in New York City. We're soon stopped at a red light, but at least we're two blocks away. The streets are mostly empty at this hour. I turn my body so I can see my band members behind me. I'm still wired from our concert. José pulls a beanie cap over his hair, nearly hiding his brown eyes. I high-five Kyla, whose tall, lean frame is wrapped in her long red parka, her black curly hair spilling out over it. She gets cold easily. We sang several songs together tonight, and I'm still in awe at how well our voices blend. The light from outside makes the purple streaks in Sayo's black hair glow red. Amira is behind them, her head bent over, glued to her phone.

"The MusEn guy texted that he wants to meet us tomorrow afternoon," Amira says. "This could be it. This could be our big break."

"We can't get our hopes up," I say, although mine are rising. "We've been here before—with Vinyl five years ago—and it didn't result in anything."

"I have a good feeling about this," Amira says. "Plus, we've been making steady progress during those five years. We're now ten years into this. We have a solid fan base. It's not like the early days, when we first started and the only people in the bar where we were playing were the other bands performing."

"Way to bring us back down to earth," I say.

"And our friends," Sayo says.

"And your mom and dad," I say. But not my mom.

A cab swerves right in front of us. I brace against the dashboard. Mr. Muscle honks.

Amira gasps. "That woman who tackled you—she's saying she's your girlfriend, and it's blowing up on social media. She says she's the Cara you dedicated 'Goodbye Cara' to."

No way!

"Goodbye Cara" was a song about my ex-girlfriend, Christina. And goodbye was good riddance. This YouTube woman clearly doesn't get double entendre.

"Look at this footage." Amira leans forward to show me her phone. "It's too intimate. You look like you're whispering in her ear, and then you look like you're arguing with Mr. Muscle that you don't want to leave her."

That's some good editing. It does look like there's something between us.

"The flashes blinded me. She grabbed me before I could even react. Can't you simply deny it?"

"I will. I'll put out a statement," Amira says. "I'm sorry. I should have hired more security."

"It's not your fault. Nobody expected that, and our fans are usually respectful." A slight chill sweeps through me. "That was crazy."

"This video is done so well. And she got it up so quickly on her YouTube channel," Amira says. "I think she planned this to get her subscribers up. She's trying to take advantage of your YouTube popularity to increase her own."

"Isn't that good?" I ask. "We've got a clear motivation for what she's doing, so it will make sense when we deny it."

"It's just that she's so public and seems to have some skill at manipulating the media. I'm your band manager, not a social media guru."

"You've done well so far," I say.

"Let me call my cousin," Kyla says. "She does social media for her company." As our van weaves through the streets of lower Manhattan, Kyla talks to her cousin, who recommends putting out a bigger story to drown this one out.

"I have a very bad feeling about this," Amira says.

So do I. She had someone there to photograph that "kiss." She uploaded this video in less than half an hour. I'd been naïve again, trusting our fans, thinking I shouldn't hire more security and interact behind a barrier. But I was torn. Our core supporters waiting out in the cold did deserve our attention.

"I'm sure it will die down," I say to reassure Amira. *Don't give in to the doubts.*

We're near my block on the Lower East Side.

There's Maddie, my neighbor, her huge Mary Poppins bag on her shoulder, an enormous parka that looks like it's completely swallowing her tall frame, black yoga pants, and black sneakers. I'd recognize her anywhere—even now, with her back to me and her hood completely up.

"You can let me off here," I say. "Get home safely, guys. And great job."

"But we're still a few blocks away from your apartment. Are you sure?" Sayo asks. "You're carrying two guitars."

Mr. Muscle stops the van.

"I need to walk off the concert. And that woman. And Maddie's there." I push open the door and grab my two cases.

"Oh, Maddie," Sayo says. And the way she says it...

No. Definitely don't think I want to probe into that.

I run to catch up with Maddie, a guitar case in each hand.

"Maddie," I yell.

She swings around as if she's going to hit me with her bag. I duck. Note to self: Do not surprise Maddie from behind.

"Oh, it's you." She pushes down her hood. Her hair is up, but brown wisps escape everywhere. She must have been thinking a lot.

"Let me guess, you were out late covering another story, unless it was a really hot date?" I ask, sure that's going to rile her up.

"Maybe I did have a hot date," Maddie huffs.

"So hot you came home alone?" I step a bit closer. "Someday, we have to discuss your definition of hot. But you do look electrified." At least her hair does.

"Ha-ha. I have a lead on a story that could really make my career. I'm interviewing another source tomorrow." She hefts her bag up onto her shoulder. It's huge, and Maddie swears it carries all the essentials.

We stroll down the street, her jumbo bag and my guitar case putting a healthy distance between us, yet we're in step. We skirt around a couple hustling home hand-in-hand. A warm yellow light spills out from an apartment above us, its curtains still open, and it looks cozy inside. I can feel myself relaxing. I glance at Maddie, but she's pulled her hood back up. I bet she's worrying her lip. She does that when she's thinking about a story angle.

We turn the corner onto Orchard Street, where we live. The glowing, round, colorful paper balloons that hang from the bare branches of the tree in front of the Sticky Rice restaurant always cheer me up. Two delivery bikes, outfitted for a cold winter with gloves encasing the handlebars, are locked together by the tree. As we pass, I see they're actually separately locked to a pole. Not together. It depends on the angle viewed. I have to believe that on closer inspection, the truth will reveal itself with that doctored video of me with the YouTube star wannabe. Similarly, an outsider might think that Maddie and I are close friends by the way we interact, but we've been neighbors for several years and casual friends—friends who hang out when we run into each other in the neighborhood. At least, I like to think that. Maddie might have a different opinion because of how annoying she finds my late-night playing. I should soundproof my living room wall, but how is she in her thirties and going to bed at ten p.m.?

We walk single file between a tree enclosure and a restaurant's plastic winter vestibule, which butts into the sidewalk, hindering the cold air from sweeping into the dining room. The sidewalk widens, and we return to strolling side by side.

"How was your concert?" Maddie asks.

"Brilliant." I smile. If only I could capture in words that wave of energy that seems to vibrate between us on stage and our fans, pulsing back and forth. How to describe it, to explain that euphoric feeling, tickles at the corner of my mind.

"Sorry I missed it." Maddie switches her bag to her other shoulder. Maddie has only attended my concerts at Craic and Laughs, her friend's family bar. She's never yet come to a different venue to see me.

"You don't look sorry," I say, gently knocking her shoulder with mine. Maddie is so fun to tease.

"I look like a sorry raccoon because you were up practicing so late last night," Maddie says.

"No such thing as a sorry raccoon," I say. "Raccoons are cute—but they are nocturnal, so I don't think that's your animal spirit. Maybe a hibernating bear?"

She flashes a quick glance at me, and there's some hurt there. I've mis-stepped, but how?

"At least I'm not a bat pretending to be a human," Maddie says.

Did I imagine that hurt look? She now looks like her usual spitfire self.

"I'm going to take that as a compliment that I'm crucial to the ecosystem," I say.

"Indeed. You're a natural pest controller," she says.

I laugh. "Anyway, I'm sorry you missed it. MusEn was there, and Amira said they seemed keen on us."

"That would be amazing," she says. "I can look forward to your moving out soon."

"Won't you miss me?" I ask.

"Not as much as I miss sleep," she says.

"Have you ever thought you put too much priority on sleep? You're young. You should be living it up."

"Like you? You work as hard as I do. Harder. You're always working on another song."

"That's not work for me," I say.

My phone buzzes. I read Amira's text, but it doesn't make sense.

"What?" I ask. "No way."

"What?" Maddie asks.

"Some unhinged woman is claiming I'm her boyfriend, and Amira says a news outlet picked up her story." I show her the article. "Amira is putting out a denial."

Maddie peers at the photo on my phone. "You don't know her? That photo looks like..."

"I know. It's manipulated. She grabbed me, and I was asking her to release me."

"Wow. That's scary," Maddie says. "I'm sure Amira will get the denial published in reputable news sources."

We reach the front door of our apartment building. We both love living here. For one, there's a former speakeasy in the basement. Maddie unlocks the door. I step forward to hold the door for her with my body. As she passes close to me, she looks up for a second. She has the biggest, softest brown eyes I've ever seen, and her cheeks are flushed from the cold.

"I need to pick up my laundry," she says. The building's laundry room is in the former speakeasy. She takes a book out of the bookcase that covers the back wall of the foyer, and the bookcase (a hidden door to the speakeasy, now laundry room) swings open. It is still the coolest thing ever. She doesn't look back as she disappears down the stairs, and the door shuts behind her. I go up the stairs alone.

She also barely tolerates me.

And Maddie is a reporter—like my ex. Christina did an exposé on what it's like to date a wannabe rock star. It wasn't pretty. So, I learned that lesson...the hard way. *Don't date a reporter.*

Chapter Two

Maddie

The sound of guitar chords being strummed echoes through the thin walls separating my apartment from Nick's.

"I'm going to kill Nick." I stick the earplugs back into my ears. They keep falling out. I hit the pillow again and turn onto my side. My sleep schedule is also off because I stayed up too late last night for New Year's Eve, celebrating at my friend Lily's party hosted at her fiancé's place.

The earplugs hurt. I take them out.

I sit up and decide to work on one of my little felted miniature creatures. I'm selling them at the New Jersey miniature show in two weeks, and I need more stock. I take out my wool, needles, felting mat, pull on my finger protectors (before I poke my fingers with the needle because I'm tired) and start working on a little black dog.

Nick's voice carries through the paper-thin wall that separates my apartment from his. He's singing about not being able to trust anyone and worried someone likes you *not* for you, but for what you represent.

That's not something I have to worry about. But it makes me sad that he does.

I know he's not dating that woman claiming to be Cara. Our wall is so thin, I'd hear any other activity. I should be grateful I only hear music.

He's singing about loneliness and feeling like you can't share your deepest feelings and fears because you're afraid that person will turn away and never want to talk to you again.

I can't help but listen.

How does he know these feelings? He's a frickin' rock star. Okay, he's not mega-famous yet, but he's getting there. He has a fan club. His YouTube channel comments are filled with comments like: "I love you," "Your music helps me to get up in the morning," "You got me through a dark place," and "Your voice is all I need." And as far as I've seen at concerts, he's incredibly grateful to them all. He takes the time to chat with them but yet maintains a cautious distance.

At least he's never had someone he dated tell him—I shake my head. I will not repeat what my ex said about my kissing ability. He also broke off our relationship abruptly. And that's the second time that's happened. While I was thinking that we were growing closer, getting to know each other's inner quirks and foibles in the short time we'd been dating, my last two boyfriends were plotting how to tell me that it wasn't working for them. I sigh. It wasn't like I'd thought it was perfect, but I'd been willing to give it a chance. Both times.

I add eyes to my miniature dog. It's done. I crawl back into bed and count sheep. It doesn't work. It's the music from next door, yes, but I'm also excited about this possible story. If I can prove corruption at the highest levels of the New York City government—that a commissioner or deputy commissioner of a city government agency is taking bribes—that will be huge. It can even affect the mayor and the upcoming elections. A front-page story about bribery will prove that I should be promoted and assigned officially to the city politics beat. Right now, I'm listed as a reporter on published articles, but I'm not assigned to any beat, so I can be given any local story to cover. I want the beat listed after my name: Madeline Hughes, Reporter—City Politics at *The Intelligencer*.

It's between Sarah (or Nemesis, as I prefer to call her) and me. There is no way I want to be left covering parades while she is interviewing the mayor about the latest headline news. Not when I've worked so hard and she's coasting on connections. Not that I don't love a good parade. And not that the world doesn't need more feel-good stories. But I became a reporter to fight corruption—to make sure the bad guys don't win.

I turn again and pull my cover over my head. Now I'm hot.

Nick's voice is still in my ears. I hate to ask him to stop when he's deep in his music magic.

But I do not function on six hours of sleep. It's almost midnight. I'm meeting my source at seven a.m. to confirm that he was asked for a kickback in exchange for contractor work at a public housing development. I'm so lucky that I met that mom, Tasha, at the library event today. As soon as she found out I was a reporter, she said that the senior leadership at the Infrastructure Department might be corrupt. This could be a huge break.

The Infrastructure Department is responsible for overseeing the city infrastructure, such as its public housing, led by Commissioner Johnson, who has a pristine reputation. But then, could it be one of the three deputy commissioners who serve under him? They are each assigned specific public housing developments. They're also responsible for licensing for commercial establishments and doing safety inspections, among many other things. That's another area ripe for bribery. I need to be on my toes later.

Now, Nick has moved to the fire escape. And he must have plugged his headphones into his amp, but he's still singing. Softly.

It's no use. I'm wide awake. Maybe if Nick talks it out, he'll feel better, and he can go to sleep. He must be exhausted too.

I get out of bed, stick on a bra, slip my feet into my big bunny slippers, and open the window that leads onto our shared fire escape.

Nick doesn't turn around. He probably can't hear me with those huge headphones.

I walk over gingerly. Bunny slippers were not a good choice for walking on these iron slats. It feels like parts of my feet slip right through the empty spaces. I stare straight at the back of his head because no way am I looking down through the slats to see how far up we are.

I reach him and gently tap him.

He whips around. "Are you serious? I'm using headphones."

"I can still hear your voice as you sing."

Nick huffs. "What about those 'super comfortable' earplugs I got you?"

"They're not super comfortable. They're instruments of torture."

"Okay, okay. Let me write one more stanza. I'm almost done."

"Fine." I lean against the wall and wait.

He turns and looks at me. "Having you drill a hole in the back of my head is not helping."

"I can't imagine why not," I say. "Access to the inner thoughts of Nick Devlin."

Nick faces me as he takes his guitar off and writes down the last few notes and lyrics. Strands of his wavy brown hair fall over one eye as he concentrates, and I clench my hands involuntarily. His hair is the kind that makes me want to run my hands through it.

He closes his notebook with an exaggerated flourish, and his deep-green eyes meet mine. Sometimes I can't believe he's my neighbor and a regular guy, because he's just so good-looking. It's to my benefit that his music playing at all hours is so annoying, or I'd probably be more gooey eyed around him.

"But why such a sad song?" I ask. "I thought your concert went well."

"I wrote a happier song earlier, but then I had to balance it out."

"Wouldn't want to be too happy. Then there's nothing to write about," I say.

"There's some truth to that. And aren't you the pot calling the kettle black, Ms. I-can't-keep-covering-these-feel-good-stories," he says. "What's your lead?"

"Absolutely confidential?" I ask.

"I'm not talking to any reporters," he says. "Except you."

Always a pleasure when Nick reminds me how much he hates reporters.

"I might have a lead on a kickbacks story." I want to jump up and down with excitement. This could be the story that makes my career. *If it's true.*

"Seriously? That's amazing," Nick says. "How did you get the lead?"

"I was volunteering at Lily's library event, reading books to preschool kids to entertain them while their moms had a networking session. I met one mom, Tasha, who had a leaking showerhead in her bathroom. Her building's property manager hired a contractor to fix it, but he made it worse. Although she complained about him, he is still doing 'work' around the housing development. Another plumber—her friend's brother—fixed her shower, and she recommended him to the property manager, a woman named Beatrice. But when he pitched his services to Beatrice, she told him he needed to pay a bribe. I'm meeting with him and another tenant who had shoddy work done by the first contractor."

"That's huge," Nick says.

"Right?" I grin.

"Alright, I'm done, and I won't keep you up any longer. Go forth and save the city from corruption." His eyes are shining at me.

Times like this, I really like Nick.

As he stands up—way too close to me—my heart buzzes, and I really hope that he can't hear my heartbeat.

I turn to go back inside, but then I remember I forgot to tell him about my research on this YouTube woman. She *is* a scam artist. And her name is not Cara.

I whirl around but too quickly. Somehow, I trip on an uneven slat, twisting my ankle. *Ow!* Pain races through me. *I'm falling.*

Ooooh.

I can see the sidewalk below through the slats, and my stomach is in a free fall.

Until I'm caught by Nick and pressed against his chest.

"Got you," he says.

I look up at him. I can't move. Pain is still shooting through my ankle. I grit my teeth. It will fade. I need to wait it out.

"Are you okay?"

"I will be," I say through clenched teeth. "My ankle."

How am I going to cover my story tomorrow? I can't believe I sprained my ankle.

Nick sweeps me into his arms and sits back down with me on the plastic crate he's added to the fire escape.

"Are you okay?" he asks again.

"I'll be fine. I need to wait for the pain to subside, and then I'll be fine."

We sit there, me cradled in his arms, as the pain slowly lessens. I gingerly turn my ankle to make sure I still can. It's not broken—just sprained.

As the pain lessens, I am suddenly very aware that I'm sitting in Nick's lap, leaning against his chest. He's all muscle. His body is so hard. I knew he was in shape, but this is a whole other level.

I'm probably squashing him. I move to get up, but he tightens his arms.

Pausing, I look up at him and then duck my head, afraid that he'll see how much I want to stay right here. In his arms. Surrounded by his warmth. He smells like cotton laundry and fresh air. He swallows, and his Adam's apple moves. I want...

But I'm a reporter. Rock stars and reporters are not compatible careers. A reporter is behind the scenes and not necessarily recognizable. I want the focus to be on any story I'm covering and not my personal life. Whereas Nick is singing about his feelings publicly and has a fan club who surround him when he plays at Craic and Laughs. I'm not the type of woman a rock star dates, anyway. Especially if the parting words of my ex about his having *no* desire to kiss me are to be believed. And the last thing I want is for Nick to realize I find him attractive. Then he'd probably feel the need to be more aloof so as not to encourage any feelings. He seems to be careful to be respectful but reserved with his fans. He might even pity me. Ugh.

I jump up, yelping as I land on my foot again.

"Really, Maddie?" Nick stands, grabbing my arm. "Don't hurt yourself just to get away from me."

"I'm okay now," I say. "It doesn't hurt as much." The pain has retreated.

"Don't collapse and fall on my guitar over there." He gestures with his head towards the red guitar leaning against the iron railing. "She's my baby. You don't want to live with the guilt that you hurt my first child. Let me help you."

"Okay," I say grudgingly, holding up my hand. "Heaven forbid one of your guitars is in danger."

"I'll carry you to your window. Do you think you can get in by yourself?"

"Yes. Don't worry. I'll ice it and bandage it up, and I'll be fine. It's not the first time, as you know." Last year, I was running for an interview, and I went flying face down on the uneven pavement. I missed the interview, and my rival at the paper, who apparently was following me, met my source first and scooped my story.

He sets me down by my open window, and I gingerly climb back into my apartment, being careful not to put too much weight on my injured foot.

"You sure you're okay?" he asks, concern swimming in his eyes.

"I've been better," I say.

"Sorry," he says.

"It's not your fault," I say.

"What time is your interview tomorrow?"

"I'm meeting the contractor at seven at Tostje's coffee shop. He has a job near the Seward Park development at eight. Afterwards, I'm meeting Tasha and the other mom with the same issue."

"Make sure you ice that and put your foot up on a pillow when you sleep. Do you need my help?"

No. My hormones will never settle down if Nick plays nursemaid.

"It's not that bad," I lie. "I don't need your help. I will ice it and use a pillow, Nurse Nick."

He glares at me.

"Oh, and I came out to tell you that woman is a total scam artist," I say. "She swindled some older couple out of their life savings and served a short jail sentence. I'll send you the link to what I found. Maybe it can help you with your denial—that she's not someone to be trusted."

"I'm sure it will die down." He winks. "But I'm touched by your concern."

Then he gives me that slightly crooked and mischievous grin—the one that makes all his fans' hearts melt. I hate that mine does too.

Chapter Three

Maddie

As I limp out my front door, I nearly jump out of my ankle brace and tightly laced black sneakers. Nick is lounging against the opposite hallway wall, two coffees in hand.

"Rise and shine," he says.

"Are you always cheerful in the morning?" I ask, still recovering from the shock.

"We have a meeting with MusEn this afternoon, so I'm psyched," Nick says. "And we're spending the morning fighting crime. What could be more exciting?"

"We?" I ask.

My orange tabby cat Sherlock, clearly taking advantage of my distraction, has escaped into the hallway and is sniffing at the mat in front of Nick's door. I pick him up and put him back in my apartment, carefully closing the door.

"You don't think I'm going to let you hobble forth alone in pursuit of justice, do you? What if you miss your big story again?" Nick says. "I will never hear the end of it. Plus, I need to help you get a raise and move out. I want a next-door neighbor who appreciates my singing."

"Good luck with that," I say.

As he slides my big bag off my shoulder, I freeze. Still, it seems I didn't reveal anything last night. He's not avoiding me, afraid to encourage my feelings.

This is Nick. Always up for an adventure.

Hoisting my bag up on his shoulder, he picks my newspaper off my welcome mat and offers me his arm.

"You're seriously coming?" I ask.

He bows slightly. "You have my escort until noon, and then I have to go."

"I hope you don't scare off my source," I say.

"I'll be absolutely mum and take notes," he says. "Not that I ever took notes in school. You might want to take your own notes, to be honest."

I wave off Nick's help for the stairs and gingerly, awkwardly, hop down with my injured foot up in the air behind me, gripping the worn wooden banister tightly. I'm *so* glad that Nick is here to witness this embarrassing descent down the building's narrow staircase. But it is probably easier without my bag bumping against me as I bounce.

"Are you sure you don't want me to carry you down?" he says.

"Definitely not," I say. "What if you pull a muscle and can't perform?"

"You're not that heavy. I picked you up last night, remember?"

Heat flushes my cheeks. I definitely remember.

Nick escorts me to the café that is about ten blocks away. Tostje is small. A long counter runs along most of the back wall with a few tables scattered in front. The tables have enough space between them that they afford some privacy. It smells like fresh coffee beans being ground and melted cheese. It's well-known in the neighborhood for its grilled cheese toasties, which it serves until midnight. The only server chats to the customers in a low tone interspersed with the clatter of spoons hitting the sides of the mugs.

Once I'm settled at a sturdy metal table in the back corner, with yet another two coffees plus a bagel breakfast for two, in case this guy is hungry, I thank Nick for his help and tell him he can leave me here now. What if his presence makes my contractor clam up? Tasha said he was nervous about speaking to a reporter for *The Intelligencer*. I pull out my copy of today's paper.

"So much for my dreams of being Robin to your Batman," Nick says.

Exactly. He doesn't see me as Catwoman. That's a good thing, right? At least he doesn't see me as a single woman with a cat. That's what I am. He sees me as Batman—*how on earth do I give Batman vibes?*—and he's the trusted sidekick. And I need to remember that.

"Great. Call me if you need my help. I'm going back to take a nap to catch up on my beauty sleep before this afternoon." He winks at me.

I look him up and down, making sure to frown, even though my eyes want to linger. "Good luck with that."

"Right," he says. "How can I improve?"

I tsk, and he laughs.

"Sparring with you is better than any coffee," he says. He blinks to say goodbye.

He walks out with that lanky step of his. He moves his body like a dancer. Mesmerizing. I pull out my pad as I sip my coffee and watch the door. Nick's head pops up in the window, and he makes a funny face at me. I shoo him away.

A tall, young guy enters; sturdy, rubber-heeled work boots hint that he might be my source. As his glance meets mine, he clocks my

Intelligencer (subtlety is not my strong point) and comes over. I offer him a bagel and a black coffee, with milk and sugar on the side. He doctors his coffee.

"Thanks again for being willing to talk to me," I say.

"I don't want my name revealed. This is wrong, but I have a good business going. I don't want to mess that up." He takes a bite of the bagel.

"Understood. I'll use a pseudonym in the article, but someone from the paper will call to check my story. I'm using pseudonyms for Tasha and anyone else too."

"Yes. Got it."

More customers enter the little shop, but most order their coffee to go. Two nannies sit at the table by the window, their voices carrying as they commiserate about getting their kids ready for the school day.

I open my notebook. "Can you tell me about why you received the impression that you had to pay bribes to get work at the Eleanor Roosevelt Houses?"

"It wasn't an impression." He folds his arms.

"No?" I resist the urge to lean in.

"Beatrice is the property manager at Eleanor Roosevelt Houses, so I showed Beatrice my work at Tasha's apartment, hoping to get more work. She said I could have this other job fixing a bathroom in 10F, but that I had to charge under ten thousand dollars, and I needed to kick back one thousand, so factor all that in."

"She used the phrase 'kick back'? That you had to pay one thousand dollars in order to get the job?"

"No, she said I needed to show my appreciation."

"What exactly did she say?"

"She leaned in and said, 'I'll expect you to show your appreciation for getting this work.' At first, I thought she meant—" he raises his eyebrows "—you know, and I think I jerked back. My woman would have my—well, you know. Anyway, she laughed and laughed and said she's gotten smarter in her old age, and money talks, even if I was a plumber and probably knew my way around plumbing. Pardon my French. And then she said, 'One thousand sounds like the right amount.'"

Wow. She really did ask for a bribe. "And then what did you say?"

"I said, 'No thanks.' I wasn't getting involved in this. I'm doing okay on my own. And I've got kids. I'm not getting involved in some dodgy sh—uh, crap." He takes a sip of his coffee. "And then she got real silent until she said, 'I hope Tasha and Dulce like their apartments.'"

"And what did you think she meant by that?"

"She was telling me to keep my mouth shut."

"Sounds like it," I say.

He finishes his bagel and takes another sip from the paper cup. He hums when he drinks the coffee. They do make very good coffee here.

"But as you know, Tasha is not going to take that lying down, and she thinks it's better to make it public—rather than her kowtowing to that dragon."

"You didn't get the job fixing the bathroom in 10F?"

"No."

I nod and wait for him to speak. He seems to be thinking about what to say.

"I didn't want to say anything, but Tasha… Tasha doesn't take no for an answer. And she's been a good friend to my sister." He shrugs his shoulders. "So here I am. But make sure it's under an alias."

"I will," I say. "Did you discuss this with anybody else?"

"I told some guys I was working with at this other job—that new building development around here at Clinton Street. And they said, yeah, everybody knows that she wants a little note of appreciation. A one-K note. Everyone knows she's a fan of Grover Cleveland."

These quotes were so good.

"Do you think they'd be willing to talk to me?" I ask.

"No."

"Do you know anyone else I could talk to?"

He runs his hand through his hair and shakes his head.

"Okay, well, thank you for this. This is incredibly helpful. I'll find some more people," I say. *But how?* I can't run a story based on one contractor's word. It seems to be common knowledge, but I'm not sure I can find anyone else who would be willing to talk.

Once he leaves, I gather up the empty coffee cups and the bagel wrappers and deposit them in the nearby garbage. I can walk on my foot as long as I don't put too much weight on it. Going downstairs is the killer.

Only now I have to go up to 125th Street to meet a disgruntled tenant Tasha lined up for me…and the 125th Street subway station is above ground with, unfortunately, a long metal staircase down. It has an escalator, but that isn't always working.

As I step out the door, there's Nick, putting away his little black book in his messenger bag.

He drops into step alongside me, slowing down to match my stilted pace. "Did you get what you wanted?"

"Yes."

"He said he had to pay a bribe?"

"Shh. Yes."

"Wow."

"I know. I thought you went to get your beauty sleep."

"Too wired to sleep," he says. "And you said I didn't need it."

I gaze at his handsome face (but at least this gives me a reason to really drink in those sharp cheekbones and his eyes—those green eyes with flecks of hazel) and sigh in mock exasperation. "No."

"Where are you meeting Tasha and the other mom?"

"At a playground," I say.

"Let's go, then," he says.

"Are you sure you have time for this?"

"Absolutely. Amira recommended I visit a hospital to meet with sick kids to restore my rep, but I'm sure a playground will do nicely."

"I'm sure the story will die down."

"I'm sure it will."

As I limp with Nick towards the playground, someone shrieks, "Nick Devlin!"

A woman is running full speed at us. Nick suddenly clasps me to his side. I look up at him, shocked to be anchored to him. His sea-green eyes smile down at me. "Before she knocks you over and hurts your foot."

The woman skids to a stop in front of us. "You are Nick Devlin, aren't you? Can I have your autograph? I saw you play at Craic and Laughs and the Chubby Cat. I'm a huge fan. I can't believe you're in my neighborhood. I saw you on the subway, and I was playing it cool. But then I called my friend, and she said I'd kick myself if I didn't get your autograph. So I ran back."

Nick releases me gently. He autographs a postcard with an illustration of his last album and takes a photo with her. I stand off to the side. Nick then excuses us, saying we're off to meet friends. His fan then thanks him and waves as we walk off.

It's a warm day for January—the temperature is in the fifties—so lots of children are running around the playground, their shrieks of joy and high voices filling the air. An open circular space with a currently closed sprinkler in the middle takes up one side of the playground, with a long lane branching out that leads into a smaller shallow pool area. Tasha was excited about now having a sprinkler nearby for the summer days. On the other side is a huge space filled with sand and several rope structures for climbing. Trees tower over the playground. Their branches are bare, but the shade will be great during the heat. A sign across the gate announces a concert to celebrate its opening on January 25th.

Tasha waves hello as I unlock the green gate to the playground and let us in. Tasha and her friend both have newborns, and Tasha told me they are currently on maternity leave. Nick locks the gate behind us, and we cross over to meet them. The blue surface is so bouncy that it cushions my sore ankle.

Tasha introduces her friend, Dulce, and her two children, and I introduce Nick.

Nick offers to play with their toddlers in the sandbox while we talk. The three of us sit on the green metal benches that line the perimeter of the playground. I'm happy to take the weight off my ankle. Nick settles down on the sand with the two kids. He's totally into it. He's helping them build roads and drive the truck as I turn to the women.

"He's mighty fine," says Dulce.

Tasha takes a photo and AirDrops it to me. "He seems worth keeping," she says.

"We're just friends," I say.

"That's too bad." Tasha shakes her head.

Yes. I can't help smiling as I watch Nick scooping up sand to create a road for the truck. He clearly likes kids. He also babysits one of our neighbor's kids most afternoons, and yet he doesn't date. This is a different side of him that I hadn't recognized before. He treats his band members as if they're his family. He's so protective of Sayo, Kyla, and Amira, like a big brother.

But the mystery of Nick Devlin is not for me to unwrap.

I focus on Dulce, who has the same story as Tasha, with a repair that left her in worse straits than before.

"But listen to what Beatrice told Dulce," Tasha says. "Beatrice is the property manager, so she's responsible for everything—collecting rents, making repairs, etc." She shows me a photo of Beatrice from the building's website.

"I told Beatrice I was going to report her to the Infrastructure Department for taking bribes," Dulce says. "And she laughed."

"Cackled, more like," Tasha says.

"She said, 'Good luck. Do you think I came up with this on my own? I pay him his cut of each repair contract to keep my job. Report me, and he's got enough connections for you to lose your apartment.'"

I hastily scribble that down. "Wow. So she implied it was someone high up in the Infrastructure Department? Did she say anything more about who it was?"

"She implied it was someone very senior who had all the power. She said, 'He runs the district.'"

It must be Commissioner Johnson or one of the deputy commissioners. How am I going to figure that out?

"Did you ever report it to the Infrastructure Department?" I ask.

"No. She seemed confident," Dulce says. "I don't want to lose my apartment."

"Beatrice seemed cozy with all the government officials who showed up for the ribbon cutting a few weeks ago," Tasha says. "They should be here again at the concert on January 25th to celebrate this new playground."

I note down the date to attend. "If it is someone senior at the Infrastructure Department, then it's probably widespread. Do you have any friends at other buildings with similar issues?"

They both shake their heads.

I ask a few more questions and then wrap up the interview. Hopefully, I can help them.

Both kids are now sitting in Nick's lap, where I was sitting last night.

My cheeks heat up. *Stop it. We're friends.*

"Can we hire him for babysitting?" Tasha asks.

"Seriously," I say. "He's full of hidden talents."

The three of us walk over to Nick. The kids clamber out of his lap and return to playing in the sand. I thank Tasha and Dulce for their help, asking them to call me if they discover anything more that would be helpful to prove this.

One child cries out, saying he hurt his finger on something sharp in the sand. We search the sand but don't find anything. I give him a Band-Aid from my bag, and he stops sniffling.

As Nick and I walk away, I offer to pay for lunch, but Nick passes because he has to get back downtown. I tell him about the allegation that someone senior is behind this.

"That makes sense," he says.

"There are three deputy commissioners, so that narrows it down somewhat." I stop suddenly. "Didn't you say your next performance was to celebrate some playground renovation?"

"Yeah, Amira booked us the gig," Nick says. "Some joint Infrastructure Department and Parks Department deal."

"Could it be this playground? The ceremony is January 25th."

"I'll check, but that date sounds about right."

As we turn the corner of the building, ahead of us a woman stops a man with a toolbox. It looks like Beatrice! I pull Nick back out of sight against the brick wall.

"That's the woman. C'mon." I slip back around the corner, holding tight to the wall. A huge dumpster next to the wall blocks her view of us and ours of her.

I pull Nick by the hand and quickly scuttle up behind the dumpster. And then I take a deep breath as my ankle painfully reminds me that I don't have full mobility.

Wow. It smells rank—as if it's holding a million dirty diapers and poorly closed dog poop bags. I hold my nose.

"The smell…" Nick gags.

"Shh." I hobble closer to where they are standing on the other side, but I also can't get too close to the side of this dumpster because who knows what it's been coated with. Other than dog piss. I can definitely smell that.

"Thanks for repairing that shower so quickly," Beatrice says. "I have another job in 11J."

The man says something, but I miss his reply because a car honks at that exact moment.

A phone rings, and Beatrice says, "I have to take this."

It seems she takes a few steps back because her voice is closer as she says, "Hi, Deputy Commissioner, how are you?"

Deputy Commissioner.

I try to peek around the edge to get a closer look at the guy she was standing with. Maybe I can follow up with him. I snap a quick picture before ducking back.

"Can I help you?"

We look up to see a woman dressed in a green suit with heels staring at us from a few feet away—probably to stay out of the draft of this odor.

"Good luck," Nick whispers.

I put my finger to my mouth and whisper to her, "Do you see a bunch of female fans on the other side?"

She looks around the dumpster. "No. Just Ms. Beatrice and that contractor, Pablo."

Pablo!

I limp away from the dumpster, and Nick practically runs ahead of me to escape the smell.

"I told him I didn't think any of his fans were about to mob us, but you know, you never can be too cautious," I say.

As she takes in Nick, she seems to believe my cover story. Nick definitely has rock star looks, with that wavy hair, along with those well-worn jeans that hug his hip bones.

"I don't like to disillusion him that we don't have to worry about fans every place we go, so I try to humor him."

Nick shoots me a look that promises retribution later.

"But as I told him, it's only Ms. Beatrice and that guy Pablo," I continue. "I forgot his last name."

"I only know him as Pablo," the woman says.

"Has he done any work on your apartment?"

"No, he worked on my neighbor's sink."

"Was he able to fix it?" I ask.

"I wouldn't recommend him. You live in this building?" She folds her arms. That question was bound to come up.

"No, I'm visiting a friend," I say.

"We should go," Nick says. "Before my legions of fans return."

We walk away, Nick offering me his arm as he realizes I'm still limping. When we're far enough away that no one can hear us, he shakes his head. "Wow. That was unbelievably smooth, Maddie Hughes."

Thankfully, the escalator is working for our ascent to the 125th Street subway platform.

"Your rock star persona is really handy for investigating," I say. "Now whenever I'm wearing a disguise, I can say that I don't want your fans to recognize me as your next-door neighbor."

"Ah yes, my fans," he says. "The hordes that follow me everywhere."

"That fan earlier was running at us like her life depended on it. Does that happen often?" I ask as we wait for the train on the outside platform.

"Once in a while," he says.

I glance at him. "I would find it hard to give up my privacy. Do you consider it a necessary evil, or do you enjoy the attention?"

"Are you asking in earnest?" he asks.

"Yes, but not as a reporter," I say. The platform shakes slightly as a subway train pulls in.

"It's not that I want to give up my privacy, but I really appreciate their fandom," he says. "They're the ones who make it possible for me to play music. And some put so much effort into promoting me. It's mind-boggling."

"That feels like the answer you would give a reporter," I say.

His mouth curves up slightly. "You are a reporter—and a very slick one, as I just witnessed. But it's also my honest answer. There are compromises with everything."

"Even with art?" I ask.

"I want to sell my art," he says. "I'm willing to make a lot of compromises if it will get me where I want to go."

"Is your no-dating policy one of your compromises?" I ask.

Nick stares at me as if surprised that I noticed. I may be focused on my career and burned out from my last experiences dating, but it seems like a waste for Nick not to be dating anyone. He shrugs, saying he has to get back downtown to prepare for the meeting with MusEn, and quickly enters the train before the doors close.

Chapter Four

Nick

Your no-dating policy. I didn't realize Maddie knew I had a no-dating policy. Not that it seems to be helping me now. I should have made it explicit, and maybe then people would believe that I'm not dating this fraudster.

That's what I said to Maddie on the subway ride back anyway, and I teased her about keeping track of my dating life. She blushed. It's the first time I've seen her blush. Cute.

But yes, my no-dating policy is one of my compromises. And for exactly this reason—I can't trust that whomever I date is not going to backstab me. And also because I *can't* make any long-term commitment. I need to put all my energy into making it as a musician and the family that I have—my band.

MusEn has rescheduled our meeting, so instead of meeting with them this afternoon, we're in my one-bedroom apartment. Amira, Sayo, and Kyla are sitting crammed together on my couch. José is sprawled out on a chair next to my guitar rack. I'm pacing back and forth in front of my dining room table. Our last album is playing low through my speakers.

Amira looks up from her phone. "MusEn wants to confirm again that you're not dating this Cara, even though you already told them that you're not. They are not happy with the press about you and her now that it's also public that she defrauded some older couple and served jail time. They're even more worried now that she's a bad association, and they don't want to spend the money to clear your name when they haven't even picked you up yet. Especially when this is so counter to your entire image of being open and down-to-earth, this vulnerable heartthrob."

The Squirrel ran an article today asking whether *I* was the hidden criminal associate who helped scam the older couple with "Cara" (whose actual name was Karigan). Apparently, the older couple had testified during the trial that "Cara" had a personable and attractive boyfriend. *The Squirrel* is alleging that it was me, without any facts, obviously, to back that up, with this horrific headline: *Was Nick Devlin the Secret Associate Who Helped Karigan "Cara" Fonston Defraud an Elderly Couple Out of Their Life Savings?*

Total clickbait. I'd like to sue *The Squirrel* for character assassination, but a lawsuit is the last thing I want to focus on right now.

"They don't believe my denial? How can I persuade them?" I ask. "Maddie showed me that article about that woman's jail sentence. As if I'd date her."

"They're wavering," Amira says. "They don't want to bet their money on someone who's already starting with this PR liability."

I fold my arms, frustrated. This psycho woman is ruining my chance to make it big? All these years of hard work, and some fraudster wants to piggyback on my success and drag me down in the process?

Not on my watch.

I don't even know this woman.

"Should I give them some sort of sworn statement?" I ask. "Take a lie detector test? Find this retired couple and have them issue a response that they've never met me?"

"The damage is already done. It's not that the label truly believes you're dating Cara," Amira says. "But now you're associated with her."

"We need a bigger story," Kyla says. "The truth—the one-line retraction—never gets the same publicity as the original headline."

Amira's phone beeps, and she stares at her screen. "Nick, you seem to be working overtime. Are you dating Maddie?"

"No," I say.

"She's sitting in your lap. And you're carrying her in your arms?" Amira asks, holding up her phone to show me the photos.

"What? Who caught that?" I stare at the images. Somebody photographed us last night on the fire escape. Wow. *That is crazy.* No privacy. Is this what becoming famous is really like?

"Tell me the truth," Amira says. "It would be good if you were dating. We could run with that. Girl next door vibe. That would be a bigger story."

"Maddie and I are friends," I say. "And she's a reporter. We're not dating."

"Wow. This woman is insane," Amari says. "She's got another video asking if you're cheating on her. How did she get that up so fast? She's racking up the views."

I stare at that video. This is like some dystopian reality.

"At least the title of the Maddie article asks if this is your real girlfriend," Amira says.

"Or am I a playboy? Keep reading." I scroll through the comments. "It's not great. I should warn Maddie."

So much for José calling me "the monk" because I stopped dating. Here I am, trying to keep my nose clean, and it's only hurting me.

"Are you sure there's nothing between you and Maddie?" Sayo asks. "Because these photos are hot."

"She tolerates me. Do you know why she was out on that fire escape? She came out to complain that I was making too much noise, and she tripped."

"She's not looking at you like she barely tolerates you," Amira says.

"She's dazed by pain," I say.

José pulls up the photo on his phone. "The bunny slippers are a particularly nice touch. She's the exact opposite of this Cara woman."

"Couldn't you guys fake date to get us over this hump?" Amira asks. "You can deny you're dating this other woman, and we can do some cute photo shoots with you and Maddie? That's even better than my previous idea of you volunteering at various charities."

"Fake date?" I ask.

"I think celebrities do it all the time for publicity reasons."

"Maddie will never agree."

"Do you even have any other female friends?" José asks. "All you do is work. Plus, it needs to be somebody we can absolutely trust."

"We can't trust Maddie. Imagine what she can do with this. *I fake dated a rock star*. It's an even better headline than *What It's Like to Date a Wannabe Rock Star*," I say, the bitterness of Christina's betrayal still seeping into my voice. "I can date one of you."

"No way," Amira says. "My parents are not going to accept my dating you. They've only recently accepted that this is a legitimate career and that you're a good guy who's not going to expose me to some seedy underworld of drugs. I'm not risking that."

"My boyfriend might have something to say about that," Sayo says.

"I don't think we can bring in yet a third woman. That's way too hard to manage," Amira says. "We've got this perfect setup here with this headline—Is this your real girlfriend? *Yes*. Gosh. And you were hiding it by living next door to each other. Trying to protect her privacy."

"In two tiny apartments. Right."

"Promise me you'll think about it," Amira says. "I have to go home for dinner."

Sayo, Kyra, and Amira depart together, leaving José, who looks like he's taking great pleasure in my current predicament.

"Should you really be enjoying this?" I ask. "This is our future on the line."

"I'm definitely enjoying this way too much, given the stakes." José drums his fingers on my table in time with the beat. "You're rusty because you haven't been dating. Where's the infamous Nick Devlin charm? You've been neighbors and friends for a while now. You obviously trust her."

She's never going to agree.

Unless I promise to move out so she can have peace and quiet next door. If we sign this deal and make some money, I could afford a fancier apartment. But this apartment is fine for what I need. This life is so up and down. I don't want to spend money when my income could dry up. Plus, where else am I going to find a place that has a secret entrance/exit? That seems all the more necessary now.

I rub my forehead with both hands. I had to get caught with the one woman who will say no. Where *is* the famous Nick Devlin charm now?

José shakes his head. "Don't you have any bargaining chips?"

"I'm looking up the cost of soundproofing right now." I google it on my phone.

Chapter Five

Maddie

I'm still staring at the photo Nick texted me with a million thoughts racing in my head.

I can't believe the paparazzi caught me sitting on his lap. His career must really be taking off.

I hope nobody at work sees this.

We look cute together.

He really was comforting me and had his arms around me.

My lips curve up in a smile. I didn't imagine that. I save the photo to my favorite photos file.

Iris, one of my best friends since high school, nudges me. People often think we're sisters, probably because we both have brown hair, although hers is straighter, and, after all these years of friendship, similar mannerisms. We also grew up together on the Lower East Side. Her dad owns Craic and Laughs, the bar we end the night at if we go out.

We're sitting at the counter by the window in our favorite dumpling place, around the corner from my apartment. Not that we can really see out the glass because it is covered by a huge menu that announces how cheap the dumplings are.

"But how can you not participate in this panel?" Iris asks.

Get it together. The alumni fundraiser panel to discuss press careers at my old middle school with news legend Twyla Jackson. And me. That's what Iris and I are discussing. Or rather, Iris is while I'm off daydreaming about impossibilities.

"Maybe Twyla Jackson can be a mentor," Iris says. "And even if that doesn't work out, it would look great on your resume."

I nod and turn off my phone. I will not be tempted by Nick. This is my career we're discussing.

Every table in this place is full—but then, only six tables fit in the front space. The construction worker next to me places his hard hat between him and us; he's eating a steaming dumpling scallion soup. I pop another dumpling into my mouth and savor the soupy filling. Another customer comes in to pick up their order.

Iris is right that I should do it, but...

"I just don't want to go back," I say. "What if that circle of classmates is there? They were so horrible to me." Mocked me. Nobody sat with me at lunch out of fear of being "contaminated" and made to suffer social ostracism too. But they were willing to call me for homework help at night. Luckily, I left them behind when I went to a different high school than they did. I've often thought about what I did that made me the target of those bullies, but I guess I was more interested in studying and refused to participate in their mean girl games. "This is part of an alumni fundraiser, so they could be there. I don't want to see them again. I definitely don't want to have to be nice to them and pretend it's all cool now."

"You don't have to be nice to them. Ignore them," Iris says. "Maybe they'll even apologize. And it's not like they can affect you now."

"I don't think bullies change personalities." *And I don't want to test whether they can affect me now.*

"Sebastian and I will come so you won't be alone. We can be rude to anybody who talks to you. Especially Sebastian."

I should do it. Even though it's open to current students and alumni, why would they bother to show up? Because they seemed *obsessed* with picking on me back then. Thinking about it now, I can see that my refusal to be mean to those they designated as objects of scorn had to be punished, or others might not respect their fiefdom. Once they found out my mom was Jill's Cookies, it was even worse. They delighted in asking me if I was chubby because I had to taste all the oatmeal cookies.

But last year, I'd written an article about Riley, a bullied high schooler who'd created a national campaign to stop bullying, and I'd been okay revisiting my experience (not that I wrote about it in the article, but in talking about it with Riley). I think one of the reasons Riley and I connected was that I definitely understood how damaging bullying is to your confidence. The article won an award, but that still had not been enough for a promotion.

"I'll go," I say. If I let the fear of them prevent me from going to this, then I really am not over them.

"Ask Nick to accompany you," Iris says.

"Nick's not going to go with me to some middle school event."

"Pitch it as something that could polish his image," Iris suggests. "We can all say we've never seen him with that woman if the press asks us any questions."

"Actually, there's a new story," I say. "And now I'm the girl-friend."

"What?" Iris asks.

She is not going to like this. She dated the lead singer of a band and caught him cheating on her. I show her the article that Nick sent me, just as Jing walks in. Jing is my best friend at *The Intelligencer*. She says hello to the owner in Chinese and then takes the seat vacated by the construction guy.

"Sorry I'm late, but Maddie, what is going on with you and Nick?" Jing unwraps her brown scarf that matches her eyes. "Are you dating?"

"No," I say, shocked. "I would tell you."

"It looks like you're dating," Jing says.

"It does," I say. *It does!* And then I deflate. We are so *not* dating.

I slide over the plate of dumplings I ordered in advance for Jing as she dumps her much more contained bag by her feet, next to my huge carryall.

I stuff another dumpling into my mouth with my chopsticks. At this point, I need to plead the full mouth excuse.

Iris looks up. "Well, now he really should attend that middle school event with you. Now that he's stuck you in this mess. *But don't fall for him.* You can say you're good friends. But even good friends should impress that middle school crowd."

Nick would definitely impress.

"How can you say no to being on a panel with *the* Twyla Jackson? She's my idol," Jing says. "You agree, right, Iris?"

"Yes. It shouldn't even be a question."

So easy for Iris to say. But the thought of seeing that group again makes my skin crawl. And it's been years. The worst was when they painted the back of my gym shorts with spots of red nail polish, and everybody laughed at me.

"It's especially perfect because of that *Variety* article," Jing says. "They can assume he really is your boyfriend."

"I can't believe he has paparazzi already. And that I was in some paparazzi shot."

"The way you're looking at each other is smoking," Jing says.

"But it's not true," I say.

"You didn't sit in his lap?" Iris asks, her head tilted, with that look in her eyes that says, *Don't think you can try to get away with this.*

Great. I'm getting investigator Iris and not best friend Iris.

"I tripped, and he grabbed me in time and then sat down with me in his lap," I say.

"See. You were sitting in his lap, and he could have dumped you on the plastic crate if he really had no feelings for you," Jing says.

And now, reporter Jing.

"Thanks," I say wryly. "The emotions you're ascribing to the photo aren't true."

"You guys are still friends, so there's some emotional care there," Jing says.

"That's all there is," I say.

"It's a start." Jing bumps me with her shoulder.

"That's all there should be," Iris says.

Does Jing also think I have a crush on Nick? I know Iris does. And if both Jing and Iris do, then what if Nick does? I don't want Nick to be worried I'm falling for him and feel like he has to pull back from our friendship.

I don't think he does. It's not like the time in middle school when those mean girls kept sending me fake notes from the most popular guy and I believed them. That popular guy was nice to me because he wanted my help with his homework. I sent him a note back "reciprocating" his feelings, and that note was photocopied and plastered all over my locker with his *UGH* on it. Actually, that was worse than the red nail polish on my shorts. He made sure I knew I shouldn't acknowledge him in any subsequent encounter.

Such unnecessary cruelty.

At least Mr. Popular failed his next English test without me to help him study.

"I'd have to bribe Nick and let him play all night or something," I say.

"You can sleep in our living room. Or my bedroom at my parents' house is available," Iris says. Her phone beeps. "Oh, we have a cyber-security incident. I have to go and check it out." She stuffs the last dumpling into her mouth and cleans up her trash. Jing and I hug her goodbye and watch her dash off.

We finish up our dinner and then wrap up again in our coats and scarves to go outside.

"Is it snowing?" Jing asks.

I nod. We say goodbye to the owner and exit. I hook my arm into Jing's and walk her comfortably back to her apartment, which is only a few blocks away from mine, so we can continue chatting. The snow flurries land lightly on the sidewalk and seem to stick.

When we arrive in the vestibule of her building, Jing turns to me and says, "Nick's a good guy. You'd have to be made of steel not to be attracted to him." She holds up the photo of Nick and me on her phone.

"I'm *so* attracted to him." It feels good to say it out loud.

"No shame in that," Jing says.

"He came with me to my interviews because I sprained my ankle when I tripped and fell into his lap." At least my ankle is better now. I iced it again last night.

"Smooth move," Jing says.

"So not smooth," I say.

"I beg to disagree," Jing says. "You ended up in his lap."

I laugh. "He blinked goodbye at me. Do you think that means anything?"

"That means *I love you* in cat language," Jing says.

I pout. "At least Sherlock loves me."

It won't be too bad. Nick will be happy to practice late at night. But he does seem to be picky about who he dates, given that he doesn't date. And he's probably not going to want to give any credence to that *Variety* report. It's not like I want to go around pretending that report is correct. I'm supposed to be a hard-hitting reporter, not some rock star's floozy flunky girlfriend. Luckily, nobody at work seems to have recognized me. *And those bunny slippers.* I'm throwing those out. My bag feels especially heavy as I climb up the worn, wooden stairs to my apartment.

Nick's door is slightly ajar. *Weird.* I unlock my door.

Nick sticks his head out his door as if my thoughts conjured him up.

"Maddie, I have a huge favor to ask of you," he says.

"You do?" This could be good.

He nods. He looks so serious. "You never replied to my text of that photo in *Variety*."

Because what should I reply? Was he horrified? Why did he send that to me? His "FYI" gave no context.

"I still can't believe it," I say. "But congratulations. You've got paparazzi. What's happening with your MusEn deal? Do they want to sign you?"

"They did." His tone sounds so dismal.

"They *did*?"

"But now they're worried that I'm a PR risk because of that woman's video. And she put up another one complaining that I'm cheating on her with you."

"But she's a total fraudster."

"Right. It's even worse that I'm now affiliated with her and that she served jail time for defrauding an older couple. The record company is concerned that the next headline will quote the lyrics of my last song about 'looking for the one' as 'looking for the perfect victim to defraud.' Or so they said." He bites his lip. "But if I could say that you were my real girlfriend..."

My heart thuds. "Your real girlfriend?"

"I'll do anything if you'll fake date me," he says.

"Fake date you." Hurray for my saying that in an even tone. Nick doesn't want to date me. He wants to pretend we're dating.

He says, "I know you can barely tolerate me, and the way you just said that... You sound less than thrilled. But this is my career on the line. And you would have to promise to not *ever* do a tell-all article. Maybe you could sign an NDA."

He thinks I would do a tell-all article. Some friendship we have. Emotional care, my foot.

"No," I say. No way. "I'm sure you can find a million other women who'd be willing to be your fake girlfriend."

"No." He shakes his head. "I can't. Not ones that I trust."

"You just clearly said you don't trust me."

"I trust you as much as I trust any reporter," he says.

At least he sees me as a reporter. Some comfort there.

"I cover the story. I am *not* the story," I say.

"Please."

"Hard pass." I slip inside my apartment and close the door. I'm not falling for Nick's puppy dog look through the opening. The fact that my entire body did a leap of joy when he said "my real girlfriend" is all that I need to know that I would not survive fake dating with my heart intact. But even more importantly, as a reporter, my job is to tell the truth. How can I be part of a fake relationship?

Chapter Six

Nick

"She said no?" José asks, his voice over the phone echoing in my ear. But he doesn't sound sorry about it. If anything, he's enjoying my predicament way too much. He already asked me twice to repeat the exact words that I used and how she responded. Meanwhile, it sounds like his wife, Elena, invited friends over for the night, because I can hear a lot of female laughter in the background.

"Serves you right for keeping her up at night playing music," he says.

"It was only until eleven p.m. Maybe, sometimes, midnight. Who goes to bed before eleven p.m.?"

"Apparently Maddie does." José says he will ask Elena if she has any suggestions, but he needs to get her alone for a minute. And he needs to make his famous guacamole dip. We hang up.

I pace around the floor of my apartment and then stare out the window. It's dark already, and the shades of the various windows across the street have already been pulled down. A cold draft makes me shiver. I pull on a sweater.

My phone rings, and I pick up.

José says, "I'm back."

"But other than that, I've been a good neighbor." I *can't* believe she said no. I thought we were friends. "I take care of her cat when she has to travel. I brought her food when she sprained her ankle."

I move away from the window and sit back down by my keyboard and guitar, staring at the framed Rolling Stones poster on my wall.

"You've been out of the dating world way too long," José says. "How could you ask her to fake date you and sign an NDA at the same time?"

"So, Big Brain, when else should I suggest that?"

"Maybe don't suggest an NDA at all," he says. "You either trust her, or you don't."

I envy José's devil-may-care attitude. I really do. Maybe that comes with the territory of being a drummer. His attitude: *Let them write what they want.* Any publicity is good publicity. Or maybe he's just smarter than me. He never liked Christina.

"Here, Elena wants to talk to you," José says.

"Nicky, darling, you should not be having this problem, but it's because you've closed yourself off," Elena says. "You need to open up more and trust. You've got to let go of what that Christina woman did to you."

"You're right," I say to Elena. But that is so much easier said than done. If anything, this only shows that I was right not to date—because I'm too easy a target to be pulled down by scandalous rumors right now. But Maddie has been living next to me for several years now and has never written an article about me. And she could definitely have written some horror piece titled "No Sweet Dreams: Next-Door Neighbor to an Up-and-Coming Rock Star," based on how much she hates when I play late. She's not going to write an article about fake dating me if she doesn't want to be the story.

"Here's José back," Elena says, telling him that I said she was right.

"I've been telling you that for ages. And she's right?" José asks.

"You wanted me to tell her she wasn't right?" I ask.

He laughs. "No. She is right. You should get back out there and date. This is the universe telling you that being a monk is not the right approach."

"I don't think that's the lesson I'm supposed to learn from this," I say wryly.

The lesson is that I should have publicized my non-dating stance. But I can apologize to Maddie for saying that I didn't trust her.

"I can fix this. I'll write up a contract that favors her and slip it under her door."

"Cause that's going to melt her heart," José says. "I always find contracts incredibly sexy."

"You don't know Maddie. She will *love* this contract," I say.

José laughs. "I'm coming over."

"Don't," I say.

"I'll bring food," José says. "Plus, Elena has her friends over, and they need some time for girl chat. Or so I've just been told." José lives about fifteen blocks away from me.

"Bring Maddie's favorite dumplings, then." I hang up.

She will *love this contract*. I open up my laptop and stare at the blank screen. I start typing:

Dating Contract

Nick Devlin and Maddie Hughes hereby agree to fake date for three (3) months. As part of this:

1. Nick will not play music past ten p.m. *ever* again.

2. Nick will also invest in soundproofing his apartment.

I don't even own this place. That seems like a lot to pay for when I'm going to have to remove it. And what if the landlord catches me?

3. We will appear in public once a week, holding hands.

4. Maddie will also show up at any appearances required by my record label, provided that she doesn't have a work conflict.

Okay, I've veered into the wrong territory. This is too much about me. What can she get out of this?

5. Nick will show up as Maddie's boyfriend at any event where Maddie requires a date, provided Nick doesn't have a work conflict.

I doubt Maddie needs a date at events. It's the twenty-first century. Uh-oh. What if Maddie wants to date someone else?

6. Maddie and Nick resolve to be exclusive for the three months.

Great. Now she has to give up dating anyone else as well. This is not a contract she's going to love.

7. Nick will cook dinner for Maddie two nights a week.

8. Nick will scoop out Sherlock's litter box every day.

José is going to die laughing when he sees this. What else can I offer?

Maddie is all about her career, but it's not like I can help her with her career. And dating a musician doesn't help her with her career. Maybe that's why she said no.

9. The terms of this contract will remain confidential.

Maddie will want this as much as me.

10. Nick will do whatever Maddie wants for three months, as long as it is not a career conflict.

What if she wants me to move out?

I rub my brow. I can move out. It wouldn't make sense to move out while we're "dating," though. Plus, I like living next to Maddie. I like the separate entrance through the deli if I ever feel like I'm being followed by a fan. I shouldn't have played music past ten. It's only that...well, I work best at night, like an owl—or bat.

But is that truly why she's saying no? This is a once-in-a-lifetime chance for me. She's always seemed reasonable.

There's a knock on my door. Please let it be Maddie, reconsidering.

It's José.

I open the door.

José hands me the bag filled with cartons of dumplings and makes himself at home, sitting right down at my table and reading the document on my laptop.

I pile the cartons of dumplings on my compact kitchen counter, my back to José so I don't have to see his reaction.

"It's not bad," José says. "It's a good starting point, anyway."

"Really?" I ask.

"Especially clause ten. That conveys your total desperation."

"Thanks..."

"Make it clear that this is a starting proposal and you're open to any of her suggestions," José says. "I don't see how she can say no to this."

Chapter Seven

Maddie

I ignore the "contract" that is currently burning a hole in my bag. Nick must have slipped an envelope under my door last night. I wish I'd read it in my apartment and left it at home, but I was sure it was going to be a "just kidding" note. Definitely *not a fake-dating contract*.

I stare at my work screen and focus on typing the next sentence in my article.

How can he not find another woman? I'm not even a good liar.

But based on clause ten, he's clearly desperate.

I need more caffeine. All that tossing and turning last night translated into very little sleep, even though there wasn't so much as a squeak from Nick's apartment. I. Am. So. Tempted. And I do feel bad that this woman is destroying his chance. He's worked so hard. And if it was a more simple—less public—request, I'd be glad to help him out as a friend.

I stare at the last sentence I typed. I figured out Pablos' contract information, because he was recorded as the contractor on a repair ticket, but when I called him, he shot me down immediately, saying he had no interest in talking to a reporter, even off the record. I save the article I'm working on and get up to get a coffee.

How could I pretend to be Nick's fake girlfriend? So many women would love to date Nick Devlin. It doesn't need to be me.

I'm about to turn the corner and enter the office kitchen when I hear my name in conversation.

"Did you see that *Variety* article about Nick Devlin? Wasn't that Maddie in his lap?" asks a voice I don't recognize.

"Yes. But there's no way *she's* dating Nick Devlin," says a voice I very much do recognize. Sarah. My main nemesis at the paper. She actually follows me around to scoop my stories. Then again, we're competing for the same senior position, so there's no love lost between us.

"She's sitting in his lap," the other woman says.

"They're obviously friends," Nemesis says. "I mean, if they were something more, would she be wearing bunny slippers? That's clearly killing any sexy vibe."

Point for Nemesis. Those slippers need to go.

"Yeah, you must be right. I mean, if the photographer had caught them kissing, *Variety* would have published that. Plus, I mean, Maddie doesn't seem like the type to attract a guy like Nick Devlin."

Yup. Another reason why it's better that Nick finds another woman to fake date.

I lean against the wall. I should leave. Haven't I learned my lesson from when I was in middle school? Listening to gossip about myself only hurts me.

"Seriously. She'd bore him by geeking out over the latest City Council hearing," Nemesis says.

"What are you listening to so intently?" Jing whispers.

I nearly jump a foot. I put my finger to my mouth. Jing presses against me to listen in too.

"There's no way they're dating," Nemesis says.

Jing frowns and looks like she's about to give them a piece of her mind.

I shake my head.

"Well, if she is, we should cover it for Page Six."

Uh-oh. I need to get out of here. I pull Jing away from the office kitchen and back to my desk, where I grab my coat and my phone.

"I'm going to meet with my contact at City Hall about this new story I have," I say. "She agreed to meet at the back steps in half an hour."

"I'll come with you. I need fresh air after listening to that," Jing says.

We leave our floor by the fire stairs, rather than the elevators. It's rare you meet someone in the stairwell.

"Don't let Sarah get to you," Jing says. "Nick doesn't date, but if he did, I bet you'd be top of the list. And Nemesis would be the absolute last woman he'd date. She's like his last girlfriend."

Like his last girlfriend. That definitely doesn't make me feel better.

Nemesis is his type?

Ugh.

Definitely not someone like me. Nail-bitten fingers, one currently still decorated with spots of brown paint from some miniature hot chocolates I made this weekend. I took a break from needle felting animals and decided to try this tutorial to de-stress.

As we push the glass doors open to exit, the cold air hits us. Our office is located two blocks behind City Hall. As we hurry away from the office, the back of City Hall is visible to the right through a chain-link fence that surrounds a parking lot. We turn and walk down the narrow side street.

"Who are you meeting?" Jing asks.

"This woman who heads up the call center. It turns out that the New York Infrastructure Department has a number to call to schedule a repair request. It assigns the caller a ticket. I'm hoping I can get access to more of those tickets and talk to those people to see if they had repairs by someone competent. If someone senior in the Infrastructure Department is involved, then it must be more than this one building."

"That's a good lead," she says.

"What are you working on?" I ask.

"An article on solar panels that you can plug in to generate your own electricity. It's cool," Jing says. She works on the business section of the paper.

"Should we get a coffee? I have some time to kill," I say.

Jing nods, and we make a wide loop around City Hall, since it's cordoned off by police barriers, and enter City Hall Park.

We stop to get a coffee at the corner food cart and catch up with Frank, the vendor. He just had a baby.

"By the way, you asked me to let you know if I overheard the Infrastructure Department deputy commissioners say anything interesting," Frank says. "Deputy Commissioner Galliano of the Infrastructure Department often gets his coffee here, and he was on the phone the other day, and he said, 'It has to look legit, though.'"

"Really?" I ask. "Do you know the context?"

"No, he paid for his coffee then and walked away," Frank says. "But he's a nice man. Good tipper."

That was interesting, if completely inconclusive.

"Well, let me know if you overhear anything else," I say.

My phone rings. My contact now wants to meet closer to her office.

Jing volunteers to accompany me the two blocks to the new location. We walk down the center pathway of the park towards the fountain. Most of the trees are bare, but there's still a fair amount of green because of the fir trees and the bushes. To the right, outside the park, is the distinctive Gothic façade of the Woolworth Building.

Jing pulls up the *Variety* photo. "The way Nick's looking at you... I still think he might actually like you. Maybe he's not dating anyone else because he does like you."

"Photos can be easily manipulated," I say.

"Sarah is jealous. Don't listen to her."

"Don't worry," I say to Jing. I give her a hug goodbye as she returns to the office, and then I loiter outside the CVS, waiting for my contact to show up, touched that Jing was concerned about me. But Nemesis was right that Nick and I are just friends. Pretending we are dating will only lead to heartache for me. But he had a valid point that he must really trust whoever plays the part of his girlfriend. And it's not like I don't want to help him.

10. Nick will do whatever Maddie wants for three months, as long as it is not a career conflict.

He must be desperate. I'm torn. And do I want to watch him dating someone else? Even if it's fake?

I meet my friends for a late dinner at Craic and Laughs. Luckily, the source I'd met earlier today had given me the list. I also need to determine any correlation between complaints and the buildings assigned to each deputy commissioner. I'm late because I was following Deputy Commissioner Galliano around. Eleanor Roosevelt Houses is in his district, so based on the *"He runs the district"* comment, it seems like he's the most likely suspect. Following him feels like a dead end. He's responsible for community affairs, and unsurprisingly, he went to a community meeting. His nickname in the press room is Gallant Galliano and based on how responsive he was to constituent concerns, I can see why.

Iris pulls out the chair next to her, and I sit between her and Bella. Bella is a romance author, and she and I can talk about writing for ages.

"Are those glasses new?" I ask Bella.

"Yes, but still red. Red for romance," Bella says, fluffing out her wavy brown hair.

"They look great," I say.

Pushing her glasses up on her nose, Bella asks us for ideas for plotting her next book because she's stuck, and we pitch suggestions.

I say, "How about a cybersecurity analyst who is investigating a security breach to save her company during the holidays but has to resist the allure of her lawyer colleague assigned to help?"

Iris pushes me, and I almost fall off my chair. We all giggle because that's Iris's love story.

Our ideas get more and more zany.

I say, "How about he's a circus performer, and he comes to New York City to perform—"

"He's an acrobat," Iris interrupts.

"Exactly, and someone tries to mug him, and she scares the guy off," I say.

"But he must go with the show," Iris says. "He can't stay in the city."

"He's the last of a long family line of acrobat legends," Bella says, joining in the fun.

I love these nights—great company, music, and food, which is what "craic" means in Irish. Iris's dad emigrated here from Ireland. The front window is still decorated with snowflakes from when my friends and I decorated it after Thanksgiving. We're sitting at one of the worn, dark-wooden tables on the side. Colorful framed band posters adorn the wall behind us. A long bar with barstools is across from us. I can't help breaking some melted wax off the beer bottle with a candle that has yet to be lit. The front of Craic and Laughs is a typical bar, but the back has been set up as a band venue re-engineered for great acoustics. A band is setting up on the stage.

The usual old-timers have claimed their stools at the bar. A bunch of new people have shown up to hear this latest band play. I admit that I checked to see if Nick's band was playing tonight before I suggested we meet here, because I'm afraid I will not be able to resist a hard sell after seeing him perform.

I tell my friends about my story lead and my plan to interview more people from the repair request database tomorrow.

"Hey... A corrupt infrastructure inspector showed up here and gave my dad a hard time," Iris says.

"Are you serious?" I ask.

"He threatened to cite my dad for a violation but muttered something about how we could find a mutually beneficial solution if my dad would give a slot to some unknown singer for her to perform. 'Give a newbie a chance.' Dad was like, 'Sorry, I'm not running a charity. And I don't have any violations.' I backed Dad up and said I'd like to see this 'violation,' and I wrangled the inspector's name."

"What's his name?" I ask.

"Demoraux," Iris says, showing me the ticket.

I'll google the guy later to find his contact information.

"Dad asked his friend who runs the Chubby Cat down the street, and he *did* have a violation, so he agreed to let her perform," Iris says. "He gave her Sunday at five, so good luck to anyone showing up at that time. She goes by only one name: Ophelia."

"Ophelia?" I google her name and do more digging as the conversation flows around me. It's easy enough to figure out her full name: Ophelia Galliano—the daughter of Deputy Commissioner Galliano. Wow. This is almost too easy. His daughter wants to be a rock star. And it turns out Galliano is in charge of the Eleanor Roosevelt playground celebration—an event where Nick plans to perform. As his date, I'll have access to them at the celebration. And if Nick really wants to be Batboy to my Batman, he can meet Ophelia and offer to give her advice on her career—and possibly figure out if her father is clearing violations for her benefit.

Fake dating might help my investigation. It's only going to be three months, so it's not like my dating "Nick Devlin" at this point in both our careers could make people think less of me as an investigative reporter.

And the relationship was going to be governed by a contract—no emotions.

And the contract was confidential.

And I'd be "dating" Nick. I take a deep breath and put away my phone.

Who can define what dating is? We will be going out on dates, and we are friends.

"Are you done researching her?" Iris asks.

"Sorry. It was too hard to pass up," I say.

"Understood," Iris says. She works in cyber-security and understands the thrill of an investigation.

"Did you move all your stuff into Sebastian's place?" Bella asks Iris. Sebastian is Iris's fiancé.

Iris nods.

"And here I was, hoping you'd be my roommate," Bella says to Iris. "Lily is almost always over at Rupert's." Lily, a librarian, is another friend of ours, who is not here tonight because she's out with Rupert at some city function. As a real estate developer, he has quite a busy social calendar. But he only wants to attend events if Lily accompanies him.

"I'm sorry," Iris says.

"You're *so* not sorry," Bella says.

"You're right." Iris smiles, a contented cat smile. "I'm so happy. He is so sweet. He makes me breakfast in the morning, and we laugh so much together. So far, moving in together has worked well."

"Are you sure you don't want to move in with me?" Bella asks me.

"I thought you were moving in with your grandma," Iris says.

"I don't know. She likes living by herself," Bella says. "So, if Nick continues to keep you up at night..."

"About that..."

The waiter brings us our dinner as the band starts playing in the back of the bar. Outside it's dark and cold, but the sparkly tea lights draped above us give a cheerful glow.

Most customers shift to the back to listen to the band, so it's only a handful of people eating a late dinner up front.

This is perfect. Bella writes romances, so she knows all about fake dating, and whatever authors think should be included in the contract terms. Iris, though, is not going to be happy about this. It's not that she dislikes Nick himself, but because her rocker ex-boyfriend cheated on her, she *definitely* does not recommend dating a lead singer.

"Did Nick agree to be your date for the press panel?" Iris asks.

"Nick asked me to be his fake girlfriend for three months to squash the media reports of his dating that scammer woman," I say.

Bella's eyes widen, and both she and Iris look surprised, their mouths slightly agape. I take a bite of my fish and chips, smirking. It's not often my friends are stunned into silence.

"You didn't agree, did you?" Iris asks, as expected.

"She should totally agree," Bella says. "You agreed, right? You're like his knight in shining armor coming to rescue him. And fake dating will be perfect—all that time spent together..."

"She might get hurt," Iris says. "What if she falls for him, with all the close proximity?"

"What if Nick falls for her with all that close proximity?" Bella asks.

"Guys," I say. "What if nobody falls for anyone and it's purely a business relationship? That's the goal. What do you recommend putting in the contract?"

"The skinship terms. What do you feel comfortable with physically?" Bella asks.

"Holding hands," I say.

"No. I mean, maybe you need a code word before you kiss and a code word you say back so that you give your approval to proceed," Bella says.

"I can't kiss him," I say. That would be so embarrassing.

"Why?" Iris asks. "Because you like him and you're afraid you'll reveal it? See?" Iris gestures towards Bella and folds her arms. I've tried to reassure Iris so many times that I know I can't date Nick and I'm not going to let myself get hurt.

"She shouldn't date a rock star," Iris says.

I feel the blush rising up my cheeks. "No. I mean, you guys know...what Matt said."

"You can't believe him. He was mad that you had to cover a story instead of going to his work event."

I shake my head. "It seems too oddly specific to be just anger. Kissing me was like 'kissing a dead fish.' And that I was so stiff. I don't want Nick to know I'm a terrible kisser. That's mortifying. What if he writes a song about having to kiss frogs?"

"There's no way a rock star will write a song about kissing frogs," Iris says. "His fans might get insulted."

"Stop referring to Nick as a 'rock star.' He's *not* like your cheating ex," Bella says to Iris. "And they've been friends for two years, and he's done lots of nice things for Maddie, like playing at the Oasis Garden for community events and getting her food when she sprained her ankle."

"That's two nice things versus playing until midnight," Iris says.

"Okay, guys. Seriously, Iris, don't worry. I know not to fall in love with Nick," I say. "If we were going to date, it would have happened already. We're friends. And for that reason, I don't want to kiss."

"First of all, I'm sure you're not a terrible kisser," Bella says. "And obviously, if you're clear that this is all business and you don't feel anything for him, he can't expect the kiss to be good."

Does Bella think I'm an awful kisser?

"I'm also sure you're not a terrible kisser," Iris says. "You froze that one time because Nick came home and you were worried he could hear you guys through the wall. I mean, that's going to put a damper on anyone—if you suddenly think your pain-in-the-butt next-door neighbor is going to tease you about making out."

"But what if you have to kiss?" Bella asks.

"Why would they *have* to kiss?" Iris asks.

"Believe me, when I'm writing a rock star hero with a fake-dating storyline, I can come up with a million reasons why suddenly they *must* kiss," Bella says.

"Maybe I shouldn't agree to this," I say.

Bella quickly shakes her head. "But that's fiction. And this is the real world. I still think you should date him. Maybe you will want to kiss him, eventually."

Iris puts down her utensils and turns to Bella. "You want them to get together?"

"You could start with the no-kissing rule," Bella says, "and let him suggest that kissing might be required, and then you can make clear that you find that a burden, so he already knows that you're not thinking he's doing you any favors by kissing you."

"That's good," I say.

"Surprise," someone says behind us.

All three of us turn and see that it's Lily and Rupert, looking dashing in formal wear. We all exchange hugs.

"We were in the neighborhood," Lily says. "I was hoping we'd still catch you here, especially because I found this book that the library had put on the discard cart." Lily is a librarian at the St. Agnes Library on the Upper West Side. "It's about the establishment of the initial Infrastructure Department. You should ask the deputy commissioners to sign it when you interview them. It would be a great souvenir of your article."

"And she hates to see a book in the discard bin," Rupert says.

"Just because it hasn't been checked out in five years," Lily says. "I want it to find a good home."

Rupert leaves to buy us all a round of drinks as Lily squeezes in next to Bella.

"What are we discussing?" Lily asks.

"Whether Maddie should date Nick," Bella says.

"I vote yes," Lily says. "I'm still grateful to him for playing at the Oasis Community Garden benefit last spring."

"I'm outvoted," Iris says with a sigh. Then she stills. "But Maddie, you can't look at the comments on social media posts. No matter what, there will be fans who *hate* you. That fan will think that she should be the one dating Nick. I had to deal with that whenever a photo of me with the band was posted. They can tear you apart. Will you be okay with that?"

"I don't know," I say honestly. "I am worried about that. It's hard to resist looking at the comments. I'll have to take a page from Riley's playbook." In my article last year about Riley, who'd created a national campaign to stop bullying, she'd explained how she took a break from social media and changed all her settings to private.

"I couldn't help looking at the comments either, but eventually I had to stop," Iris says. "But if Nick actually makes it, it will be even worse than anything I experienced."

"Remember, we'll break up before he becomes a big deal," I say.

"If you're doing this—which I don't recommend, but okay—make sure he has to be your date for that press panel," Iris says. "And it should be reported that you broke it off, not him."

"He's never going to agree to that," I say.

"He might," Iris says. "Then he can write lots of songs about being brokenhearted and betrayed."

"Great," I say sarcastically.

Chapter Eight

Nick

The mood in my apartment is the definition of glum. It's like a blanket of hot air has weighed down everyone in the room. The hiss of steam piping in from the corner radiator is the only thing that fills the silence.

Amira is sitting at my small dining table with her laptop, trying to rustle up some positive PR, but mostly she's staring at her phone as if willing it to ring.

José alternates between restlessly tapping out some rhythm on the table and texting with his wife, because every once in a while, his mouth tilts up in a smile. Both reviewed all their phone contacts for suggestions of anyone else I could date, but I couldn't see myself dating the women they suggested—even if just fake dating.

No response from Maddie. Really?

I shake my head and focus on the last line of lyrics I wrote:

I thought you were my friend...

That's so not original. I cross it out.

Even José thought this proposal was going to work. At least he's not rubbing my "She's going to *love* this contract" in my face.

Meanwhile, MusEn seems to have disappeared off the face of the earth. So much for "we want to wrap this up quickly."

"I cover the story. I'm not the story." That seems to be her main objection.

But José and Amira are taking this much more seriously now that MusEn is doing a vanishing act.

"Amira, you must have some idea of how he can persuade Maddie to date him—as a woman," José says.

"Because all women are the same," Amira says sarcastically. "What does she like?"

"What she wants is a breakthrough in her investigation, but I don't know how I can help with that. I have all her usual favorite things here. Gourmet cat food for Sherlock, new pens, a new notebook, and dumplings. Plus, peanut M&M's for those nights when she doesn't have time to eat."

"That's really good," Amira says. "I'm impressed."

"Still, I thought she'd do this as a friend," I say.

My phone rings. It's Maddie. I pick up.

"Okay," she says. "But I have some additional terms I want in the contract."

I punch the air. "Yes!"

"I'm coming upstairs now," she says.

"She said yes, and she's coming home now. You guys should go," I say.

"There's only one way out," José says. "We'll have to pass her."

"That's good. It's not only Nick's career at stake," Amira says. "What should we plan for your couple debut?"

"That's too soon. Let Maddie call the shots," I say.

Amira and José grab their stuff.

"Don't say anything about our couple debut," I say to them. "You might make her change her mind."

They rush out the door as I stand there waiting in the doorway with my bag of gifts and the dumplings.

I hear them saying "thank you" to Maddie on the stairs and Maddie demurring that it's fine.

It's more than *fine*. It's a huge frickin' deal.

Maddie comes into view, and I want to hug her. The rush of emotion I feel is insane. It's relief, right?

She smiles at me, and it's her usual open smile that makes me relax when I see it.

"Thanks again." I hand her all my gifts. "I bought these to help persuade you."

"Dumplings? Yummy." She looks inside the other bag of gifts. Her eyes light up as she views its contents. "It's scary how well you know me. But you might not thank me when you hear my terms." She puts the two bags behind her back. "But you can't have these back."

"I've already conceded that I'll do what you want."

She passes by me to unlock her door, and I smell the fresh peony scent of her hair. That fragrance is now the title of one of my songs.

She clears the table of papers and her laptop as Sherlock winds around my legs.

"I'll give Sherlock this gourmet food," I say, opening the can.

"You've corrupted my cat," she says as she re-heats the dumplings.

"Desperate times call for desperate measures," I say over my shoulder as I reach for some plates. Maddie has bright, colorful plates Our apartments have a similar layout, so I know my way around her apartment like I know my own—except that mine is filled with guitars and other instruments and has a separate bedroom. And my plates are chipped relics from my childhood that my mom gave me when she moved upstate.

"Hit me with your terms, Maddie Hughes."

Maddie smiles slightly. She's toying with me. "And let these dumplings go to waste when they should be eaten hot?"

We sit down at the table as Maddie sets the steaming dumplings in the middle. She helps herself first as I distribute the drinks.

I'm in the middle of chewing when she says, "No kissing."

I nearly choke. *What?*

"No kissing?" I ask.

She nods.

I blink. "But what if it's absolutely necessary?"

"Why would it be absolutely necessary?"

"I don't know. But the fact that you're making this a provision means you could see a situation where it might happen." I pull my chair closer to hers. "Why don't you want to kiss me?"

A flush appears on her cheeks. I lean in closer.

"I promise you, I'm a good kisser," I say.

"How do you know?" she asks, looking earnestly at me.

Is this an actual question? Am I getting reporter Maddie about to grill me about how I'm a good kisser? Does she think I'm not a *good kisser*?

"Because I've never had anyone suggest we stop."

She seems to consider this evidence deeply, staring off into the corner.

I add, "And when I'm kissing a woman, she grabs my shirt or—"

"I get it. Have you kissed anyone in the past two years?" she asks. "Maybe you're rusty."

Rusty? No way.

"Are you worried I'm rusty?" This is getting more and more nuts. "I promise you, I'm not rusty. It's like riding a bike. It's not something you forget. But if you find me rusty, I'm willing to practice with you until I get better." I grin.

Maddie's blush deepens. "I just said 'no kissing,' and now you're suggesting we practice it. Do you *want* to kiss me?"

I take in her big brown eyes asking me this and her very pink lips. Sometimes, I would definitely like to kiss Maddie. Especially at times like now. "I have no objection. And practice makes perfect. If you really want no kissing, of course, I won't kiss you. But what if it's some situation where everyone is tapping glasses or something and people will think we're not dating? Can't we have an emergency clause that allows it?"

"Okay. But then we need a code word, and we both need to say it before any kiss happens."

Now, I *really* want to kiss her.

"Great. What's a good code word?" I ask. "Pucker up?"

She laughs.

"Yeah, that doesn't seem like a good one if it's going to make you laugh," I say. "How about *Thank you*? Because honestly, thank you."

She hides a smile. "That sounds good. I will add that."

She drafts the next clause:

Clause 11. There will be absolutely no kissing or physical contact other than hand-holding, with the sole exception that if there is a situation where one person believes that if we don't kiss, we will be perceived as not dating, that person may say "Thank you"—

"But we might say thank you in another context, so maybe 'thanks much' is better," I say.

She revises the clause:

—that person may say "Thanks much," and if the other person agrees, he or she will also say "thanks much," and then the parties may kiss.

"Do we need to put our code word in this contract?" I ask. "Let's write 'on terms discussed.'"

Maddie nods and types the change:

Clause 11. There will be absolutely no kissing or physical contact other than for hand-holding, except on terms discussed and agreed to.

If Maddie and I do ever kiss, the code words I want her to say are: *Please don't stop.*

"But that's not all of it. I have two more conditions."

If "no kisses" was the first condition, I dread hearing the next.

"You have to help me with my investigation." She explains what she learned through Iris.

"Happy to," I say.

"Also, you have to be my date to this press career panel I'm doing at my middle school," she says.

"You need a date for that?" I ask.

"Yes. Some of the girls I went to school with bullied me—they'd make fun of anyone who sat with me for lunch. They were very creative. Every day it was some fresh hassle. One time, one of them sat behind me and unzipped my schoolbag, so my belongings fell out when I picked it up to pack up after class. You know, things like that. But this panel is a good career opportunity for me. And they might not even be there, even though alumni are invited."

I hope they show up so I can show that Maddie is worth a million of them.

"If they are there, it'd be nice to show up with you as my boyfriend," Maddie says.

"Are you complimenting me, Maddie?"

"Don't let it go to your head," she says. "In fact, when we break up, I should be the one to break up with you."

"That's harsh," I say. "How can you already be thinking about ending our relationship?"

"I already overheard Nemesis saying there's no way you'd date me, so I don't want her to be proved right when you dump me."

"Nemesis—the one who stole your story after you twisted your ankle?" Poor Maddie. She was grumbling about this woman, Sarah or her "Nemesis," when she was laid up last year with a sprained ankle and I brought her food. Who are all these people attacking her? I thought I had it rough. But now I'd like to give Nemesis a piece of my mind.

"Yeah."

"Of course you can be the one to break up. Why would anyone really want to date a musician? We travel all the time, and we work nights. Strangers pretend to be our girlfriends. You'd have to be really sure of your relationship. Iris can give you a million reasons why you'd break up with me."

She winces. I'm sure Iris is dead set against this fake-dating plan. That was a nasty break-up last year. I know her ex-boyfriend and his band from playing the same clubs. I know Iris, though not well, from playing at Craic and Laughs, her dad's bar. Her ex is now banned from performing at Craic and Laughs, and I don't blame Iris's dad.

Not that I'm anything like Iris's ex. I would never cheat on someone. Not when that's one of the reasons my mom left my dad. That, and the fact that he wasn't interested in being part of a family. My mom pretended she no longer cared about my dad, but I saw the way she'd sometimes check out who he was dating online.

"Is that why you haven't been dating for the past two years?" Maddie asks.

"That's the main reason. I can't promise any stability. Why would I do that to someone I cared about?"

"Mom, why isn't my dad here?"

"Because he's a musician, Nick. He has to travel to play gigs to make money. We have our own apartment, I have my job, and you have friends at school. Living in hotels or on a tour bus is not a life for you and me."

I'd definitely learned that lesson at a young age. Suddenly the dumpling I'm chewing doesn't have any taste.

She didn't say—*and he doesn't want us*. I learned that lesson later.

"Because we're both writers, we should agree that we will try to be nice to each other when if we break up."

"Agreed," I say.

Maddie bites her nail. "I'm not sure we need to add these last clauses to the contract. I trust you."

"Anything else?" I ask.

"The confidentiality clause," she says. "I already told Iris, Bella, and Lily, and your bandmates know, so we should exclude them. And I will have to tell Jing and my family as well."

"And my friends Luca and Tristan know as well."

"Oh, and you need to make sure I'm seated next to the deputy commissioners at your Parks Department concert," she says.

"How am I going to do that? Like I have control over seating."

"I'm sure you can insist on your girlfriend sitting with the rest of the dignitaries. I read somewhere that some band has a whole list of requirements, including that they get M&M's—but no green ones."

"You would remember that detail about M&M's. And they do that for safety reasons. Because if there are green M&M's, then maybe something else on the safety checklist was also missed." I lean forward. "Should I insist that all my concerts provide M&M's backstage for you?"

Maddie's eyes widen, her gaze briefly drops to my lips, and she pulls back to put some distance between us. Hmm. She's *not* immune to me.

"I'll do my best to get you seated there," I say. "Do you want to add that to the contract?"

She shakes her head. "No, I trust you."

I am oddly touched that she does, so much so that she said it twice.

"Let's also remove fake from the first line," she says. "I don't want to be involved in anything fake. This is a dating contract."

"Agreed."

She prints out two copies, and we each sign them. I photograph the final copies. It feels oddly formal, especially when she places the original in a folder in her desk drawer.

"My spare key." She hands me a key.

I look at it, confused.

"For when you're cleaning Sherlock's litter tray, remember? Every day."

"Right."

"A huge contract benefit," Maddie says.

Great. Scooping the litter is the winning contract clause. Not dates with me.

I disappear into my apartment and return with my spare key, which I hand to Maddie. "You can also have my spare key. In case I ever get locked out, I can knock on your door."

Our hands briefly touch, and we both pull back as if shocked.

"What's our backstory of how we came to be a couple?" Maddie asks. "People tend to ask that question."

"We met as neighbors. We were friends at first, and then we started dating about two months ago, but we didn't want to be public about it to preserve our privacy."

"But how?" Maddie asks.

"How would you like it to happen?" I ask.

"I'm not a romance writer. I should've asked Bella," Maddie says. "Let's say we were watching a movie late at night, and then I snuggled into you, and you kissed me."

That's so *wholesome*. Maddie and I have never watched a movie together. And the times when I've hooked up with someone in the past—before Christina's tell-all—usually started in a bar, after a night of performing and then drinking in celebration.

I glance at Maddie. She's nibbling her lip as Sherlock purrs in her lap.

Maddie is direct and can be so practical that I've always thought she was jaded about love and romance...

"Let me text Bella," Maddie says.

"Okay, but it has to be realistic," I say. I read one of Bella's books after Maddie forced me to come to Bella's book signing to make sure there were lots of people in the audience. (There were. I'd been impressed.) The romantic hero was perfect (or flawed only in the best ways) and definitely a man written by a woman.

"She says that it has to be that you sang me a song on the fire escape to tell me your feelings."

"That works," I say. "We can use 'Together Forever.'"

Our walls are so thin that I would have heard if she'd brought someone home. Why isn't she dating someone? I have my reasons for staying single. What are hers?

Chapter Nine

Maddie

Nick holds my hand as we are escorted into the MusEn conference room to meet Ashley, the MusEn producer, and convince her that we're dating. My stomach is doing somersaults. *What if she doesn't believe us?*

"This is Maddie Hughes," he says, and it feels like he says that with pride. "The woman I'm dating. My next-door neighbor. As I said over the phone."

"He's not dating the other woman," I say.

Ashley narrows her eyes and tilts her head. "She's definitely more in line with the band's image."

What does that mean?

Ashley says, "Down to earth, open, honest, and vulnerable. I definitely like the *girl next door* vibe."

That wasn't the image I'd thought I conveyed. I'd even dressed up for this meeting with a pants suit. But compared to YouTube woman, I'm definitely down to earth.

"How did you start dating?"

We share the story we prepared, and Nick seems to really enjoy embellishing it with tiny details from our real interactions. I can't stop staring at him. He also explains how I used to complain about his playing late at night and so he'd dedicated a song to me. He ends with, "Maybe that was the start of my feelings."

She snaps her finger. "This is great. We'll run with this. You'll need to go out tonight, and I'll arrange for some photographers to capture it."

"Do we need to identify Maddie?" Nick asks. "She's a reporter, so she'd prefer not to be the story. It's one of the reasons why we kept our relationship secret."

"I doubt her name will remain secret, but we will try running with she's not a celebrity, so please respect her privacy. That might be good. It might add a little mystery. And it will be a great contrast to this 'Cara.' It will show Maddie is not using you for added publicity."

Now we're having our first "date." Although we discussed going to my favorite dumpling place around the corner from our apartments, Nick pointed out that we probably want to keep that place secret for us. I hadn't thought of that. I am getting a new perspective on what it's like to be a public person, and it's not pretty. Ashley chose an already popular place that we wouldn't normally visit.

We're eating at a sophisticated restaurant in midtown with dim lighting and a brown and beige décor theme. It feels like we should whisper when we converse and that any loud laughter would be frowned upon. This is *so* not my life.

So far, there's been no sign of any reporters or photographers. The meal is delicious. I ordered yellowtail snapper in a curry sauce with black rice. Nick had one bite of my dish and said we have to come back so he can order that next time.

"Do I get to ask my burning questions about you?" I ask.

"Only if I get to ask mine," he says.

As if he has burning questions about me.

I agree.

"Why did you choose that photo of the bar Pickles as your first album cover?" I ask.

Nick tilts his head. It's clearly not the question he expected, but I've learned that these types of indirect questions can sometimes tease out more of a story from someone who definitely has walls, as Nick does—and for good reason. He clearly wants to keep part of his life private.

"Do you remember that bar, Pickles?" Nick asks.

"Barely," I say. "But Iris immediately recognized it when she saw your cover. She said her dad wanted to model his bar Craic and Laughs on it because it had such a wonderful atmosphere—a feeling of good times and lively conversation—and so many amazing musicians played there."

"Exactly. In high school, I used to hang out around there to hear the musicians, and the owner, Joey, took pity on me and invited me to watch the dry run sessions. I learned so much. I was also lucky that I was already 6'2" by 9th grade, so I looked less like a kid. I felt like it was my home away from home. And Joey..." He pauses and seems to swallow. "He was a good man. A good role model."

The waiter refills our water glasses.

"My turn," Nick says. "Why are you single?"

"Dating in New York is not exactly easy," I say, surprised by his question and flattered that he seems to think I should have my pick of boyfriends. "I'm focused on my career right now because I really want this promotion. It's hard to schedule dates when I might get a call to cover a story or I'm spending most evenings trailing infrastructure deputy commissioners."

"How's that going?" he asks.

"Nothing so far. Ward and Pommer both usually go straight home. Pommer sometimes picks up his young kids from school first and takes them to a playground in the park. Ward sometimes stops at a library on the way home, so he must like to read," I say. "Gallant Galliano often goes out to dinner with his wife or to community affairs events around the city."

I need some sort of break in this case.

"Galliano has the most complaints in his neighborhood for repairs that don't work, but Beatrice threatened Dulce enough not to report anything, so Dulce didn't report the repair issue, so that could also be a sign that he's not the one taking bribes, because he actually has complaints. In the districts where tenants, like Dulce, are being threatened not to report any problems, then the numbers will be lower."

"Can you break the data out by who has the most repeat complaints?" Nick asks. "Because Tasha's situation is where it wasn't fixed properly the first time."

"Good idea. I'll try crunching the data that way," I say.

We finish our dinner, and Nick pays the bill. He opens the door for me, and I step out into the cold night air, Nick following. I pull on my mittens.

Nick tucks my hair behind my ear as I look up at him. *I wish this was real.* "Do you want to walk home? Didn't you bring a hat?" he asks. "It's crisp out tonight."

The way Nick is looking at me... His eyes have this tender look to them that makes me feel like I'm being warmed by a bright sun. I don't feel cold.

How does he do that? How can he fake it so well? Am I looking like that at him?

Flashes blind me. Nick pushes me behind him.

"Is this the one?" yells a reporter.

"Are you dating?" yells another reporter.

"She's a private person, so please respect her privacy," Nick says.

"Pull up your hood, zip up your jacket, and cover your face with a scarf," Nick whispers to me as he uses his body to shield me from view.

I do that and then peer out from the depths of my hood. It's going to look like he's dating a stuffed coat jacket, but I appreciate the effort he's making. From my viewpoint, I make out a small group of people—half reporters and half photographers.

"Will you give us an interview if we promise not to use her name?" another one asks.

"I'm happy to answer your questions, but please leave my friend out of it," Nick says.

"Friend or girlfriend?" a new female voice asks.

Nick stiffens next to me. "Christina."

His ex. Great. I'm looking like Big Foot, and his ex is interviewing him. I can't really see her because of the flashes going off. My eyes are still adjusting.

"It's business," she says. "My boss obviously assigned me because I have some expertise on the subject matter."

"Here I thought that would be called a conflict of interest," Nick says.

"Nick, you've expressed in some prior interviews that you're not interested in dating right now," another reporter says. "What's special about your 'friend'?"

We should have practiced more. *What on earth is he going to say?*

"I realized that I looked forward to catching up with her after a long day, and I missed chatting with her when she was traveling, so there was that," Nick says.

Aww. That's sweet. *If so not true.* He was always asking me when I was traveling, so he could practice late. Our conversations when I was home often consisted of: "Nick, I'm going to bed now, so you need to be quiet."

"She's fun, but also level-headed, and she has her own career, so she is definitely not dating me because I'm a musician," he adds.

"Or so you think," Christina says.

Nick takes a step forward. "Don't engage," I whisper and wrap my arms around him, burying my face in his back. He stands still.

"That's why you kept your relationship private initially," the other journalist who has spoken already says.

At least this guy is offering a softball interview.

"Exactly," Nick answers.

"Most women would want to make any relationship with Nick Devlin public. Why didn't you?" another reporter asks.

"I said I'd answer questions," Nick says. "Not her."

"But your label went public with the fact that you're not dating the YouTube star because you're involved with someone else."

"Yes," Nick says. "I'm not dating that woman. I had never even met her before that night."

"Did you both agree that it should be public?" asks another reporter.

That's a question that can be twisted if I don't answer. They can write that Nick answered yes, while his date was silent. At least the flashes have stopped going off.

"Yes," I say, still from behind Nick's back.

I feel Nick nod in agreement.

What are *they going to think at The Intelligencer?*

I add, "Of course, once this other woman claimed to be his girl-friend, I wanted to set the record straight that Nick was not dating her."

"And I really appreciated that she was willing to say that publicly, but we're also hoping that once we set the record straight, we can have our privacy back," Nick says. "I don't want this to hurt her career. I'm sure she'd prefer to be in your seat rather than here." Nick places his hands over my mittened ones. My bright-red mittens that Iris knitted for me. What if they become some weird meme?

"I'm sure she's quite happy being with you or, as the case may be, giving you a back hug." Christina sticks her recorder in my face. "Here's an easy question for your 'friend.' I'm sure many women envy you as his girlfriend, but what specifically attracted you to him?"

Does Christina regret giving him up? Did that article give her the break she wanted? How could she hurt him like that? It makes me want to defend him, in my own way.

I release Nick's back and take my place next to him, on the other side, away from Christina. Nick turns to me and, very earnestly, putting his hand up to shield his mouth from view, whispers, "You don't have to do this."

I nod and face the reporters but keep my hood and scarf up, which means I'm practically yelling to make my voice heard.

"He's a good guy," I say. "I like that he's open and honest about his feelings."

"But Maddie, I'm in the groove. Can't you put your earplugs in? This could be my next hit."

I don't dare look at Nick because I'm afraid he'll look skeptical.

"He's good at communication—maybe because he's a songwriter."

Christina makes a scoffing noise out loud. She did refer to him as a "fortress."

"He's also very supportive of my career," I say. "He's made so many sacrifices to support me."

Nick makes a choked noise next to me.

Another female reporter looks like she's about to ask me to detail his sacrifices. Also, as much as teasing Nick is fun, he *has* been considerate *at times*.

"He's really sweet, but you can probably tell that from his lyrics. I sprained my ankle about a month ago, and Nick bought me groceries and made sure I stayed off it," I say. "And honestly, how could I say no?" That is the crux of the matter. Nick has worked so hard for this opportunity, and our fake dating makes sense as the solution. It is only three months—and then we'll return to being friends, and the contract will remain a secret between us.

"You sound like a changed man," Christina says to Nick.

"I learned from my mistakes," Nick says.

"Seriously." The other female reporter gazes dreamy eyed at Nick. "So can we ask if 'Fevered Dreams' is about Maddie?"

Nick starts.

Poor Nick. "Fevered Dreams" is about liking the girl next door—*the girl next door*? I turn to look at his face.

"You wrote that about two months ago, right before you guys got together, right? Did that song give you the courage to tell Maddie you liked her?"

"Yes," Nick says.

What? My eyes widen. But it does fit so well into the narrative.

"You didn't realize that?" the interviewer asks me.

I should have stayed hidden behind him.

"I didn't," I say.

"It was supposed to be a secret that I fell first." Nick pantomimes looking crushed. "But she knows 'Peony' is about her. I've told her never to change her shampoo because I love that scent." He squeezes my hand again.

I stare at him. *No, I did not know that.* Is he making this all up? The cameras flash again. Not that they can really see my face since it's still covered by my parka hood. But I guess they've now caught the stuffed coat looking at him.

I turn back to face the reporters and catch that one confirming with the photographer that he captured that shot.

"And 'Together Forever' is the song I sang to tell her I liked her," Nick says.

Okay. Finally, the story we agreed upon: Nick sang "Together Forever" to tell me of his feelings—on the fire escape as we were sitting out there one night chatting.

She asks some questions about that, and then Nick says we have to go, as he hails a free cab. He shields me again as I climb into the taxi. He gives the address of the 24-hour deli on Allen Street that has the back entrance into our apartment building on Orchard Street. The deli is also owned by our landlord, and its supply room has a back door that leads into the laundry room of the apartment building, which has an entrance on Orchard Street. Only the tenants have a key. The laundry room used to be a speakeasy bar with several exits and entrances in case it was raided. To enter the basement laundry room while in our building, one pulls a book out of a bookcase that covers the back of the foyer entrance, and the bookcase door swings open, but it can be bolted from inside the laundry room. Our landlord loves showing it off to tenants once they've signed a rental contract.

"We can lose them in there if they follow us," he says.

I pull down my hood and unwrap my scarf.

He texts Amira to let her know that the press did show up and we gave an interview, but they definitely took photos of us at the beginning before we were aware of them.

I hate photos of myself. I have a much more positive image of myself in my head, and that always gets destroyed when I see myself in a close-up—bags under my eyes, freckles spotting my nose, mascara clumped, and of course, I forget to hold in my tummy. Not that I need to remember when I'm wearing an oversized parka.

Still, it's only worse knowing that trolls will tear me apart online. I feel like throwing up at the thought.

Nick pulls me close in the cab and looks into my eyes. "Are you okay? That wasn't so bad, right?"

"No, but really, 'Peony' and 'Fevered Dreams' are about me?"

"'Peony' is about you. Doesn't your shampoo smell of peony? I like it."

Shocked, I touch my hair.

He winks, and I can't help but smile back. Then he raises one eyebrow, doing his mock imitation of a dashing duke from when he caught me reading a regency romance on the fire escape last summer.

"Are you trying to make me laugh?" I ask.

"Yes. I love your laugh, and you look especially pretty when you smile," he says.

Those words hang between us. The air feels weighted and like we're in our own bubble. He flushes and looks away. He looks like he didn't mean to say that out loud, and I wonder if he meant them for real.

Because I think he did.

Nick *loves* my laugh and thinks I'm pretty. My smile widens, and I feel like I've been lit from within—like I'm one of those lava lamps that is now glowing with bubbles of happiness floating through me.

The cab makes a jerky turn around a corner.

Nick turns his head to look out the back window of our cab. "Are we being followed? I wouldn't put it past Christina."

I look out too, but I can't tell. It's a bunch of cars, taxis, and black sedans, but nothing identified as a news van.

"Did it bother you to see Christina?" I ask Nick.

"Definitely not," he says easily and chuckles. "She must hate having to cover me. It's not that she wants to cover hard-hitting news like you, but she definitely doesn't want to write a story on an up-and-coming rock star, even if that was her original angle. She wants to be on the red carpet."

Did Nick find that attractive?

That cold water reality of Christine and how much we differ returns me to my mantra: Don't fall for Nick.

This is fun and flirty, and I am so, *so* tempted to give in to these feelings. But Nick is not for me. I'm not going to be seen as a hard-hitting reporter if I'm the known girlfriend of the lead singer of Orchard Folly, especially if Nick makes it big. But that might also be a benefit because they might discount me and give me more information. *No.* They probably won't take me seriously and give me an interview to begin with. This is just for three months to help each other out, and then we'll remain friends and go our separate ways. My shoulders slump. That thought is not cheering me up. How could Christina give up Nick for an article she had the choice to write? They were actually dating. Nick was her boyfriend. If he was my boyfriend— No, we're just friends. *Stick to the facts, Maddie. You're a journalist. Not a fiction writer.*

Chapter Ten

Nick

I lean back against the wall of the dance studio. A full-length mirror on the front wall reflects my loose-fitting shirt and pants back at me. When Maddie hugged me from behind when I almost told Christina off…it felt like such a boost of support. When Maddie looked up at me yesterday in the cab after I told her she was pretty when she laughed… I wanted to kiss her. I take another swig of water from my water bottle to cool down.

Especially now that I know she's not interested in dating anyone else. No lost love is waiting in the wings.

This is not good. I need to keep feelings out of this. This is a business deal. I can't date anyone. Maddie is someone who wants a family and deserves a partner who is there for her full-time, not someone who is traveling and "married to his music," as Christina so aptly put it.

I can't believe Christina had to cover my new relationship. But I realized last night that I was over her completely. I like Maddie so much more, even as just a friend, than I ever liked Christina. Christina was attractive at first, and she was driven like me, but she doesn't have that moral core that Maddie has. I never felt I could fully trust her because of the way she talked about getting stories and how she'd do anything. And I was right in the end.

The photos of Maddie and me in the news articles look like I want to kiss her. Most of them are titled some variation of "Nick's New Love", and the reception is about as good as it can be. Sure, a few disgruntled fans question what I see in Maddie, but the majority of the comments are about how happy we both look. "Cara" is quiet. But that only makes me nervous. Is she gone now for good, or is she planning some new approach? She increased her follower count, and I'm hoping she'll now move on to a new story. That would be too easy, right?

I was being honest in the interview when I said Maddie makes me laugh. Even now, my lips curl up. Maddie mocked me during that interview. I "support her career"—when she's been yelling at me for a year that she can't function on limited sleep—and I'm "so emotionally open." That's the first time a "girlfriend" has said that. Most of the time, any woman I date gets frustrated: *You're holding back, Nick.*

Yes, I hold back. Because my relationships aren't meant to last long term. And we both agree to that up front. I've always been honest before starting a relationship. I always say that if I ever make it, I'll have to travel and be on the road for months, and that's not a life for a family. But the fact that I say "family" seems to make any woman I date think I'm considering having a family, and then they don't hear the rest.

It's why I stopped dating. That, and Christina's lovely tell-all article about me. I'm surprised one of the reporters didn't quote her line in the article that "he literally gets up in the middle of the night and starts scribbling on scraps of paper" and ask Maddie if I still do that. Maddie could have definitely added her own stories about how I write at all hours of the night—whenever the muse hits. Dating a wannabe rock star is not all roses.

I finish gulping down my water. MusEn wants two choreographed dance routines, and they're providing two backup dancers to perform with me while a backtrack plays. I'm in the studio with the choreographer and my dance captain learning the steps. It's like learning another language. They finish conferring about what to do next and ask me if I'm ready to go again. I nod. It's cool to see how the choreographer has interpreted my lyrics and the musical score into physical movements. At first, she clearly thought I was hopeless, but she was kind enough to say, "Fake it till you make it." But now I've memorized the first half, and a bit of respect has formed in her eyes.

I will do anything for this break—almost. I haven't worked this long to mess up now. If they want me to dance, I will dance.

She presses play, and the song starts up again. I tap my foot to the beat, already bouncing with my knees. And we're off.

Knee up, scoop, two-step, *pas de bourrée* (which I initially pronounced as parbolle), slide...

We're in sync. It's amazing. I grin at her in the mirror, and she gives a thumbs-up.

I mess up again in the second half, going left when I should have gone right.

"You'll get it," she says. "You still look like you're concentrating too hard in the first half, but we'll practice it enough that you'll feel more comfortable."

She shows me the steps again.

"Remember, in this part, you're singing that she's turned away, so you hunch your shoulders, you feel rejected. But then you straighten up when you decide you're going after her. Right? Isn't that what the song says?"

I nod.

"Feel that emotion and put it into your body as well as your singing," she says.

Feel the emotion as if I were pursuing Maddie.

"It all makes sense. Like you said, I need to keep practicing." I'm used to putting all my emotion into my singing. Adding choreography is not easy. But I can't admit that. I have to believe her when she reassures me that it will become muscle memory. I should be able to put the emotion into my body as well as my voice.

"It's good you're in such good shape already," she says.

We spend the next half hour working on the second half, and I think I've got it.

"Yes!" She high-fives me. "This routine is going to drive your fans crazy."

"I have a girlfriend," I say. Who knows if this conversation will be reported anywhere?

"Your girlfriend is a lucky woman."

If only Maddie agreed.

"That's it for today," the choreographer says. "Keep at it tonight, and then we'll learn the next one in a few days."

As if I've got any more energy to practice at home tonight. I don't *feel* like I'm in good shape. Every muscle aches.

I rush out the studio door. I don't want to be late for my babysitting gig. Three times a week, I'm responsible for picking up ten-year-old Dylan from school. I teach him guitar for an hour and then supervise his homework or playdates until his mom comes home at five. It isn't a huge deal, especially since he lives in the same apartment building as Maddie and me. I don't charge much, but it makes me feel good to help a single mom out. I know how hard my own mom worked.

I make it to the schoolyard in time, and soon, Dylan is sitting at my table doing homework while I set up a security camera on the balcony. As much as I hope that the Cara-wannabe woman will move on, I don't trust her *not* to try to get access to our fire escape to photograph us in our apartments. Who knows what story she next wants to feature on her YouTube channel.

There. Done. I confirm the video stream is working and watch a pigeon poop. Lovely. We need to install a fake owl. And maybe some sort of noise deterrent.

My phone rings. It's Luca, one of my best friends. Perfect timing. He works in security.

"Are you and Maddie still coming over for takeout?" he asks. He lives in SoHo, about a mile away from us, so it's about a twenty-minute walk via Grand Street.

"We are," I say. "She should be home soon, and then we'll come over." I offered to pick up Maddie from work because of that one work rival, but Maddie seemed horrified at my suggestion. She wants to keep work and her "dating" life separate.

"Home soon. You guys are already basically living together," Luca says.

I snort. "Except that we're very much *not*."

I don't even have permission to *kiss* Maddie. And in the cab, when Maddie was looking up at me with those big brown eyes and her hair felt feathery soft, boy, did I want to taste her lips. I think I distracted her from clocking my feelings by asking if we were being followed.

The no-kissing clause seems to be driving my mind crazy. I don't think I felt desire this deeply before we signed that contract.

I shake my head. I've missed whatever Luca said, so I ask him to repeat it. And then I wish I hadn't because he suggests we date for real.

"Yeah, that's not happening," I say. Especially after Maddie's wholesome suggestion of how we got together. I change the topic by asking him my questions about setting up the camera. He confirms that it's done correctly.

A knock sounds at the door, and Dylan runs over. It's his mom, Stacy. She thanks me as Dylan tells her about how I let him play my electric guitar. His mom and I smile at each other over his head.

"Are you going on tour soon?" she asks.

"Yes. They're lining up the dates now," I say. "But I've found a replacement for you. You know the family who owns the bar down the street? One of his daughters says her co-worker is looking for work after her morning shift at the day care, so she could pick up Dylan and look after him until you come home from work. If you trust her when you meet her."

"That would work well," she says.

I hear Maddie's footsteps on the stairs, and then she comes into view on our landing.

"I'm glad you guys are dating," Stacy says. "I always thought there was something there. You two seem so well-matched."

Maddie's step falters for a second, but she recovers quickly. "How so?"

"You seem to communicate well," she says. "You're both invested in your careers. While that could be an obstacle, it could also work out for you."

Maddie, Luca, and I all help ourselves to dinner from the various takeout containers on the steel counter in Luca's kitchen. His apartment is an ode to functionality and minimalism. And fancy gadgets. The three of us take our full plates and sit at his round glass table on his "ghost" chairs. I don't know how he lives with translucent acrylic chairs. They're completely transparent. I'd probably end up killing myself if I lived here, because I'd search for a snack in the middle of the night or a piece of paper to scribble on and end up tripping over a chair and falling into the table. But to each his own.

"Aren't you going to show us your new routine?" Luca asks me.

"No," I say. "I don't need to embarrass myself in front of you guys tonight."

Luca casually slings his arm around Maddie. Maddie doesn't look like she minds. Apparently, Luca doesn't need to invoke clause eleven for physical contact. He *is* a good-looking guy.

"You mean, you don't want to embarrass yourself in front of Maddie?" Luca asks.

"That, too. I also need to rest up for tomorrow." I look at my notes on my phone. "And frankly, now that I look at what I scribbled down for the choreography: 'Arms/legs up, jump, side to side, turn and swing, swing,' my notes are not going to help me. I feel like I've missed the basic class and vaulted straight into expert experience."

"That's so cool that you're going to be doing choreographed dancing at your show," Maddie says. "I'm impressed."

That's something.

Luca gets up and brings what's left of the partially filled food containers to the table so we can help ourselves while seated.

"What's happening with your investigation?" I ask.

Maddie fills Luca in on her research to date, after swearing him to secrecy. Luca owns his own security company, so I convinced Maddie he could be a good resource. A bribery case might involve high stakes with desperate people. But I can't say that to Maddie. I don't want her to think I don't believe she can handle herself, even if it scares me to think of one of those guys coming after her if she gets too close to the truth.

"I found several other people who had shoddy repairs with a similar story to Tasha's friend by looking through the repeat repair request tickets filed with the Infrastructure Department, so there's a pattern. Also, I convinced my boss to allow me to do a *Meet the City Agencies* article series, both because it's helpful to know, but also as a way for me to interview the deputy commissioners, so I'm meeting with them tomorrow."

"She's on fire," I say. This story could be Maddie's big break.

"Tonight, I'm reviewing my repair tickets spreadsheet to see who else to follow up with," she says. "I was able to crunch the data as you suggested, and Pommer has the most repeat calls."

"If they're taking bribes and facing criminal charges if discovered, that could be dangerous," Luca says.

My gaze meets Luca's to convey my thanks. I'm worried about Maddie pursuing this story for that exact reason. But it would be a career-defining scoop.

"Shouldn't you guys move somewhere safer than your current apartments?" Luca asks.

Wait. We didn't discuss moving.

"What do you mean?" I ask.

"Stalker woman might be able to figure out your address. I'm not sure the security is up to par, even if you did install that camera, Nick. Now that you're taking off."

"You've never mentioned it before," I say.

"I'm worried about Maddie, not you," Luca says. "There's been an uptick in break-ins via fire escapes this spring."

"Have you seen Maddie fight?" I ask. "You should be more worried about the burglar. I'm still scarred from when Maddie invited me to her ju-jitsu ceremony awarding her a brown belt."

"My friend Iris made us all take classes," she says. "I can definitely take stalker woman."

"Can you?" Luca asks. He looks intrigued.

I frown. Maybe introducing Maddie and Luca was not a good idea.

"You think I can't?" Maddie asks Luca.

Nope. I don't want Maddie and Luca showing their jujitsu moves—or any moves—to each other.

"You can show him using me," I interject. Pathetic, I know.

Luca leans back and smiles like he's figured something out. Great.

"I believe you," Luca says. "Nick here isn't bad either. I've taught him a few maneuvers. You guys can practice together." Luca winks at me. He does know how to read a room, as his career in security depends on it. "I'll do the dishes. Let me bring out the mat."

He would have a mat handy.

Maddie turns to me and leans close. "You should show me." That whiff of peony drifts by. It's not my jujitsu moves I want to show her.

But better me than Luca.

"Show me your move to get out of a grab from behind. I'll grab you," Maddie says. "But don't actually throw me. I just ate."

"Okay," I say.

We both stand up and move away from the table. Maddie grabs me from behind, her arms wrapped around me, her chest pressed against my back. All that softness... My mind goes blank. Absolutely blank.

"Nick?" she asks.

Right. *Focus.* I drop lower and step out so the gap between my legs widens, bringing Maddie off-balance, clinging to my back. I swing my left foot behind her. And then I grab her lower legs, pushing my hips forward so that all of a sudden, Maddie is fully off the floor and about to be tossed over my left thigh.

"I'm not going to throw you because that's kind of a nasty throw." I put her down gently.

"That's cool," Maddie says. "I'm adding that to my repertoire. Let me try it on you."

Maddie stands with her back to me. Normally I grab across the chest, so I hesitate. Luca snorts. So glad we're amusing him.

I grab her low around the waist. She drops down, stepping her right foot to the side, and then steps behind me with her left foot and grabs around my legs but doesn't try to pick me up.

"Got it," she says.

She then shows me her under-the-arm move. When she butts her head into the crook between my shoulder and neck, I forget to focus on keeping my balance. I fall easily into her when she sweeps against my foot.

"You're not putting up any fight," Maddie says. "I'd then flip you over my shoulder."

"I'm worn out from the hours of choreography practice," I say weakly.

"Let me show my Osotogari move," she says.

When she first grabs my arm and directs me to fist her shirt near her neck and then moves me to the side, almost as if we're in some dance, our arms locked together, all I can think is: *I want Maddie.*

Until she sweeps my leg out from under me and I'm on the mat.

She kneels down next to me. "Are you okay?"

No. Her lips are so close to mine.

Luca coughs. "Still. You guys can always bunk here if you think you need more security. I have an extra room."

I scramble back to a sitting position because lying down with Maddie leaning over me is testing my self-control. "And a comfortable couch. Or so I've heard."

"It's a good thing that Tristan is not here to hear you rub it in," Luca says. "You should introduce him to Maddie since they're both reporters."

"Who's Tristan?" Maddie asks.

"He's a reporter for the Washington bureau of *The New York Carrier Pigeon*, but he's moving back to New York to take over the family business."

"*The New York Carrier Pigeon* family empire, you mean. You know him?" Maddie asks. "I haven't run into him yet, but I'm sure I will."

"We're friends from playing high school travel league soccer to-gether," I say. "He's a good connection for you to have."

"How come you haven't mentioned you know him before?" Maddie asks me.

"Because..." I can't answer that question. I could have intro-duced them last weekend when Tristan was in town. But Christina couldn't stop talking about Tristan after the three of us had dinner. Tristan even revealed, after we broke up, that she'd hit on him. What woman could resist him? He had it all, especially for someone interested in reporting. I should introduce them, but not anytime soon. As two reporters, they might click. Maybe when this contract is over and this possibly proximity-fueled desire has faded.

"Christina liked him a little too much," Luca says oh so helpfully.

She raises her eyebrows. "I heard he's quite competitive. And we're working for rival papers. I'm not sure we'll be friends."

"My money is on you," I say. Maddie has an amazing network of connections. I met her at City Hall once for lunch. We had to stop every few minutes to say hi or catch up with someone while walking in the park, including the street sweeper, the hot dog guy, and a few people who looked like they were living on "their" bench. Those relationships take time to build. Tristan is kind of aloof.

"Nick hates to ask for favors," Luca says. "On his own initia-tive, Tristan ran the article yesterday morning interviewing that elderly couple where they acknowledged that Nick was not Cara's boyfriend."

I didn't even think to ask Tristan.

"Our friendship is not about favors. He has too many people who ask him for favors. It was a surprise to me when he ran it," I say. "I thanked him for clearing my name."

"As he said, he ran it because it was the truth. But it doesn't seem to have been picked up by any other press. Still, I think Nick and I would both feel better if you carried a whistle. I can also offer you a spray." Luca unlocks a cabinet filled with gadgets and hands Maddie both a whistle and a small spray device.

"Why do you keep your pens in there?" Maddie asks, pointing at a box of pens. "Is it disappearing ink?"

"They're recorder pens. Do you want one?"

"Definitely. That's so cool," Maddie says.

I should have thought of buying Maddie a pen recorder. Luca explains some of the other gadgets, and Maddie looks fascinated. I should *not* have introduced Luca to Maddie, but at least he's a good guy. Definitely a better prospect than I am. Unless he returns to being a bodyguard.

We walk out the door into the cool night air. At least this winter has been relatively mild, other than a few freezing nights. Maddie is wearing her huge parka, all the new toys from Luca stuffed into the inner pockets. Her parka apparently doubles as a substitute bag.

Crosby Street has a different feel than where we live, particularly with the brick-paved street. This street in the SoHo Cast Iron District maintains the feel of the old industrial and artistic SoHo.

As we walk to Grand Street, we pass by the hollow cast iron columns and the huge windows that allow sunlight to permeate the far depths of the floors that characterize the west side of the street.

Maddie says. "That was fun. You were right. It was a good distraction from my nerves about tomorrow's panel presentation."

"I didn't expect you to be so nervous. Is it because you're worried that those women will be there?"

"I haven't seen them since I left middle school," Maddie says. "I think I'm over it, but I hated them so much."

It's hard to imagine Maddie hating anyone. One of the things I like about her is that she's such a positive person. But then, I can't understand anyone bullying Maddie either.

"How did you cope?" I ask.

"I mostly escaped into reading at lunch so I didn't feel alone. Then I found Ms. Philips, who supported me when I said I wanted to start a newspaper. I retreated to her classroom during lunch to work on the paper, so eighth grade was much better. And then high school was amazing. I met Iris and other friends, and it was great to be among smart kids and appreciated for wanting to study and learn."

I escaped into music, and she escaped into reading. We're more similar than I realized. Grand Street is quiet now, with only a few people hurrying down the street. We're in Little Italy now, and a huge cannoli sculpture decorates the side of one corner building. The customers sitting in the restaurants look warm and cozy.

"Did you like high school?" she asks.

"High school was better than middle school and elementary school, that's for sure. At least parents were no longer expected to show up to all our activities," I say. "With my mom working full-time to support us, she couldn't take off to make school meetings or come to performances. I always felt like the other kids pitied me. Luca's mom kind of adopted me and would try to play that role sometimes. That meant a lot to me." I look down. "I loved dinners at Luca's house. It was so chaotic and warm with his four siblings. And his mom always seemed fully present, really listening to us."

"And you didn't feel your mom was?"

"My mom was doing the best she could, and she managed to support us all on her own," I say. "But boy, did she hate when I joined a band in middle school, because she was worried that I would pursue a futile dream of being a rock star like my dad and not take academics seriously. And all I wanted to talk about was the band—which didn't reassure her. It was absolutely a topic I learned not to bring up. It would put her in a terrible mood."

"That must have been hard not to talk about what you're passionate about," Maddie says.

"At least since she often worked late, I had free rein to practice at home," I say.

"The neighbors didn't complain?" Maddie asks with a mischievous glance at me.

"They did." I grin back at her. "But I learned to practice before they got home from work. That still gave me plenty of time. I've tried to do that for you too. I try to practice during the day when you're not there. I'm sorry I practiced past eleven."

"I'm sorry I gave you such a hard time," Maddie says.

We share a look of mutual contrition and acceptance.

We pass by the stores with signs in English and Chinese as we amble farther into Chinatown. As we wait for the light to change, someone exits the bar behind us, and the jazz music from inside reverberates through the quiet night air.

Most of the stores are closed at this hour, bright graffiti decorating the aluminum fronts covering the front entrances. One market with fried chickens hanging on hooks in the window beckons passersby inside with the offer of a warm meal.

"Do we need a code word for these bullies?" I ask. "So I know to be rude to them if they approach?"

Maddie smiles at me. "You can't be rude to them. That might harm your public persona. It's okay. I can handle it. But I'm touched you offered."

"I'll tell Luca to be rude to them," I say. "The code phrase should be 'Have you seen Riley?' because of that article you wrote last year."

"Luca's not going to come, is he?"

"Of course he is."

"But I just met him."

"He liked you," I say. Even if he did try to be my wingman.

We both detour slightly to pay our respects to the tiny lion sculpture that guards Lions Gate Field, Maddie patting his head. The clouds are low enough in the sky that the bare brown branches of the trees look like they have been tufted with cotton balls. My hand brushes against her hand once—one feathery touch. I could suggest we hold hands. *No.* I need to proceed slowly.

Her brow is already furrowed, like she's thinking about her story and her spreadsheet. She glances at me, and I smile at her.

It's so easy with Maddie. I can't quite believe I'm sharing all these details, but I trust her. She won't betray me.

Chapter Eleven

Maddie

I run into Nemesis as I exit *The Intelligencer* building on my way to interview the deputy commissioners. Their building is around the corner on Broadway. I move to pass her, but the sidewalk space is narrow here because of the scaffolding.

She stops me and asks, "Where are you going?"

"I'm interviewing the deputy commissioners for my *Meet the City Agencies* series idea."

"Everyone will be buying copies to read that," she says sarcastically. "You must have some other angle."

"Looking to poach my idea again?"

"I didn't poach it," she says.

"What do you call following me to discover my source and then beating me to the interview because I had a sprained ankle last year?" I ask.

"Ideas don't have a copyright," she says.

"No," I say, wishing I had some snappy comeback. "But it helps to have your own."

"I don't need your ideas. I'm off to meet my dad, the editor of *The Big Apple*, and I'll probably see your deputy commissioners at *The Big Apple* event this evening." She tosses her hair and leaves.

As if I could forget who her dad was.

The scaffolding provides some shelter from the cold wind as I hurry down the street. My phone beeps with another friend texting me about the photo of Nick and me, saying that we look so cute. The photos of Nick and me in the *Variety* article came out better than I expected. I look like I'm in love with him. So that's good for our fake-dating charade. Last night's conversation during our walk home made me like him even more. That's *not* good. I didn't know all that stuff about his mom not supporting his career. It feels like he's trusting me more and opening up more, and our relationship is shifting. But that could also just be what I want to believe. I'm going to end up with a broken heart. I know I told Iris that I could do this and protect my heart, but not when he shares stories about growing up and introduces me to his best friends.

And his look was so very male when Luca hugged me, as if the hug bothered him. But maybe that was his big brother nature emerging. I shake my head. It definitely wasn't. His look had been intense, and his green eyes had darkened. I shiver at the memory.

And yesterday when I stuck my head into the crook of his neck, he smelled so good. I wanted to touch my lips to his skin. And the way he swallowed then, and his Adam's apple moved... *Remember clause eleven of our contract. No physical contact.* Nick seemed completely distracted, or he really was worn out from dancing. He put up so little fight when we were practicing jujitsu.

The bright brass doors of the Ted Weiss Federal Office Building gleam in today's sun. Around the corner, large white columns frame the windows of the city building that houses the offices of the deputy commissioners. An old green clock with *The Sun* in white letters protrudes from the façade. *The Sun* was a newspaper published from 1833 to 1950 that had the famous editorial, "Yes, Virginia, there is a Santa Claus." This is newspaper history right here. The columns remind me of court buildings and give me renewed inspiration to pursue justice. *Infrastructure Department* is etched in gold on the glass doors. I clear security and take the elevator up to their offices, giving my name to the assistant. She gestures to take a seat.

I cross my legs while waiting in this small reception area.

My boss was clear that Commissioner Johnson had a reputation for being committed to cleaning up corruption and had worked in city government his entire career without so much of a whisper of impropriety. She seems to doubt that he or the deputy commissioners can be involved in this. But I have to come to my own conclusion.

Commissioner Johnson finally comes out to meet me, and we retreat into his office, where he provides me with a department overview. He explains that all the deputy commissioners have buildings assigned to them and are responsible for the day-to-day details, such as repairs. Deputy Commissioner Galliano is responsible for the area that includes the two buildings with kickbacks that I've identified. But that would be too easy. It's like the rule that you don't date your roommate. So much for that rule, now that I'm fake dating my next-door neighbor.

Next, I meet Deputy Commissioner Ward. He's in his fifties, with a round, pleasant face, thin brown hair, and a slightly heavy build. His desk is covered in stacks of paper, but he offers me a drink as I take a seat. The walls are covered with framed old maps of the city. As he pours me a cup of tea, I admire his collection of miniature New York street scenes that fill his bookcase.

"These are amazing. This looks like the bodega around the corner from me," I say. "And it even has a miniature bodega cat."

"I made it."

Wow. I look at the details he caught—the way the space is filled to the brim in true bodega style. It must have taken hours to make all the products to stock the shelves. *Could an artist with this kind of eye for detail be the corrupt commissioner who is fine with shoddy work for families?*

"The cat looks so realistic," I say. "I've always been impressed by the patience it must take to add the fur. I make felted cats as a hobby, but it's nothing like this."

"I should clarify that I bought the cat at a miniature show. I made the diorama."

"It's amazing," I say.

"I like to capture these scenes of New York before they disappear," he says.

"I think that desire to capture places as memories is one reason why miniatures remain such a beloved hobby," I say.

He nods. "It certainly gives me great satisfaction. I feel like I'm back in touch with my inner kid. It's a great stress reliever."

He shows me a scene of a former club on the Lower East Side. It reminds me of Nick's last album cover, with its photograph of Pickles. It made me so happy that Nick had someone looking out for him, sort of like my teacher who "adopted" me. I shake my head. I need to focus on this interview, not replay my conversation with Nick.

"You really capture New York," I say. "Are you working on anything now?"

"An alleyway." He gestures for me to take a seat. "With a dumpster and graffiti. It's coming along nicely."

I take out my pad and ask him a bunch of general questions to set him at ease. He's worked at the Infrastructure Department his whole career, while Commissioner Johnson moved here from the Department of Transportation to be "anointed" the commissioner. I finally turn to my more relevant questions.

"So obviously one area that might be of concern to our readers is repairs," I say. "What happens when an apartment in a city housing complex needs repairs—like maybe the electrical wiring needs to be repaired, or someone needs a new refrigerator?"

"Well, they can log a complaint via the 311 system, but it's now handled at the building level, so they can also speak directly to the property manager."

I know that a property manager is basically the equivalent of a landlord for private housing.

"Is that recent?"

"Yes, as of a few years ago," Ward says.

"And what does that mean—that it's handled at the building level?"

"Each property manager of a building decides upon the contractors for contracts under $10,000. They know the contractors and what's needed by the tenants. There's less bureaucracy then."

"Do you have oversight still?"

"Sure. But it's the same old story. We have limited resources. We still have all the major renovations on our plate. I was initially opposed. I thought it was more efficient to centralize it, but reluctantly, I've become a supporter of it. The project managers should have that kind of autonomy. And this building stock is old. It helps to have a contractor who's familiar with each building and its idiosyncrasies."

I ask him how he exercises oversight. He explains that he checks the repair complaint system and often talks to the property managers, who must submit a report of authorized repairs and status. I ask a few more questions, but nothing in his responses strikes me as suspicious. I ask him if he'd be willing to sign my history book about the first Infrastructure Department, and he does. We chat for a few minutes about our passion for making miniatures. I ask him if I can include this interest in his profile, and he seems pleased. He agrees to my taking a photo of his bodega scene. He stands and groans.

"Age. I'm getting stiff," he says. He escorts me to Deputy Commissioner Galliano's office, murmuring to me that I should be sure to ask Pommer about playgrounds.

As I take the seat offered in Deputy Commissioner Galliano's office, I take a quick look around. A happy family photo is on his desk, and the young woman in the picture is Ophelia. I checked out her Spotify page. Galliano has sandy brown hair, smiling brown eyes, and a similar body build to Ward. I can see a family resemblance between him and Ophelia. He comes across as personable and charming—he's nicknamed Gallant Galliano for a reason—and if Ophelia is anything like him, that will help her when she has to entertain a crowd.

Deputy Commissioner Galliano also seems passionate about working in government. His shelf is filled with public service awards. He's the one mainly in charge of licensing and permitting. I ask him about how that works and then fight to keep my eyes open while he delves deep into the intricacies of permitting. Definitely no story material here.

"Why did you decide to work in city government?" I ask.

"I wanted to give back to this country. My parents were political refugees, and I came to this city when I was twelve. And although it was hard, it meant I could live without fear that my mom or dad was going to disappear overnight. My dad got a job in construction. He'd complain about bosses cutting corners. I wanted to work in this department to make sure construction sites are safe."

This all sounds legitimate. And not like someone who is going to take bribes for shoddy repair work. I've already confirmed that his father was a construction worker, so that checks out.

"Why did you decide to be a reporter?" he asks.

"I wanted to make a difference in people's lives, and my mom always said I ask a lot of questions," I say. "And covering a story is like solving a mystery or putting together a complicated puzzle. It's fun. Plus, I'm not one for staying in an office."

"Yes." Deputy Commissioner Galliano smiles. "That's one of my favorite parts of this job—that I'm out and about, checking on buildings and construction sites."

"Do you check in on repairs?"

"If we get complaints." He explains how it's handled at the building level.

"Are there complaints about this being handled that way?"

"All systems have their wrinkles to iron out," he says.

"So there are some complaints?"

"Yes," he says.

"Complaints about the system or about repairs?" I ask.

"Both," he says.

"What happens next?"

"We address them."

We discuss a few more aspects of his job, I ask him to sign the book, and then he drops me off at Deputy Commissioner Pommer's office.

Pommer's desk is covered in architectural drawings. Pommer himself is tall and thin, with an angular face. He's in his mid-forties and seems fit.

"I know the rats are a problem," Deputy Commissioner Pommer says into the phone as he waves me to the seat in front of him. "I've talked to Sanitation, and they're rolling out the new garbage cans, but obviously we also need to do something about the current population living in your building." It sounds like someone is screaming at him on the other end. "No, of course it's not acceptable to have a rat in your bathroom. We'll arrange for the exterminator first thing."

The person on the other end yells loud enough for me to hear: *"It's obviously dead now. The super killed it."*

"You don't want the exterminator?" asks Deputy Commissioner Pommer in a dry voice.

The person says something.

"Yes, it probably has friends," Pommer says. "But you know, it's best to call your super about this. They're the ones who arrange for the exterminator. But I will let them know as well."

Screeching erupts from the handset.

Pommer replies, "Last month, and it had no effect? Yes, I will look into it. Yes, I am impressed you have my number. How *did* you get my number?"

He listens and then says, "Yes, it *is* good to have friends in high places. I will definitely look into it." He hangs up and turns to me. "Sorry for the delay, but constituents have to come first."

"As they should," I say. He seemed thrilled to chat with that constituent.

"I'm Deputy Commissioner Pommer," he says.

"I'm Maddie—"

"The girlfriend of Nick Devlin. I know who *you* are."

He says that in such a patronizing tone.

And...here it is already. Someone is defining me because I'm dating Nick. I didn't expect it to be so soon or from a government official.

I straighten in my chair. "I prefer to introduce myself as a reporter for *The Intelligencer*." And, hopefully soon, a city politics reporter.

He huffs. "I doubt that's your preference, but let's get this over with. What questions do you have for me?" He leans back in his chair.

"Based on my research, you're spearheading an initiative for modernizing playgrounds. Can you tell me more about what's going to change?"

He blinks. "How could you know that? Did Commissioner Johnson suggest discussing that topic?"

"No," I say. "I saw you at the community board meeting for that district, and you left right after the playground matter was discussed. You put out a request for playground modernization proposals, and I read it."

Take that.

"I see. You have done your research." He steeples his fingers. "We're working on a new playground. We're coordinating with the Parks Department to make sure enough trees are planted so that there's shade on the really hot summer days, and we're also using this new type of playground surface that's blue so that it doesn't absorb heat like the black surface of old."

"That sounds great," I say.

"I think so. We're celebrating our first park with this design at Eleanor Roosevelt Houses on January 25th," he says. "You should come so you can see these innovations in person for the article. But then, maybe you already know, since your boyfriend is playing at that event."

This is perfect. I don't even need Nick's official invitation. But still, it's better to go as his date.

"I'd love to see it," I say. "In fact, I'd love to write an article about these new playground initiatives. Would you be open to doing a follow-up article focused on that?"

"Definitely," he says, seeming to soften towards me. "Here, this is a book I co-authored on this topic with a park designer. I suggest you read that first."

"Will you inscribe it for me?" I ask. "I was also hoping I could get your signature on this history book about the first Infrastructure Department."

He signs both books, adding a note that parks are the lifeblood of the city in his co-authored one.

"How come you didn't join the Parks Department?" I ask. Parks Commissioner Pommer sounds good with the alliteration.

"I'm ashamed to admit that I only became deeply interested in parks and playgrounds after I had kids," he says.

We discuss some other improvements they're making, and then I bring the conversation back to repairs. He repeats what Ward said—that the stock is old and not always easy to repair and that it's best done at the building level.

"And do you spot check the repairs?"

"When necessary," he says.

Isn't that the opposite of spot checking?

"How is that defined?" I ask.

"When there are an above average number of 411 complaints."

"What's average?"

"I don't have that figure at the ready." His phone rings. "I'm sorry. I have to take this. I hope you have what you need."

I'm dismissed, and I'm still not sure how to figure out who is taking bribes.

As I leave the building, I call the number for Demoraux, the corrupt inspector. I finally tracked it down. I wanted to call him after the interviews so the deputy commissioners didn't have any cause to cancel them. He picks up after the first ring.

"Is this Demoraux?" I ask.

"Might be. Who is this?"

"Hi. This is Maddie Hughes of *The Intelligencer*. You've been fining a lot of bars in the East Village lately. Is this part of a new enforcement effort?"

Click. He hangs up. I guess he wants to do this the hard way. But I *will* speak to him.

It's off to the panel at my middle school now.

My middle school's auditorium hasn't changed. I remember walking on this stage to receive an award for starting our first newspaper and how proud I felt.

And not only is Nick in the first row in the audience, along with all my girlfriends with their boyfriends, but Nick persuaded the band and Luca to show up as well. An army of supporters has filled the room.

The mean girls who tormented me don't seem to be here.

The panel starts off great. Twyla Jackson, whose career I've been following since I first became interested in journalism, immediately sets both the moderator—the twelve-year-old chief editor of the school newspaper—and me at ease. Twyla and I have an instant rapport, and we play off each other's strengths.

The whole talk lasts about forty-five minutes, and then we take questions from the audience.

"What's your advice to aspiring journalists?" the moderator asks as her last question of the evening.

After Twyla gives her answer—to remember to be skeptical and to reflect the diversity of America in your stories—I say, "It's hard to narrow down my advice. First, talk to people and try to make as many friends as you can in all walks of life, because that can give you a lot of different perspectives and expand your horizons. It gives you practice in getting people to open up. You also never know when this connection might come in useful. I was covering a bill at City Hall last year, and the city council member had left for the night, so we thought the bill was dead. But at 6:05 a.m., one of my friends in the neighborhood called me—he runs the coffee truck outside City Hall—and he let me know that the city council member's car had arrived at 6:00, along with the mayor's car. I was the first reporter on the scene and found out that they'd renegotiated some points, so it was going to be passed. That was a great scoop for me and our paper. *The Intelligencer* ran the story that the bill was being passed while the other papers were reporting it as dead. And my other tips are don't put your phone on silent, and don't expect to get much sleep." I wink at Nick as I say this, and he smiles at me.

The moderator thanks us for a great discussion. *I'm glad I did this.*

Nick stands up to clap, and he looks so proud of me that I almost tear up. Twyla and I chat for a few minutes as we remove our microphones.

"It was a pleasure to meet you," she says. "Feel free to reach out for lunch or a late breakfast if you ever want to commiserate about lack of sleep. I can't have dinner out because I get up at four o'clock for the morning show."

I can't imagine how she gets up that early in the morning every day and then goes on live TV. It's impressive.

"I'd be honored to meet up." I gesture to Jing to come over, and I introduce Twyla to her. The three of us chat a bit more about being a journalist, and then Twyla has to leave.

As I venture out into the seating area, I'm soon surrounded by my friends. There's definitely a heady feeling being surrounded by Nick and Luca—two tall, attractive guys—and my girlfriends. I feel so protected.

"Way to knock 'em dead, Maddie," Nick says, patting me on the back.

And then I see her. The one who started the bullying. The one who first decided that I should spend middle school as an outcast. My body flushes cold. I look away. She circles around us, staring at both Luca and Nick in a calculating way. I owe her nothing, so I turn back to my conversation with Jing. *Good luck breaking into this circle.*

But I underestimated her gall, just as I often did in middle school.

She taps me on the arm. "Maddie, I'm so glad to see you succeeded at your dream of being a reporter. We all knew Maddie would be a success." And she scoops her arm through mine, her nails digging into my skin.

I freeze. *She's actually touching me.*

My mind goes blank.

I stare at Nick. A quizzical expression crosses his face. His brow furrows. But it's his eyes, full of concern and support, that bring me back to myself.

I jerk my arm away from her.

I ask Nick, "Have you seen Riley?"

"We should find her." He holds my hand and tucks me close into him. He turns us around to walk away as Luca speaks up.

"You'll excuse us," he says. "The van is waiting outside for us and the rest of *Maddie's friends.*" He emphasizes "Maddie's friends." When I look back as we reach the exit, past my whole group of friends trailing behind me, she stands alone.

Like I used to stand on the lunch line. She used to threaten anyone who ate with me with social ostracism. I quickly learned who my true friends were.

Still, I feel no joy in leaving her there alone.

Nick slips his arm around my waist and whispers in my ear, "Forget her. Just think that she made you a stronger person."

But I'm not. I froze again. She was still able to affect me. I'd thought I would be impervious to her. *I'm not.* I'd thought she couldn't affect me anymore. *She can.* A tear of frustration escapes my eye. I should have said, *We were never friends.* I should have excused myself from her company. I should have prepared for this.

Maybe I should look at the comments on the articles and posts about Nick and me dating. Iris said not to look, but maybe I need to. I need to see if I can handle them, because if I really want to have a relationship with Nick, I won't always be able to ignore the trolls and the rumors.

His possessive look when Luca hugged me, the way he looked so proud when everyone was clapping, and how quickly he pulled me into his embrace earlier today, I feel like there might be the possibility of something real.

Nick clasps my hand, and the warmth of it grounds me. I grip it back tightly. This is my life now. This group of friends and my career. I was on a panel with Twyla Jackson! And she treated me as an equal. We might even have lunch!

My phone beeps. It's Demoraux, confirming that he is willing to meet me tomorrow. I show Nick that we're on for tomorrow. This could be my big break.

It's true that I froze. But she's my history. What I need to determine is... Can I handle a future with Nick as a famous rock star with the trolls that will attack me? Am I stronger now? More sure of who I am? Will that be enough? Because I'm falling for him.

Chapter Twelve

Nick

Maddie accepted my offer to come along with her on this interview with the corrupt inspector because he wants to meet in a seedy-looking bar. Luca said this place can attract a rough crowd and to be careful, so I'm relieved Maddie is allowing me to tag along. That has to mean something, right? She trusts me.

This is definitely a step forward in our relationship. She always wants to handle everything herself. Or she truly thinks this is dangerous. Luca's parting words were "duck and weave." He said at least I'm fast on my feet, with all the dancing and exercise I do. He gave me a whistle. Some help he is.

I tighten my scarf and wait for Maddie outside the subway station. A cold wind sweeps down Fulton Street, fresh off the East River. The World Trade Center looms over the street if I look west. This corner has some thatched roof outdoor café set up, vacant at the moment, which promises that spring weather is coming soon, even if it doesn't feel like it.

Seedy bars are not my thing. When I was thirteen (and becoming "a man," as my mom said), my mom tried to find my dad because she thought he'd want to know me and that I might need him. And we searched for him in some disreputable bars—huge men with black leather and tattoos and the smell of pot smoke and stale alcohol are what I remember. I hated the way people would stare at me when my mom and I entered. And she'd tell me to wait by the door in her sight while she checked out the back. I didn't like her going into those places—I worried about her. I even thought maybe my mom had cooked this up as an elaborate scheme to deter me from wanting to be a musician. But she found my dad. He wanted nothing to do with us. I was relieved when he moved back to Nashville, and she realized once again that we didn't need him.

I check my phone to make sure that Maddie hasn't texted me with a change of plans, because it's now five minutes past the hour.

It's impressive Maddie managed to convince the inspector to meet for an interview. She said that he'd hung up initially but then called her back. He wanted to know how she'd been able to track him down. She told him, and he seemed to change his mind. She's a good reporter. It was good to see her getting some recognition for that at her middle school event.

But Maddie *freezing* like that—I've never seen her react that way before. I didn't even need the code word. I couldn't care less if that woman outed me as rude. I wanted to pull Maddie away from her.

Has Maddie seen the comments online under the recent article about us? Or the photos taken of her leaving *The Intelligencer* one night? I hope not. Some are cruel.

Is he dating the Pillsbury Doughboy? Why is she always dressed in that enormous parka?

Is she carrying a dead body in that bag? Or just a lot of makeup to make her look passable?

What does he see in her? I give them three months.

Three months is right. At least it will be Maddie breaking up with me. And I have a feeling I'll be able to make them believe I'm heartbroken.

But these trolls...

One more reason *not* to date someone who wants to be a famous musician.

And then there's Cybergirl's comments: *What does* she *see in* him? Rock stars are not to be trusted.

Why do I have a sneaking suspicion that Cybergirl is Iris? But good for her for supporting Maddie.

Should I tell Maddie not to look at the comments? I don't want her feeling hurt. But if I tell Maddie *not* to look at the comments, then I fear her reporter instincts will take over and she'll think they're bad and she needs to look at them.

"Nick!" Maddie walks up, smiling. She puts her bag down and opens her parka for a minute to take out the pen recorder. I take a moment to appreciate Maddie dressed up in wide-legged black pants and her tailored black jacket. She usually wears jeans or yoga pants and a sweater, so I'm guessing she wants to look more imposing to this guy. But other than that, her eyes are bright and open, unclouded by doubts or pain. Not like yesterday. Even at the restaurant we all went to for dinner after the panel, she seemed relaxed and over it. But I didn't imagine her freezing—or how tightly she gripped my hand.

Maddie offers me her hand, and I hold it. She pulls it into one of her huge pockets. "Your hand looks cold."

"I forgot my gloves at home." Maddie's hands are so soft and tiny. I should forget gloves more often. "Are you sure my hand isn't too cold?"

"Yes," she says.

"Looking stylish," I say.

"A leather jacket?" she asks. We walk briskly towards the bar, which is several blocks away. "I didn't even know you owned a leather jacket. Are you trying to blend in?"

"Every rock star wannabe owns a leather jacket. And yes, I thought it might be best to try to blend in. You obviously decided to go with the opposite approach." I sweep my hand to indicate Maddie's pantsuit.

"I thought it best to remind him I work for a reputable paper," she says.

"I agree with that approach," I say, regretting that I didn't also wear a suit. "I didn't know this was the Strangelove dress code."

"You're the muscle, so you're perfect." She winks at me.

Something melts within me.

I pull out my phone. "You need to say that again so I can record it."

She shakes her head, and her ponytail swings behind her head. "Nope."

"But don't worry, I'm still wearing sneakers in case we have to make a fast getaway," she says. "Here we are."

A red neon light *STRANGELOVE BAR* sign blinks on and off, as if it's conserving energy to keep going for another night. The two windows are grimy, so we can't see the interior.

When we walk inside, it's practically pitch-black, and the walls are covered in graffiti. Not only the walls, but every available surface—the chairs, tables, and even the cash register. The musty smell doesn't help either. Nor does the headless mannequin also covered in graffiti stationed at the end of the long bar.

Maddie stops briefly next to me. "I think my heel just caught on some sticky spilled beer."

"You always take me to the nicest places for our dates," I say, teasing.

"Not everyone can find the types of places where we can date without your fans catching us," Maddie says.

"I hope these are my fans—and not my anti-fans." I stare at the two big, tattooed guys at the bar. They thankfully ignore us, more focused on their shot glasses. Another man is slumped with a drink next to the mannequin. He raises his head to call for a refill.

The only other customer is sitting at the very last table in the back and dressed in black, barely visible, except that someone opens the bathroom door next to him and the light reveals his hunched-over shape.

"I'm going to ask Luca for the spray next time I see him," I whisper to Maddie.

"Is now a good time to tell you I forgot to bring it?" Maddie asks.

"No. Not a good time," I say. What do I have? Me, my phone, my whistle, and my backpack with Maddie's gift and probably guitar picks. But I thought Maddie's bag had everything. Should I call Luca or Mr. Muscle and see if they know any security guys in the neighborhood?

"Just kidding," she says.

Maddie strides up to the table with her hand out. I actually don't like shaking hands anymore. I thought I had it tough shaking fans' hands, but this is a whole other level.

The man half-rises to shake her hand but keeps his cap low on his head, hiding his face.

"Who's your friend?" he asks in a gravelly voice that sounds as if it's been burned by years of smoking. "I thought you were coming alone."

"My boyfriend," Maddie says brightly. "We're having dinner after this. I haven't been to this bar or area before, so I thought I might as well check out the neighborhood." She looks around as if we're having tea at The Plaza. "He can sit at another table if you want."

The man shrugs.

We both sit down, although Maddie places a handkerchief from her bag on the seat first. That bag really does have everything. Except for an extra protective cover for me. She takes out a notebook and what I hope is the pen recorder.

"How long have you been an inspector for the Infrastructure Department?" she asks.

"Two months," he says.

"What did you do before?" she asks.

"Is that relevant?"

Yes. I want to know if you were a boxer—or a hired assassin.

"It might be," Maddie says. She must be used to hostile subjects.

"I got the job, so I had the necessary qualifications," he says.

"What made you want this job?" she asks.

"Why does anyone want a job? The pay and benefits seemed alright," he says.

She asks a bunch more warm-up questions, but he doesn't seem to be getting any friendlier. I leave to order drinks because the bartender is glaring at us. I give the bartender double the amount of the bill. Maybe the prospect of high tips will keep him on our side. I place two sodas on the table and another beer for this guy and sit back down. He raises his glass to me.

Maddie clicks her pen. "Are there any pay incentives to find violations?"

I guess we've moved past the warm-up.

"No," he says.

"What's your connection to Ophelia?" she asks.

"I don't know anyone named Ophelia," he says quickly.

"That's not what I heard," she says. "Nor what the evidence shows."

"What evidence?" he huffs.

Maddie pulls out a piece of paper. "Here's a list of bars that were cited for violations in the past month and yet cleared upon a second inspection by you once they offered to let Ophelia play. Funny how they match. And the bar owners tell me that's not a coincidence—that you said you'd 'overlook' these issues if they gave Ophelia and her band a chance."

He stares at her. "How did you figure that out?"

Go, Maddie. I should have brought popcorn. I finish my Diet Coke. Maddie hasn't even touched her soda. She's completely focused on this interview.

"I have my sources," she says.

"Are they going to admit that they were willing to pay a bribe?" the inspector asks.

"Sometimes it depends on who comes clean first," Maddie says. "Or who shares who's behind the scheme."

"It's pretty obvious who's behind this scheme, isn't it?" he asks, a sneer disfiguring his face.

"Too obvious," Maddie says.

He shrugs. "It's not like it was a big ask. Most of them offered her some completely dead time spot."

"Are you saying Deputy Commissioner Galliano is behind this?" Maddie asks.

"I'm not sayin' anything."

"Nothing? And here I thought you might be the key." She leans back, seeming more relaxed.

He shakes his head.

Maddie sips her drink. Finally. I was beginning to worry that she knew something I didn't and that I wasn't supposed to drink any beverages here.

The silence lengthens.

The Maddie silent treatment. It's not fun. He shifts in his chair.

Ha. Even tougher men than me can be brought down by the Maddie silent treatment.

He looks at me. "You like her? This isn't safe."

"That's exactly what I'm worried about," I say. I'm probably not supposed to say that.

"Definitely not safe." He holds up a napkin and rips it in half. "You should quit while you're ahead."

I pick up the napkin he ripped and rip the two parts in half. "You touch her, and you will regret it. You tell your boss that."

We stare at each other. He drops his gaze first.

"Okay, I'm glad we've made that point," Maddie says. "Are you safe?"

He starts. "As long as I keep my mouth shut."

"Then why did you meet me?"

"He wants to know what you know." He points to the paper.

Should Maddie have shown him what she knows? She doesn't look upset. She knows what she's doing.

"I have a pretty good case for Galliano," she says. "You should tell him that."

"I will." That sneer is back.

"Well, I appreciate you taking the time to talk with me," Maddie says. "If you want to share anything else, please let me know." She hands him her card.

"Are you guys really going on a date now?" He fingers her card.

"Of course," Maddie says. "Any places you recommend around here?"

He barks out a short laugh. "You're interesting, lady." He points his finger at me. "And it looks like you're not just a pretty boy."

"I grew up in this neighborhood when it wasn't quite as gentrified," I say. "As did Maddie. Give your boss our best."

We leave and walk outside. I take a big breath of fresh air.

I turn to Maddie. "It's not safe."

"He's just trying to scare me off," she says.

That may be. In my experience, growing up as an initially scrawny kid in this neighborhood and a "pretty boy," people often bluff and threaten, but if they're serious, they get to it and don't have an introductory meeting. But Maddie going up against that guy or his friends makes me worried.

We walk briskly down the street. All the stores are closed with grates down on this block. The windows are also dark, as if there is no point in paying for electricity when only rats visit this area at night.

"That didn't give you pause at all? It definitely made me want to get out of there." I hold Maddie's hand and set a brisk pace to put distance between that guy and us. The next few blocks are also deserted, with just a traffic light blinking red and green amid the shadows created by the lamplights. This street is all office buildings with abandoned shops underneath.

We finally reach a block where the stores are lit up. We pass a group of college students out for the night, discussing what bar they want to go to next. We're back among people.

"There's a cool place if you want to walk up near the South Street Seaport," Maddie says.

Normally, one of the great things about being friends with Maddie is that she is always up for trying new experiences and can always suggest cool places to go. But right now, she's avoiding the topic.

I turn and face her, reaching out to hold her other hand as well. "Really, though, Maddie. Are you taking his threats seriously?"

Her gaze meets mine. "I'm taking it seriously. I had extra jujitsu practice sessions before I agreed to meet him here, and I also talked to our paper's security about the best protocol. And I brought you. This also isn't my first time experiencing this. You have to trust me."

"Okay," I say. "I'm out of line."

"No, I appreciate your concern." She squeezes my hand. "I'm really touched that you came along and that you're worried."

I nod. "I'm relieved you've talked to your paper's security." She knows what she's doing. "So, by 'cool,' you mean the opposite of the last bar, right?"

"By cool, I mean a family-run Neapolitan pizza place by Pier 17 that a fellow reporter recommended."

"I'm in."

As we enter, we're welcomed warmly, and we are shown to a table in a brick-walled nook. The floor of dark-blue hexagon tiles adds to the feeling of comfort and cheer. It's clean and crowded with waiters making their way between the tables carefully carrying large wooden paddles with wood-fired pizza. I'm starving.

"This is a much more public place. We should act like we're dating," I say. "Can I hold your hand across the table?"

"Thou'st may," Maddie says.

"Thou'st are the one who did set these courtship rules," I say. "Your wish is merely my command."

As we study the menu, Maddie suggests we share the dishes so we look "lovey-dovey."

I narrow my eyes at her. "Is it because you can't decide and want to try mine too?"

She shakes her head. "Where is your sense of romance?"

I lean my head on my hand and stare into Maddie's eyes. She blushes and averts her gaze.

"Okay, yes, I can't decide," Maddie says.

We narrow down our choices and place our order. The waitress fills our glasses with water. Another good thing about dating Maddie is that we're both in the same budget range—the tap water range.

"That was helpful, though," Maddie says.

"Do you think it's Galliano?" I ask. "He definitely implied it was Galliano behind this."

"He did." Maddie leans closer to the table and flutters her lashes at me. "And so, I think it's not. It's too obvious. I shouldn't have said that, though."

"Your collar is slightly crooked," I say. "May I?"

"Yes," she says.

I reach out to straighten the collar on her jacket as we maintain eye contact. It's like I'm not even breathing. She raises an eyebrow. As I pull my hand back, she runs her hand through my hair. I feel like a cat that wants to lean into her hand and butt against it, asking for more. She blushes again.

"This is going to get messy if we eat the pizza with our hands," she says.

"Let's ask for cutlery," I say.

She laughs.

We are just friends. We should revert to safer terrain.

The waitress serves us the platter of bruschetta that we ordered, and we each take one. It's very good.

"Interesting that he acknowledged that giving Ophelia playtime wasn't a big ask," I say.

"That's just it. If I'm the deputy commissioner and I've worked my whole life to get this position, why would I then risk it to get my daughter put into dead time spots? The fact that Demoraux knew that she was being slotted into dead times supports my theory that it's not Galliano."

"That's a good point. Of course, she can still say she played at all these well-known clubs. It's not like you put the times on your resume."

Maddie eats another bruschetta. "Hmm. That's true. But is that significant enough?"

"No. Not enough to risk your career."

"I think it's an attempt to muddy the waters and make it look like Galliano, which means it's one of the other two. But Ward spends his spare time making miniatures, and Pommer seems devoted to building better playgrounds, so it's hard to imagine they're corrupt. I need proof, but this inspector interview solidified my feeling that it's not Galliano." Maddie bites her lip. "Especially Demoraux's sneer at the end. But now I need to figure out if it's Ward or Pommer."

"Follow the numbers, as we say in accounting."

"Would you be willing to review numbers for me, or do you hate it too much?"

"I don't hate it. I enjoy it in moderation—it's so orderly. It's not my passion, but doing the books for various small businesses helps pay the bills." I had a dual major in college of accounting and music—so that my mother didn't die an early death, as she put it. "Have you found more people who have had faulty repairs?"

"Yes. I have the human element angle," Maddie says. "I just interviewed a mom with a newborn, and the kitchen sink had been turned off because of a leak. Imagine having to cook with water from the bathroom with a baby."

Our pizzas arrive, and my mouth waters at the smell of melting cheese and tomato. Maddie ordered broccoli and sausage, and I ordered the chicken and vegetables. I serve Maddie and then take my first slice.

"I thought you'd have to eat lettuce and grilled chicken. Aren't you going shirtless?"

"Luckily, I seem to have inherited an amazing metabolism."

"Lucky," Maddie says as she purses her lips around her straw.

I should not be looking at Maddie's lips.

"I'm glad that you don't want to eat lettuce and grilled chicken." I need to keep this conversation on track and not let my mind wander off where it seems to want to go: shirtless me and Maddie's lips.

"I feel like I burned off enough with the adrenaline of that meeting," she says. "Enough talk about this case. Do you feel ready with the dance routine?"

I nod. "It's the most amazing feeling when I'm dancing in sync with the backup dancers. I wouldn't have thought it would be, but I'm totally into it now."

"I'm impressed." She hands me a small package. "I bought this for you online as a thank-you."

I unbox it, and it's a miniature guitar on its own little stand. "Wow. Thank you."

"And see, underneath is a 1/12 scale notebook for songwriting. It opens."

"Are you encouraging my songwriting?" I ask, touched.

She nods, blushing.

"I bought you a gift too." I open my backpack and pull out the hat wrapped in tissue paper.

Maddie unwraps it. "A Sherlock hat! Wow! I love it!" She hugs it. "I'm so impressed."

Take that, Luca's spy gadget closet.

She puts it on, tilting her head for me. "How do I look?"

"Adorable."

"I should look intellectual," she says.

"That too." I take a photo and show her. It fits her.

She crooks her finger to indicate I should come closer.

"Thanks much," she says.

Is Maddie going to kiss me? Across the table at a pizza shop? That's one way to keep it contained.

"Thanks much," I say, waiting and very much wanting.

She leans over the table and kisses me quickly on the cheek with the faintest brush of her lips.

She's killing me.

We bike back home, me singing the set songs to Maddie. Okay, it's not quite the same prep as running on a treadmill while singing, but it's a start. Especially because Maddie is heckling me and trying to make me mess up. We return the Citi Bikes to walk the last few blocks to our apartment building.

Maddie stops suddenly and looks into an eyeglass store window.

"You need glasses?" I ask.

"That Citi Bike with the guy with the red helmet—wasn't that guy behind us when we first started biking?" she asks. "Don't turn around."

I try to check him out of the corner of my eye. "How can you tell?"

"He doesn't have any deliveries. I thought it was weird that he didn't have any bags on his handlebars. I thought he must be returning home or to the restaurant after a delivery, but he drove so slowly behind us."

"Let's go in that bodega and see if he's still outside when we leave," I say.

She glances at me. "Thanks for not thinking I'm crazy."

"I'm the one with the crazy fans. We can't be too careful. We should probably go to the Allen Street deli and use the back-door entrance into our apartments too."

The bodega door chimes as we enter. Every shelf in this bodega is packed. The first row is cookies, chips, and crackers, and all types of immediate snack foods, with the flowers in buckets to the side, stored inside for the night. The second aisle holds all the canned goods you could possibly need on the spur of the moment, while the third aisle holds yet more dry foods on one side and refrigerated items on the other.

I pick up some M&M's for Maddie, and we find ourselves in front of the cookie section. Maddie pauses in front of the chocolate cookies and reaches for a pack.

"I shouldn't," I say. "My metabolism has some limits."

"I shouldn't either, then." Maddie puts the cookies back. "Apples?"

"Thanks. Apples it is."

Someone is yelling outside. We peer through the glass front in the slight space between the advertisements. A guy in shabby clothes, ripped sneakers, and two hats is yelling at the top of his lungs that the aliens are coming. We wait for a minute to see if it looks like he's going to leave soon, but he's clinging to the lamppost as if it's feeding him electricity.

We pay for our purchases and exit the store. On the plus side, the Citi Bike guy seems to be gone. But he might have been scared off by the homeless guy.

We turn and quickly walk away. But he follows us, yelling, "Beware! The aliens!"

We jog. But he picks up his pace.

"Time to pretend the aliens have arrived," Maddie says to me. She twists her body back and forth and waves her arms up and down on either side.

I do the same, adding a loping gate.

"Oh, well done." Maddie laughs quietly. She screams, "*EEEE!*"

I jump in surprise.

"*EEEE!*" I yell and look behind us. He's stopped, and now he's walking backwards, away from us. Then he turns and runs down the street.

"Sometimes you have to out-crazy the crazy," Maddie says.

"And here I thought I might get to see your jujitsu moves in action," I say. "You don't see anyone else following us, right? We're actually safe now to go straight home?"

"I don't see anyone. You?"

"No," I say. *Is this going to be my life now?* Am I going to have to worry about crazy fans and lose all privacy? Lots of celebrities live in New York City, though, without any problem. New Yorkers generally take pride in ignoring VIPs. Ms. Cara-wannabe is a one-off—someone who's trying to use my popularity to boost her own.

Wait.

"Isn't that the Citi Bike again—same red helmet?" Maddie asks. "Let's take the back route into our apartments."

"Okay, but first I want to get a photo." I head straight for the guy on the bike, clicking photos with my phone.

The guy on the Citi Bike finally sees me, stops short, and then turns, speeding away.

I return to Maddie. "I'm going to ask Luca if he can provide extra security for the parks concert."

"Did you get a good look at his face?" Maddie asks.

"Let's see." I show Maddie the photos. "Oddly, it seemed like he was focused on you rather than me."

She widens the photo so she can see the person's face.

"That's Nemesis!" Maddie exclaims.

Chapter Thirteen

Maddie

Nemesis! She's trying to scoop my story again! She must have followed me from work. Hayden, our new "boss"—while my usual boss, Felicity, is out on medical leave—must have given Sarah the same lecture he gave me, that I need to up my game before the new recruits come in June, all fresh from journalism school. But she and Hayden are close, so I thought he only gave me the lecture. He then assigned me a sure-to-be-riveting story interviewing the Head of Sanitation about how they are preparing for an upcoming snowstorm. I handed that in yesterday so I'd have the weekend free for the miniature show I plan to sell at.

Sarah probably saw us enter Strangelove, but neither Nick nor I saw her there. Did she wait outside? Did she see us with Demoraux? What if she interviews Demoraux? My blood runs cold. She might scoop me again. *No.* Then she would have followed him and not us.

Is she trying to prove that we are *not* dating? Or figure out what I'm investigating? At least we looked romantic at dinner. So romantic that I almost believed it myself that we were dating. At least I finally had the chance to run my hand through Nick's hair. And the way he looked at me made my stomach quiver. Was that real or part of the charade? And I'd been so tempted to kiss him. Clause eleven strikes again. I had to remind myself that this charade is not supposed to make me want to kiss him.

Once we're sure she's gone, Nick and I continue on to our apartment building, entering through the deli entrance just in case. He waits at my door for me to unlock it.

"So…" he says, sounding a bit awkward. "See you tomorrow for the mini show?"

I nod, pleased that he remembered and that he even suggested that he come along. "Yeah, see you tomorrow."

I smile and then step into my apartment and close the door softly behind me, blowing out a quiet breath. I pick up Sherlock and bury my face in his soft fur. I know I'll be replaying tonight's dinner in my dreams, but that's what dreams are for.

Nemesis was not on the bus with us to New Jersey today for the mini show. Only dealers are allowed in this huge hotel conference room right now to set up. Nick is next to me, unpacking my felted miniatures to sell and arranging them on my table. I glance at his profile. He's so attractive, but he's also such a good guy. He really likes discussing my investigations. He has good insights. A heaviness fills me that this dating relationship isn't real.

The friendship is solid. That's what counts. And I'm at a mini show. Honestly, for someone who loves minis, a miniature show is pure heaven. I'm not going to let thoughts of Nemesis ruin it. Plus, I'm with Nick. He'd agreed at dinner last night to be my wingman because it's hard to man the table all by myself. Last time, someone actually *stole* a miniature silver tea set off a dealer's table. It's a day with Nick and a mini show. I smile.

I sneak another peek at him. I can't quite believe he's here with me.

I set out a little box of minis priced at twenty-five cents each for kids to buy. When I was a kid, I loved finding miniature treasures at vendor tables.

"I can tell you want to check out all the other tables, so go ahead. I'll watch this," Nick says.

"Thanks so much! I can't spend much, so I want to take a quick run around so I can think about what I want—what I absolutely love—before the show opens," I say.

Nick smiles at me. "Have fun."

This huge room has been filled with rows of tables, each with different vendors selling miniatures. One table has handcrafted metal miniatures, like trash cans, kitchen sinks, and ranges. They're so realistic and detailed but way out of my budget. Prices start at three hundred dollars. Another craftsperson is selling the most beautiful flowers. So many choices! I narrow my picks down to a miniature teddy bear and an orange cat that resembles Sherlock. I quickly buy those and return to my table.

The show door opens, and a wave of excited voices rolls over the room. The first person who reaches our table studies my little animals, picks one up, puts it down, and scurries away.

"Ouch," Nick says. "I didn't realize you face rejection in your mini endeavors."

"All creative pursuits need a thick skin," I say. The puppy she put down seems cute to me. I pat his fur and place him next to the other little dogs.

Nick glances at me, seeming to appreciate that I get it.

Luckily, that customer seems to be the odd one out, and our table is soon swamped.

"Surprise, surprise," a voice says. One I recognize. I look up to see Deputy Commissioner Ward with two folded Fresh Direct bags under his arm. Those bags are huge when open. He must be planning to buy so much. He really is into the miniature scene.

"I didn't expect to see you here selling," he says.

"I like making my little felted animals, so I might as well make some extra income," I say.

"Do you have an Etsy store?" he asks.

"No. I only participate in this show because then I can plan stock for it. My schedule is not that predictable, and I'd be afraid I couldn't fulfill Etsy orders on time if I suddenly had to pursue a story."

Nick handles another customer while I focus on Ward.

"You take your reporter career quite seriously," he says.

"Of course." Did I give him the impression I didn't?

He narrows his eyes and stares down at my table as if absolutely gripped by my display. "This squirrel. It will be perfect for my park scene. I must have it."

That's quite a strong statement.

"Do you take cash?" He pulls out his wallet.

"Of course." I fill out a receipt with the sales tax and hand it to him. He hands me the cash, and Nick stores it in our little metal cashbox.

"I can't convince you to take requests?" Ward asks.

"Not usually," I say. "But I have a mailing list, where sometimes I email my subscribers to see if anyone has any requests—when I'm not that busy at work." I point to the sheet of paper on a clipboard. He writes his name and email address there.

"Is there something you want right now?" I ask.

"No, but when I'm in the middle of creating a scene, I have so many different needs," he says. "Are you buying anything?"

"I bought this teddy bear." I don't share that I bought a cat too. He can't use a bear for a street scene, but what if he says *I must have your cat*?

"So far, I've only bought this microphone stand and boom stand for Deputy Commissioner Galliano. He's always promoting his daughter Ophelia, so I thought he'd like it," he says.

Interesting. Could Galliano be the right one after all?

Nick wraps the squirrel in tissue paper, places it in a box, and hands it over to Ward.

"I'm off," Ward says. "Wish me luck. I have a long list of what I need for my next scenes."

"Good luck!"

As he disappears into the crowd, Nick teases me, "Do you want to follow him?"

I smile but then say, "Do you think I'll get some insights based on his purchases?"

Nick shrugs. "Probably not. But interesting that he paid in cash."

"Right. Who pays in cash nowadays? Unless he's receiving a lot of cash that he needs to get rid of." He paid with a $100 bill. I stare at Nick.

I feel a jolt of electricity when his green eyes meet mine. I blink. Does he feel that too? Can it be this strong and just be me feeling it?

Focus on the investigation.

"I'll try to meet up with him if he looks like he's leaving," I say. "Maybe I'll get some clues if I engage him in a conversation about his job when he's in this setting and less wary."

"Sounds good."

It feels so easy with Nick here. There are not that many young people. Although most of the older female customers give him an extra glance of appreciation, the focus remains on the miniatures. One young woman, though, has stopped by our table five times and talked to Nick exclusively. She has yet to buy anything but says she is having trouble deciding and then leans in to ask Nick what he thinks. He seems happy to humor her.

But when he does become really famous? He won't be able to do something like this. Obviously, this isn't quite the thrilling experience for him that it is for me, but won't he miss being able to do normal things?

"I'm starving," Nick says.

"Don't worry. I have snacks in my bag." I offer him a choice. He takes the healthier granola bar, while I eat the M&M's.

"Impressive," he says.

My phone beeps. I check it and see that it's Hayden. Hopefully, he liked my article.

"You made a face," Nick says. "What's the message?"

My shoulders dip. "Hayden assigned me a story—top ten best things to do in New York City for Valentine's Day. He wants it on his desk by midnight Sunday. I thought I was done with these types of stories, but I guess I have to prove myself all over again. I hope Felicity comes back next week."

"We can research that together," Nick says.

I reach out and squeeze his hand. "That will make it more fun. Are you sure I'm not taking too much of your time?"

"Remember, this helps people think it's real," Nick says.

Yes, I need to remember that. This is all a façade. But it's definitely messing with my head. I keep forgetting this is an act. Hopefully, the friendship part is still real. That can last forever—although if Nick marries someone... Okay, that thought hurts. I need to stop thinking about this.

"We should take the 3:00 bus back. I'm almost out of stock, and I should research this. I'll text my girlfriends to see if they have any ideas. Lily wants to take Rupert to this super romantic café for Valentine's Day. And Bella must have some ideas since she writes so many romances." I text them.

"Ward's leaving," Nick says sharply.

I look up quickly. Ward is at the exit, his two Fresh Direct bags now full. That's a lot of purchases.

"Go," Nick says. "I'll pack up what's left."

"Thank you."

I make my way quickly through the collectors crowding the tables, out the front door, and into the lobby of this New Jersey hotel but slow down as I reach Ward so I can make it look casual.

"Already on your way out?" I ask.

"I've spent way over my budget." He lifts his bags. "If only I could resist."

"What are some of your favorite purchases—my squirrel excluded?" I ask.

He stops by a couch in the lobby, deposits his bags, and takes out a box. "Definitely these metal garbage cans. But I also had to have the whole metal kitchen to make a restaurant. And I commissioned the closed-lid plastic garbage cans Pommer wants to mandate—to prevent rats. They will be perfect for a New York City street scene." His phone beeps. "My ride is outside. Good luck with your sales."

"I can't believe Ella's Café is closed," I say. "Lily is going to be so disappointed." Ella's Café on the Upper West Side had been billed as one of the top romantic spots in New York City for Valentine's Day the last three years. It was an entirely pink shop with tiny little tables and either loveseats or two armchairs facing each other for seating. But what had made it really special were the flowers. It smelled of orchids when you walked through. I'd included it on a top ten list for best places for proposals in one of my first articles.

I stare at the pink door with the huge "Closed for Renovations" sign. Above it is a pink awning with the name written in purple lettering. Colorful cloth flowers frame the window.

"Let's go meet my friends at Banter & Books," I say. "At least it's Salad Saturday, so we can get dinner too."

We walk down West 74th Street past all the picturesque brownstones. One tree still has a witch decoration left over from Halloween. We turn at the corner to walk up Amsterdam Avenue towards Banter & Books. We pass by Levain Bakery, but I don't dare suggest we buy cookies since our last conversation when Nick turned down the snacks.

"Are you sure you don't want to include Strangelove on your list of romantic places?" Nick asks. "At least it has love in the title."

"I'd be afraid to send anyone there." I shudder. "But now I wonder if Sarah thought we'd actually gone on a date there." I think again of my list for the next article. "I can't believe that the bumper cars on ice are also no longer available, but at least I now have renting an igloo at Bryant Park, Drag Me to Joanne's, the Pink Pier, a picnic in Central Park, sharing an electric blanket, Love Pong—which sounds pretty cool with the Ping-Pong and tarot card readings—visiting the Reliquary Arm of St. Valentine's at the Met 5th Avenue Galleries—"

"That one is definitely a little odd," Nick interrupts.

"True, but a trip to the Metropolitan Museum is always a good date," I say.

"Is it?" Nick says.

"You disagree?"

"No, I like visiting the Met. My favorite rooms are the Armor Room, the Egyptian tomb, and the Japanese garden. Oh, and you can't beat the view from the rooftop garden."

"Still, it seems on point for Valentine's Day, given that it's his holiday, even if it does seem a little macabre if it used to hold his arm bone, but you know, it's original."

"It's definitely original," he says. "I've never seen that on a Valentine's Day top ten list."

I laugh. "Hayden gives me the impression of liking more conventional ideas. I need five more ideas. Don't you have any?"

"I'm not sharing my best ideas with your readers. I'm saving them."

"That makes sense. That's always the toughest part. Sometimes I don't want everyone else to find my favorite places too." We pass by the back of Beacon Theatre, where they've roped off part of the street as they load band equipment in through the wide doors. Nick looks over as if he wants to figure out who's performing tonight. His desire to be the band playing there radiates off his body. But then his walls come up, and he focuses on the taco restaurant across the street.

"Do you ever feel like you don't want to share your emotions so publicly?" I ask. "Your songs can be so raw."

He glances at me, his gaze narrowing. When he does that, he looks so cute. "Off the record, right?"

"Always," I say.

"Sometimes I write a song, but I'm not ready to share it because it makes me feel too exposed, so I wait until it feels right. Do you ever have that when writing articles?"

"Not yet. I do try to convey emotion in my stories because I want people to feel moved when reading them. I want people to be upset when they read about what happened to Dulce with her bathroom or this mom with the newborn and to feel it is wrong." I pause. "I haven't had to write an article about myself where I share my feelings publicly. I don't know if I could do that. I would feel exposed." A target for bullies.

"I'm not the story," Nick says.

"Exactly," I say.

"But I'm definitely invested in your story," Nick says.

As I turn to look at him to figure out if *that* means something more than friends, I hear my name being called.

It's Jing and Iris, coming up the block. We wait outside Banter & Books for them to join us. Bella's latest romantic comedy book is displayed in the window. I hug them hello.

I open the bookstore's door, immediately enveloped by warmth. Hanging plants and shelves filled with books line the whitewashed walls. Bright book covers and green plants give such a cheerful, welcoming vibe. It feels like a cross between a café in Provence and a greenhouse. French-blue settees and armchairs scattered around form little nooks for private conversations or reading. Around each cluster of chairs is a mass cane, an Areca palm, or a peace lily, providing some additional seclusion. At the back is a conservatory with a small, free library, where people can exchange books.

We grab a table by the side and place an order for four salads.

I catch up with Iris and Jing while Nick leaves to order four hot drinks. I'm tempted to tell them immediately what Nick just said, but he'll probably be back too soon before we can discuss it. Plus, Iris wouldn't approve. I need to ask Jing later if she thinks it could mean anything.

"Nick looks like he likes you," Iris says. "When you guys were walking ahead, we watched for a while, and he seemed so intent on whatever you were saying."

"He did?" I ask.

"Yes," Iris says. "I'm sorry I was biased because of my whole ex experience. I shouldn't tarnish Nick with the same brush because he's also a musician. Nick has certainly demonstrated over the past few years that he's a good person. Lily reminded me about Nick playing at the Oasis Garden Concert. I remembered how I'd asked my ex to play there that day, and he told me he had to prioritize paying gigs. I should have known then."

"I understand." I rub Iris's back. She's much happier now. Now I can discuss Nick's remark! "As we were walking up here, we were talking about writing and conveying emotion, and I said I don't write about myself, and he said he was 'definitely invested' in my story. But maybe that's a friend thing to say."

"That seems more than a friend thing," Jing says. "I mean, he said 'invested.'"

"Right," I say. "'Interested' would mean nothing."

"Okay, you wordsmiths, but what also counts is that he's here and that he went with you to your mini show," Iris says.

Nick turns and walks back with the tray of drinks, and we are all suspiciously silent as he puts the drinks and our salads down.

"Am I interrupting a good conversation?" Nick asks.

"Always a very good conversation." I pat the seat next to me. "They're trying to think of truly romantic dates."

We distribute the salads around the table and eat.

Bella suddenly appears at our table. "Sorry I'm late. I had to get down my latest ideas. What ideas for your column do you have so far?"

I tell her my latest ideas, minus visiting St. Valentine's arm.

"Sebastian and I walked around Central Park in the last snowstorm, and it felt magical," Iris says. "I like the picnic idea."

"Because ultimately it depends on who you're with," I say.

"That's what I was going to say," Bella says.

"Should I share what we did last Valentine's Day?" I ask Jing and Iris. "That was my favorite Valentine's Day ever."

"What?" Nick asks.

"We did a Valentine's Day scavenger hunt, where clues are sent via your phone," I say.

"How did you find out about that?" he asks.

"I was searching for scavenger hunts in New York City," Iris says.

"What about a private yoga with puppies session?" Jing suggests. "That seems fun."

"Oh, I like that," I say.

"I am planning to send my couple to Mochi Dolci for Valentine's Day in my next book," Bella says. "You enter the speakeasy in the back through a pink phone booth. It's cool."

"What about the Kimoto Rooftop in Brooklyn?" Iris suggests. "It has a great romantic ambiance. But that could be because I was there with Sebastian."

"Perfect." I call to confirm it will be open for Valentine's Day.

"Did you get Nick's opinion?" Jing asks.

"I like to go dancing," he says before I can say that he didn't want to share his best ideas. "My friend is spinning tonight at some club that just opened up. We could check them out."

"That would be great," I say. "Do you guys want to go dancing?"

"I just realized I forgot to feed the cats," Bella says. She elbows Jing, who elbows Iris. *Not subtle, guys.*

Okay, clearly Bella thinks this is an opportunity for me. Still, she's a writer, and that's the best excuse she could give?

Jing and Iris look blankly at each other and then both say at the same time, "Laundry."

"It's my laundry and romantic comedy movie night," Jing says.

"With me," Iris adds.

"Do you want to go too?" Nick asks me. "I wouldn't want to interrupt a girls' laundry night."

He totally knows. Those are the lamest excuses ever.

"No." I kick them under the table. "I did my laundry already. I'm good."

Nick must totally think I like him.

"I'll text my friend and find out where it is." He texts his friend and then chuckles. "The Laundry Room."

"What?" I ask.

"The new club is called The Laundry Room," Nick says. "Are you guys sure you're not coming?"

"Not unless they actually have washing machines," Iris says with a straight face.

Chapter Fourteen

Nick

I clasp Maddie's hand and pull her into the side of the crowd by the DJ booth at The Laundry Room, which is literally in a former laundromat. My eyes are still adjusting to the dim light, but the laundry machines that line the side walls look like they might still work. But I'm not planning on calling Iris and Jing to join us. The club has a good feel, and this song has a great beat. How have I never been dancing with Maddie before? But then, we've gotten so much closer in these last few weeks. I've seen her dancing in the audience at my concerts at Craic and Laughs. She's a good dancer.

Crimson curtains block any light from the front windows, and a disco ball twirls above the dance floor.

"Thank you again for coming to the mini show with me," she says, swaying to the beat.

Yesterday, Demoraux threatened her. Did she really think I was going to let her take a bus to New Jersey by herself and be at some public show?

Okay, given that a significant percentage of the population was over fifty, I might have overreacted. Apparently, a mini show might be the safest place she could be. But at least Maddie seems to believe that I'm doing this because we need to be together for publicity purposes. I don't want to lead her on when I can't commit to a relationship because of my career.

I spin her around and then dip her, holding her in my arms. Our gazes meet, and that flare of attraction simmers, making my breath catch. I know that we can't be more than friends, but I wanted an excuse to touch her, to reassure myself that she is going to be okay. And if whoever is behind this corrupt scheme is watching, I want them to believe that we are dating and that they will regret it if they harm one hair on her head.

The music changes to a slow song. It helps to know the DJ. I pull Maddie tightly against my chest and hold on to her. She rests her cheek against my heart. A light flashes, but I'm not mad about it. At this point, being seen together in public is a good thing if it will make any foes think twice.

Maybe.

I wish Maddie would look up at me. Then again, maybe it's good that she doesn't. My eyes would probably reveal too much.

Another flash of a camera. I turn so that my back protects us from the location of the flashes. It's probably friends taking photos of each other, but I want to protect our privacy as best I can.

The beat picks up. My friend said he thought he could only get away with one slow song. But that's all I needed. I hug her tightly and feel her relax against my chest.

Bubbles float over from bubble blowers on top of the washing machines.

The next song is "I Gotta Feeling" by Black Eyed Peas. We break apart and start jumping up and down, waving our hands. Maddie smiles at me. This is what I needed—to release the tension from yesterday and the emotional roller coaster of the past months as I worried that we wouldn't sign the record deal.

Maddie follows my moves, and that feeling of satisfaction from dancing in sync comes back three-fold when it's the two of us who are in rhythm. I move closer, and Maddie shimmies right up to me, just out of reach, inches apart. Her gaze meets mine, and the simmering heat flares up between us. Kissing Maddie would be *so good*.

My phone buzzes. I ignore it.

It buzzes again. It could be an emergency. I pull it out of my pocket. My mom. She'd be proud of her timing. The song switches to "Pink Pony Club" by Chappell Roan, and I whisper to Maddie that it's my mom and I have to take it. We leave the dance floor and go into the back hallway, where it's a bit quieter. I call my mom back.

"Were you planning to tell me that you were dating someone, or did you feel like I should learn it from the news?" my mom says.

I didn't think to tell her because I'm not actually dating anyone.

"I'm sorry," I say. "It's been a whirlwind. And I know how you feel about my dating."

"Is this serious?" she asks.

Maddie is standing right next to me, but there's no way she can hear my mom's question. Especially with people now singing along to the lyrics in the room next to us. Still. What I want to say is that this is the most serious dating of my career—that I need this to be a success so the record label believes me. And so, since Inspector Demoraux said it's not safe, whoever is behind this also believes this is real so Maddie will be protected because they know I will come after them.

"That's quite a long pause," my mom says. "While you think about it, why don't you bring your girlfriend up to visit me? The first weekend in February would be good. I want to meet her. And it's been a long time since you visited."

My mom wants to meet her? My mom doesn't think I should date if I want to be a musician. But this would be another good excuse to spend the day with Maddie. We definitely won't have to worry about any ambiguous threats while we're upstate.

"I'll see if she's free," I say.

"Okay, I can tell you're busy at a club, so I'll let you go. Call me," she says before hanging up.

I turn to Maddie. "My mom wants to meet you. She saw the article. Would you be willing to drive up with me the first weekend of February when I visit her? There's also this great place I'd love to show you. It's a small hike, but..."

"But we're not..." Maddie whispers and then gestures with her hand in some sweeping motion that seems to indicate I can finish that sentence on my own.

"Don't worry. She never expects my relationships to last," I say.

Maddie looks like she wants to argue the point. I wish I could kiss her to distract her. I hold her hand instead and lead her back into the main room, where Abba's "Gimme! Gimme! Gimme!" is playing.

My mom's call was perfect timing. This is a night for dancing with Maddie, and things had been getting a little too heated before the interruption. It's best that we stay as friends. That way, I can always see her, and I won't have messed up something fragile.

Chapter Fifteen

Maddie

I'm still floating from dancing on Saturday night with Nick. I thought something might have happened that night because there was definitely electricity on the dance floor, but we separated at our respective apartment doors. He practically ran inside. His side of the wall was then completely quiet. I missed the noise.

I feel more alive and like I'm sparkling with him. There is an attraction simmering beneath the surface. But I think we both recognize that we want to keep our friendship, and this is a three-month contract with no permanence. Especially when both of us need to focus on our careers. Speaking of which, the newspaper bullpen is humming. I check my email to see if Hayden has responded to the draft article I sent late last night. He has and wants to see me in his office.

I should give Hayden a chance. Just because he and Nemesis went to the same college together and are always bonding over school ovonto dooon't moan ho'o not going to bo fair to mo.

He's on the phone when I enter his office area. His desk is bare. Today's vest is dark blue, and his tie is light green. He seems to alternate between bow ties and wide ties.

He speaks in a measured tone, deliberate. I always speak quickly, like a New Yorker.

"I went with Sarah's article," he says.

"Sorry?" I ask. *What does Sarah's article have to do with mine?*

"I also asked her to write an article on the top ten places to go for Valentine's Day," he explains. "And I chose her article."

"What? Why?" I ask. Is he some Roosevelt aficionado who believes in competing kitchen cabinets?

He repeats my "why" back to me, but very much in a tone of how dare I question him. "She gave it to me early on Sunday morning—not late on Sunday night."

"I thought you'd want me to visit the places I'm recommending—so I could convey the atmosphere," I say. "As it was, with only the weekend, I was only able to visit The Laundry Room and Kimoto Rooftop at night. Luckily, I've already visited most of the other places."

"Nice try," he says. "Didn't you visit The Laundry Room for some paparazzi shots with your rock star boyfriend?"

My stomach clenches. *I don't want to be the story.* "No. I went to get a feel for it so I could describe it accurately. Nick accompanied me because, obviously, it's much more fun to go together than for me to go on my own." I make sure to enunciate each word in the next sentence to match his speaking style. "Those weren't paparazzi shots. Those were random social media posts by fans published on Instagram and YouTube." And he calls himself a reporter? *Check your facts.*

"Felicity mentioned that you had a story you were covering that could be ground-breaking and to not assign you too much work," Hayden says. "What's the story about?"

As if I would trust him not to give it to Nemesis.

"I'm not ready to discuss it yet," I say.

"We could brainstorm some leads if you're stuck," he says.

Right.

"I'm working on the leads Felicity and I discussed, and she was clear that I should not share this story with anyone," I say. "It doesn't seem like she shared the subject matter with you either."

He leans back. "Remember, I may be your permanent boss if she doesn't come back."

As if I could forget. This is not going well for me. But maybe it's good that our animosity is out in the open and we don't have to tiptoe around, pretending that we like each other.

"I look forward to sharing the full story with you when it's more developed," I say.

"It seems you have some time to do an article on the Chinese New Year parade while you 'develop' this story," he says. "Here's Sarah's article."

I scan it quickly. We have some similar items, like the igloos, but most of her ideas are more typical—and expensive, like a dinner for two at Le Rock on Rockefeller Center with a visit to the Top of the Rock observation deck. And she's included Ella's Café.

"Ella's Café is closed." I hand him back Sarah's article. I'm surprised Sarah made such an egregious mistake and didn't check her recommendations. But then, I've never been put head-to-head with her before.

"It is?"

"Yes, I went there on Saturday, and a sign on the door said *Closed for Renovations.*"

"It's good I had you write an article too, then," he says. "Which one should we add from yours?"

That's his response?

"Here. Check that the others are open." He hands me back Nemesis's article and walks away.

My mouth hangs open. This is how he envisions my role? Felicity has to come back. Or I really have to write a breakthrough story. Hayden clearly does *not* have *my* interests at heart.

But who is corrupt? Let's hope I uncover some clues at the concert on Saturday.

I'm excited for Nick's first concert under the MusEn label, and I'm relieved that it's not that cold this late Saturday afternoon. A stage has been temporarily constructed behind the playground in the basketball court area. I'm escorted to the VIP pit. Up on the stage, Nick looks intent as he checks the equipment with Amira, who is dressed in a black hoody and black pants like a tech person. Nick and I stashed our own tech person disguises for later in the backstage area.

Nick's threadbare jeans hang low on his hips, and his black T-shirt tightly defines his chest and his flat abs. I pull my own stomach in. He looks amazing. He also brought Mr. Muscle and another guy as security this time. Mr. Muscle is near me, apparently so he can get a feel for the crowd.

A few silver-haired people of importance sit in a row of chairs in the front, but most of the space is for standing.

I maneuver to a spot right by all three deputy commissioners. José's girlfriend and Sayo's family are also here. Nick is pointing at some cord that needs to be taped more securely on the stage to a tech person.

Our eyes suddenly meet, and he smiles. I wave back. Then he talks to another tech person and points at me. She nods, climbs down from the stage, and hurries over to me, weaving through the crowd.

"Nick wanted you to have this." She hands me a baggie of only green M&M's.

I hold it up for Nick to see, and he gives me a thumbs-up and then disappears behind the curtain to the backstage area.

More people join the expectant crowd. The MC strides out and announces a female pop group as the first act. Pommer is texting the entire time. Ward is chatting with his neighbor, an elderly woman who, based on their conversation, seems to be quite active in the neighborhood. The only one enjoying the concert is Galliano. Next to him, his daughter moves to the music. Her dad says something to her, and she shakes her head.

I move closer to them.

She says, "Dad, you can't introduce me. I want to make it on my own merit."

"*I'm* not introducing you to the Parks Commissioner. Pommer is. And I told him he absolutely can't mention that you're my daughter. I respect your decision," he says. "And there's not much I can do, anyway. What does my work have to do with becoming a rock musician?"

"Are you investigating why I got that offer to play at those clubs?" she asks. "I appreciate the opportunities, but those owners seemed like they'd been forced to do it."

"Yeah, I really don't understand why," he says. "I'm investigating. That inspector quit, and I can't track him down."

Hmm. He was saying he respected her decision to not use his influence, but he was still getting Pommer—such a fan of rock musicians, I think sarcastically, remembering his reaction to me being Nick's girlfriend when I first met him—to introduce her to the Parks Commissioner, presumably to get her on the radar for future concerts. But most interesting was that she was suspicious of the offers to play at those clubs. And if he wasn't the one behind those offers, then who was? Was he really investigating the offers? Did Demoraux really quit and disappear? That seemed like an excuse. Galliano was still the most likely party behind those offers. Are there two separate kickback schemes?

"Believe me, with the recent threats of cost-cutting and Commissioner Johnson warning us that they plan to reduce the number of deputy commissioners to two, I need to figure that out," he says.

The deputy commissioners are competing against each other for their jobs?

Is that why the commissioner is so keen to do this series of articles on his department, so he can get some good publicity and, potentially, support in the public eye? And maybe forestall these cuts?

This gives Pommer and Ward a motive to frame Galliano.

I back away before Galliano turns around and realizes I've been eavesdropping.

Nick comes on next, and I am transfixed.

They perform two songs while the crowd dances to the beat, and then Nick pulls out his earbuds and introduces the band, talking to the audience. He seems relaxed as he develops a rapport with them. He has the crowd totally in the palm of his hand.

It makes me so happy to see him experiencing his dream.

He slips off his guitar for the next song. It's my favorite—a high energy pop song. Two backup dancers join him on stage. Behind him, a video of a starry night plays.

I hope he can do it. I bite my lip as they start.

Yes!

He's actually dancing in sync. And singing!

He swings his hips back and forth and sweeps his hand across from thigh to thigh. And I feel like all the women in the pit swoon along with me. The sweep is so sexy and suggestive while not being remotely improper.

I can't believe we're even friends.

He winks at me.

That brings me back to the night of dancing at The Laundry Room and being held tightly by him. I fan myself.

The woman next to me looks over and says, "He's definitely taking the chill out of the air."

I nod. I certainly feel warm.

Nick and the two backup dancers do a cha-cha-cha and a two-step back while singing the last line. And then his set is over. He looks at me, and I give him a thumbs-up. He's so good.

Next is a blues group, and it's a bit more mellow.

Finally, the sun is setting as the concert ends. Galliano prods his daughter to join Pommer, who is talking to the Parks Commissioner. Nick enters the VIP pit area and, per our agreement, talks to Ophelia. At least he's made that connection. I stand near Galliano, but he's glad-handing the various constituents.

Suddenly, Pommer's head whips around. I follow his gaze to see who had caught his attention.

The property manager for Eleanor Roosevelt Houses, Beatrice, has joined us in the pit, and she's talking to Ward.

Go time.

As if Nick senses my thoughts, he looks at me. I head backstage as he excuses himself. Backstage, we quickly change into the black tech gear we stashed here with the rest of the band's equipment. I pull my hair tightly back. We both put on roomy black hoodies, pulling up the hoods and face masks. I whip out sunglasses.

"And I'm supposed to be the rock star," Nick jokes.

"Don't you have your own?" I ask. "This is years of investigative expertise. Watch and learn."

"I'm definitely learning something." Nick's cell rings.

It's Amira, per our plan.

He holds out the phone so we can both hear her.

"Ward and Pommer are with Beatrice by the south side of the park, so head that way with the backdrop," she says. "I'll direct you through your headpiece."

"Got it." Nick puts in his air pods and slides his phone into his pocket. "I'll cough when we need to stop."

We each heft one side of the 10x8-foot wooden stage frame with their band name on it. The only things you can see are our sneakers and black pant legs underneath it.

We leave the tent and head south, Nick leading us.

He coughs.

We stop and put the stage frame down.

"Are you talking about work on a day like this?" Pommer asks.

"Yes. The turnaround time for these new contractors is taking too long," Ward says. "I'm noting it now before Commissioner Johnson asks me to write it up formally. I'm doing Beatrice a favor by telling her this in person so she can fix it before she receives a formal complaint letter from Commissioner Johnson."

"Yes, I appreciate the heads-up," she says.

The sound of drilling hides the next bit of conversation. *Why are they allowed to drill on weekends?*

We pick up the frame again. It will look too suspicious if we stay too long, anyway.

We carry it to the truck, where Amira and José help us load in. Amira suggests I sit in the front because I might be able to watch the rest of their interaction. I clamber into the truck's passenger seat.

Beatrice hands Pommer a book. I'm too far away to see the title.

Ward is also holding a book—he wasn't before.

Did she give them both books as gifts? I need to see the titles. Maybe she slipped money into the books.

I exit the passenger side and slip behind the truck in front of ours. Keeping to the street side of the truck, I inch back up to where the three of them are standing.

"One of our tenants recently passed away, and her son asked me if I wanted any of the books. He knows how much I like to read. I saw this and immediately thought of you," Beatrice is saying.

I peek through the space between the cars and take a photo. I then enlarge the photo for a better look. The title is something with playgrounds. And the book for Ward is *Streets of New York*.

"I can't accept gifts over fifty dollars," Pommer says.

"It didn't cost me anything," she says. "Otherwise, it's probably going in the dumpster. That's where most of the books went. I saved some for our laundry library and donated some to Housing Works, but the son has no interest in doing that. There's only so many of them that I could carry."

"Let me look at how much it costs and give you a check," Pommer says.

"Mine is under the fifty-dollar limit," Ward says. "Thanks so much for this New York history book."

"But those books add up, don't they?" Pommer asks.

Ward looks over, and I pull back behind the car. I can't see or hear them now because the drilling has started again. My phone buzzes in my hoodie pocket.

> Nick: *They're walking away now. Both carry-ing books.*

> Nick: *Something dropped out of Ward's book*

I take a chance and peek around the car. It's something long and rectangular. It could be a thin envelope—or a bookmark.

I want to run up and talk to them to get a closer look at the books. Is it a hollowed-out book that holds the bribe money? I wait until they disappear out of sight and then scurry over to pick up what dropped. It's a bookmark for a book titled *Caper Crush*. Not an envelope with money.

Beatrice knows both Pommer and Ward well enough that she gives them tailored book gifts. Galliano had no independent inter-action with her, but he may be afraid to interact with her in public if he's the one getting the payments. Galliano also knows about the quid pro quo payments, and it doesn't seem like his daughter is in on it.

These books add up. Did Pommer mean something by that? No way Ward is getting his cut in books. Those were not rare books. But

Ward did stop by the library a lot when I followed him. Are Pommer and Ward in it together? They could have ganged up on Galliano.

These seem like clues, but I need to figure out what they mean.

Chapter Sixteen

Nick

The goal: look like a loving couple out on a date. My label has "leaked" to some paparazzi that we'll be dining at Ciel on the Upper East Side. Several social media posts have alleged that we broke up because they haven't seen us out together since the night we went dancing. Someone posted a shot of me huddling with Sayo after rehearsal and claimed I had a new girlfriend. But thankfully, a long-term fan posted that it looked like Sayo and me walking together.

This goal might be harder than the MusEn publicist imagined, because Maddie is clearly frustrated that she doesn't yet have a break in her investigation. Hopefully, the soothing bistro ambiance of this restaurant works its charms. Small round tables are set up across a black and white–tiled floor, with large green trees interspersed between, and a bar along one side. An enormous copper hood commands the corner with a grill underneath (the specialty is grilled steak), with another bar with stools surrounding that cooking area. On either side of the bar mirror are vintage French posters on the white-tiled walls. We're seated on a huge, circular, deep-green velvet couch surrounding a table. A candle flickers in the votive in the center. Maddie seems to absorb the décor and puts her phone away.

Our waiter hands us our menus and then asks if we'd like tap or bottled water, flat or sparkling. We both say "tap" at the same time.

"This is the utter opposite of Strangelove," I say.

"Don't say I don't take you to the best places," Maddie says.

"I think that's my line…" I tip my head to point out the crystal chandelier glinting above us and the green velvet couches.

We're seated in a corner with some space between us and the surrounding tables. I'd asked for as much privacy as possible. I don't have to make it easy for the paparazzi. I want to be able to talk to Maddie freely.

I promptly reach across the narrow table to hold Maddie's hand, lacing my fingers through hers. I like holding her hand. There's something about the way Maddie relaxes a bit when I do. She's so hard-charging, and yet, when our palms touch, it's like she wants to stay in this moment.

"I can't study my menu if you're holding my hand," she says.

"Why not?"

"It's distracting."

"Distracting?" I ask. "In a good way or a bad way?"

She smiles at me. "Both good and bad."

"How so?"

"It's comforting. Your hand is always so warm. And I like the way I can feel where your skin is rough from playing the guitar. It makes it feel more real." She pouts. "But it's distracting when I need to study this menu."

Maddie's pouting… Is she flirting with me?

"Maddie, what a surprise to see you here!" a voice intrudes upon our conversation. "You must introduce me to your *boyfriend*."

The woman says the word "boyfriend" as if she can't quite believe it. Maddie also doesn't look thrilled to see this woman. Is she one of the bullies from middle school?

"This is Nick," Maddie says. "Nick, this is Sarah."

Nemesis?

No way. She looks different without a helmet and face mask.

Sarah introduces the man she's with as her boyfriend.

I stand and put out my hand. "Nick Devlin. You work with Maddie, right?"

Sarah looks surprised. "Wow. I didn't think you'd know my name."

"Well, sometimes we talk about work," I say. "And obviously, I've met Maddie's *close* friends, like Jing."

A corner of Maddie's lips kicks up on my emphasis of the word "close," and then she compresses her lips back into a straight line.

"I like coming home to Nick and getting his perspective on whatever I'm working on," Maddie says.

Sarah looks back and forth between us. "You're a dark horse, Maddie."

Maddie shrugs but doesn't seem to take umbrage.

"She's a thoroughbred," I say. "I'm the one who's fortunate because Maddie agreed to date me."

I cringe inside. That sounds so cheesy. I sit, a little embarrassed.

But Maddie gives me such a warm smile, and she reaches for my hand this time.

"We seem to be superfluous," says Sarah's boyfriend.

Maddie and I both say that it was nice to meet them and turn our attention back to each other, as he pulls her away.

"Thank you," Maddie says simply.

"I can't believe she said that in front of me. And I meant it," I say. "Thoroughbreds are smart and hardworking with an even temperament but also spirited."

A faint blush stains her cheeks.

"You last likened me to a bear. I seem to be improving."

"Bears are also very intelligent and social, but they do like to sleep, so that was a compliment," I say.

Maddie tilts her head, as if considering this, but then nods. "She seems to be our main stalker. I can't believe she followed us to this restaurant. Are they seated so they can see our table?"

"Yes, and Sarah is the one facing us," I say.

"That's too bad," Maddie says. "She'll probably study us to see if we're really dating. But that was so great that you knew she was a colleague, and brilliant job on mentioning Jing. Well done."

Now it's my turn to look pleased.

We study the menus and give our orders to the waiter.

Maddie is wearing this light-green scoop-neck dress, and she looks really pretty. I mean, she always looks pretty, but that scoop-neck collar is driving me insane because it shows off her creamy skin. I want to feel if her skin is as soft as it looks.

"Do you know where or when the paparazzi will photograph us?" Maddie asks.

"No," I say. "We'll have to be romantic all night." That's my plan, anyway.

"Do you have any romance game?" she asks.

"Are you doubting me?"

She nods. "Other than singing love songs to someone, because I'll grant you that, I'm not sure romance is your specialty."

"Why would you think I can't be romantic?"

"It's not like you could think of a particularly good cover story for how we got together, and you haven't dated in a while, and..."

"Counting with your fingers as you itemize my flaws is definitely not going to look romantic in a picture," I say.

Maddie drops her hand and flushes. "You're right. Sorry."

I lean forward. "I'll pretend you were enumerating all the things you want to do to me later."

Now she really blushes. I chuckle.

"Still, not exactly romantic," she says.

The waiter places our appetizers in front of us. I pick up one of my gougères and say to Maddie, "Here, try this. Isn't feeding you romantic?

"Mm." She bites into the cheesy filling. I have to look away when she gives a murmur of satisfaction. Maybe being romantic right now is not such a good idea.

I eat one too.

"I'm not sure about feeding each other, to be honest, but I can give it a try," she says. "Isn't it a little childish?" She cuts off a bite of her asparagus-gruyere tart. "Here." She reaches over to feed me.

I dart a glance over to Nemesis's table. "Nemesis looks transfixed."

"But maybe that's because she thinks it's cheesy."

"It is cheesy." I reach over with my thumb and wipe a bit of cheese from Maddie's mouth. Her lips part. I trace her lips so lightly and so gently with the other side of my thumb.

I lick the cheese off my thumb. Our glances meet and hold, and the air feels heavy between us. I reach out again, unable to stop myself. I tuck a loose strand of her hair behind her ear.

I have to pull back. And it feels like we're being stared at—either by Nemesis or the paparazzi. This isn't what I want—my love life dissected or offered up to the press for their entertainment. Not for Maddie. She has the softest hazel-brown eyes. They'll tear her apart.

What if she gets that bitter edge my mom has whenever she talks about my dad?

A black extended camera lens from behind one of the potted shrubs aimed at us snares my corner vision.

I pull back. This is a three-month fake-dating gig. That's all it can ever be.

Chapter Seventeen

Nick

This is a bad idea. It seemed brilliant when I asked Maddie to meet my mom—the perfect excuse to ensure I'm with Maddie and can protect her. But after the Ciel dinner, I should have thought of an excuse as to why Maddie couldn't come, even though she seemed excited to go. But how could I disinvite her suddenly? She'd inevitably find out I'd visited my mom without her.

I didn't think this through—on so many levels. My relationship with Christina shifted after she met my mom. My mom couldn't stop pointing out the negatives of dating a rock musician. Christina probably conceived the idea for her article that weekend. I'm not sure if my mom is actively trying to undermine my dating life, or if she just has so much resentment against my father that she can't keep it in.

I merge into the next lane as we head upstate in the band's van.

"Was Sarah friendlier to you at work this week?" I ask. Hopefully she's not trying to curry favor with Maddie now.

"No," Maddie says. "Do you worry about that?"

"Yes," I say.

"That's terrible," she says simply.

"It is. I'm not famous yet, but even so, people can be so obvious that they are befriending me because maybe I'll become famous and be good to know."

"I don't think I have to worry about that happening with Sarah," she says. "But I was out of the office most of the week following Deputy Commissioner Galliano. It all seemed aboveboard, though. He attended one tenant meeting where they complained about repairs, but interestingly, other tenants vouched for him that he would fix everything. I also went to jujitsu classes every morning this week. I'm so sore."

"You followed him? Did he know?" The inspector said this wasn't safe, and she's following the main suspect around! At least she's practicing her jujitsu.

"I don't think so. I borrowed some wigs from my friend's uncle. He works in theater, so he has everything. He also gave me eyeglasses and stuffing to change my body shape, etcetera. When you are famous, I can introduce you."

"This sounds like something I must see. Do you have a photo?"

"No," she says.

"Oh, I definitely want to go on an undercover mission with you." It makes me feel better if Maddie is dressed as someone else. Maybe she's not in danger, then. "Can I come on the next one?"

"Sure," Maddie says. "Does that mean I get to be in charge of whatever you're going to wear?" She's wearing her evil grin.

"Be kind," I say. "We're almost there."

We exit the highway.

"I'm sorry I'm pulling you away from your investigation." And there was the perfect excuse that I was an idiot not to use.

"A walk in the woods will be good," Maddie says. "At this point, I'm not getting anywhere with what I'm doing, and I need to step away. Some of my best ideas come when I'm walking, so I'm looking forward to our hike."

"It's not a full-on hike," I say. "It's a walk to a waterfall."

"That sounds good too," she says.

We turn off at the exit, and I pull onto a dirt path with a hiking trail sign. A bunch of cars are parked here. We exit the car, and both of us attach ice cleats to our boots because I know the path will be slick.

"These are cool," Maddie says. "This is a whole other side of you."

We walk carefully down the path, each finding a stick to use for balance. It's about a quarter mile, the snow and ice crunching under our feet, and then the wooded path opens up to this lake with an amazing waterfall. The white water rushes down, and the whooshing sound is soothing. I take a deep breath of the fresh pine-scented air.

"Wow," Maddie says.

"I know," I said. "My mom showed this to me when she first moved here. I come here sometimes when I'm feeling blocked."

"Yes, I can see why," she says. "It makes me feel like it's all going to work out."

I watch Maddie take it all in—her face glowing, her cheeks pink from the cold. I want to stay in this moment, being here with her as we absorb the beauty of this winter wonderland. Snow flurries float down. Maddie sticks out her tongue to catch one. I feel such a yearning for this—a lifetime of these moments with her. I swallow and look back over the lake to find my center again. Music. The wind whistles through the trees.

Eventually, we walk back to the car, not needing to talk, appreciating the nature around us.

We remove our cleats, and I put them back in their bag. It's only a few miles to my mom's house.

As Maddie clips in her seat belt, she turns to me. "I don't really feel comfortable lying to your mom that we're dating. Can't we tell her the truth?"

Bringing Maddie to meet my mom is such a bad idea. I should have told my mom that Maddie was in the middle of a work assignment and didn't have time to meet. Why didn't I do that?

Maddie repeats her question.

"It's okay. I don't think she's actually excited I'm dating someone. She probably wants to warn you about the pitfalls. Then when we break up, she can say she told me so." I pull out of the parking lot, heading back onto the country roads.

I bite my lip as I make another turn on these narrow country lanes. I hadn't wanted to admit that, but it will be obvious when we meet my mom, so it's better to prepare Maddie.

Maddie turns to face me. "C'mon... I'm sure your mom wants you to be happy."

"She wants me to be happy...doing marketing or accounting," I say. Maybe a tinge of bitterness slips through. "I would tell her, but her roommates can't keep secrets. That's how the fact that Christina and I were dating leaked. I was talking to my mom about Christina, and the next thing I knew, there was an article in *The Squirrel* titled 'Who is Nick Devlin dating?'"

"She has roommates?"

"She bought the house with two female friends. They fell in love with the house on some group trip up here. They all have hobbies, and each has a hobby room."

"That's cool," Maddie says.

"She's happy," I say. "And I'm happy that she's happy." I glance over at Maddie. She's got that look when she wants to ask a million questions, but she's wrestling with herself to decide what the best approach is.

"What is her hobby?" Maddie asks.

She's decided to back off for now. I don't doubt she'll ask me more questions later. But once she meets my mom, she'll understand what I meant. I've met Maddie's mom in the hallway, and they seem to have a more normal mother-child relationship, if a little strained because Maddie doesn't want to take over her cookie business.

"She knits, but her friend makes minis. That's why I told you the mini knit sweater was a perfect gift for her. Not that you needed to bring a gift."

"I can't meet your mom and not bring a gift," Maddie says. "How do you know for sure it was her roommate?"

Maddie hasn't backed down.

"Her roommate apologized. Otherwise, I wouldn't have known."

"Your mom doesn't miss New York?" she asks, changing the subject.

I point to the bag in the back. "She misses some things about New York. She sends me a list of food to bring up. But she loves the fresh smell of the countryside. And the views. You'll understand when you see her house."

We've arrived at my mom's Victorian house, which sits at the top of the hill, close to the main street of Catskill. It's an over-the-top huge house with nine bedrooms, with each of the three women having two bedrooms leaving several spares for guests, like their visiting children or grandchildren. There's a wraparound porch on the first floor, perfect for reading books or writing lyrics, and then a second-floor balcony that provides a river vista. The views are absolutely stunning when the sun sets and the leaves change.

Still, I was shocked when my mom first fell in love with this house. I thought she'd want a modern, utilitarian house, not one with nooks and crannies (and lots of maintenance) and history. So much history. It was the home of a judge. I can't say I'll ever truly understand my mom.

My mom meets us as I park the bus in the driveway next to their backyard, most of which is covered with a vegetable garden. I hug my mom hello. She feels smaller—shorter and frailer—every time I do. We break apart. My mom is definitely checking Maddie out. I put my arm around Maddie and pull her closer to me.

"I feel like I've had a courtside seat to your dates, there's been so much publicity," my mom says. "I was sure it was merely a publicity stunt, but here you are."

Maddie blinks.

"It's not a publicity stunt," I say.

"I thought you'd decided to fly solo, Nick?" my mom asks.

My mom has to be the only mother who's not actively seeking grandchildren. Actually, she just really doesn't want me to pursue a career as a musician.

"That was the plan, but then I met Maddie," I say.

"You're next-door neighbors?" she asks. "Was the article correct?"

"Yes," I confirm. "That's how we met."

She nods but gives Maddie another once-over. As I grab the Orchard Folly-labeled bag, filled with specialty food items she requested from the city, she seems to glance at the band name. I probably should have packed it in a different bag.

"It seems like a big deal that MusEn picked you up," she says.

"It is a big deal, Mom." Dad was never picked up by a legit label.

"It's great. He's finally getting his break," Maddie says.

"Do you actually believe that?" my mom asks. "Aren't you worried you'll lose him if he makes it big?"

Maddie stares at her. Her brow wrinkles as if she can't quite make sense of my mom.

My mom's open hostility toward my career is a shock to most people.

"No. I support his dreams, like he supports mine," Maddie says. "I'd be more worried that I'd lose him if he didn't make it. I'd worry that his creative flame would die, and he'd become bitter. And then he wouldn't be the Nick I know, who's so passionate about making music."

She gets me. How does she understand me so well?

"You're not worried about him being swept up in the fame?"

"He's pretty level-headed. You probably had a lot to do with that," Maddie says. "I think he knows what's real and what's not." She gives me a pointed glance.

"What about the fact that he'll have to travel?"

"My sister is married to a lawyer. Believe me, that's not better. He works until eleven every night and works most weekends. And his routine doesn't include dancing to stay fit."

I very much appreciate the way Maddie's eyes flicker over to my chest, with a definite heat of approval in her glance.

"Plus, I have my own career, and I often work nights or week-ends," she says.

"Oh, so you don't plan to have kids?" my mom asks.

I can't believe she's going there. *We will drop them off here.* I think she's half afraid that's my plan.

"Not at the moment," Maddie says. "We've only just started dat-ing."

"I got pregnant on my first date with Nick's dad."

"Mom!"

"Although, I guess it wasn't really a date," my mom says.

"We're taking every precaution," Maddie says.

Yes, like not even kissing.

"Do you want kids?"

"Someday, but obviously, we'd have to both be financially secure," Maddie says. "But my mom and my sister run a cookie business, and it has a daycare for employees, so I can drop them off there. That's what my sister does. It's pretty much a child's dream to be living in a cookie factory. At first, anyway. My mom would be happy to see them. She spends more time there now than in the kitchen."

I want to delve into that "*At first, anyway.*"

"That's good that you have a plan. Would you like some tea or coffee? Let me take you on a tour of the house first," my mom says. "Nick mentioned that you make miniatures. You will love our miniature room."

Maddie seems to have passed whatever test my mom has with flying colors.

"Oh here. I forgot to give you this," Maddie says, and she hands my mom the little present.

My mom unwraps it, and she does indeed love the miniature knitted sweater.

She takes us on a tour of the house. First up is her knitting room, which has a bookcase full of yarn and a comfortable rocking chair.

Next, we visit the miniatures room, so titled because it's literally a miniature town, and meet my mom's roommate, Christy. Her other roommate is away this weekend, visiting a friend.

"Wow, you even have a bookshop, a coffee shop, and a Christmas store," Maddie says, staring at the red, white, and green shop.

Christy beams with pride. "I couldn't decide whether to make a house for Santa Claus and Mrs. Claus, but then I decided that I have so many Christmas miniatures that I really needed a shop."

"Oh, and you created a secondhand shop too. I haven't seen that before," Maddie says.

"Same thing. I made some things for my mini club, and they didn't fit in anywhere, so I thought a secondhand shop would be perfect."

"What is your mini club?"

"We meet once a month at someone's house and make miniatures. You're welcome to join us, if Nick wants to bring you up here on the third Saturday of the month."

"That's why you seemed so familiar with miniatures at the fair," Maddie says to me.

"I told you my mom's roommate had a mini town," I say.

"I'm sorry I missed that New Jersey fair," Christy says. "Several of my friends were dealers there, but my boyfriend had an operation earlier that week, and I needed to be around. Do you have a website?"

"No," Maddie says. "With my work schedule, it's hard to create enough stock. I do this one show, and periodically I email my list to see if they have any requests."

"Well, I know so many people in the mini community. If you ever want me to put out the word, let me know."

"Have you ever seen this work before?" Maddie asks and shows a photo of Ward's bodega.

She peers at the image. "I know that artist. He has an Instagram page."

"He does?" Maddie asks.

"It's not under his real name, obviously, but sure. Let me find it," she says. "He spends a fortune on miniatures." She shows Ward's Instagram handle to Maddie.

"Wow." Maddie shows me one of the posts. "Look at this miniature deli. It really captures a New York City deli. And the signs are even electrified and blinking on and off."

"I wanted to get an electrified one, but they were too expensive," Christy says. "Even I couldn't justify spending that much for my miniatures."

"That must have been a lot, then," says my mom wryly.

We next see the library. Maddie immediately finds the photo of me at twelve, awkwardly holding up my math medal.

"He's very good at math," my mom says. "He could have a stable career in accounting or something else math related."

My mom's back at it.

Christy glances out the window, and gestures for us to look out too. "The snow is coming down thick and heavy now. They're expecting several inches."

"You guys should stay the night. The roads might be icy and slippery," my mom says. "And it's not that often that I get to see you."

But that would mean we're sharing a room. And a bed. My mom doesn't have any rooms with twin beds.

My mom looks out the window. "It's already several inches deep. It looks like it's going to be hard to drive with limited visibility. I won't sleep if you go."

How am I going to sleep if we stay?

Chapter Eighteen

Maddie

Nick seems reluctant to stay, and I can't tell if that's because of his relationship with his mom or some other reason. I can't read him. Am I supposed to say I need to get home or that I'm okay with spending the night? Icy roads make me nervous as well. I vote to stay.

We retreat downstairs to the living room, and his mom stokes up the flames in the fireplace. The living room has one large couch with two comfortable-looking armchairs and a huge flat screen TV. On the back wall is a bookcase filled with DVDs.

I offer to help make dinner with his mom, but Nick says that he and his mom like cooking together, and I should keep working on my article. I give Nick and his mom some alone time and retreat to their library to work on my latest article. But my thoughts keep flashing back to Nick. *"I support his dreams, like he supports mine."* How could I say something so corny? I hide my head in my hands. That probably convinced his mom that our dating is a publicity stunt now. Except that then we'd have a better script, and it wouldn't be me saying sappy things like that.

I had looked into Nick's eyes at that moment and thought, *Am I the only one feeling this connection? Am I out here by myself, living in my own fantasyland?* It was the same when we had dinner at Ciel and the night we went dancing. I'm falling so hard, and I don't know how to stop liking him.

I sigh. That slight blush that stained his cheeks when I said that he was fit... It made my heart flutter.

Then I think about his mom, which makes me think of his dad. Did his dad even try to be a father? Or did he disappear immediately? Is that why his mom is bitter?

Or did his dad change over time? Won't Nick change at some point? He'll no longer blush when a woman checks him out. He'll expect it.

This isn't real, I remind myself.

But why did he want me to meet his mom? Why didn't he say he was busy? Or that I was busy?

He said he can't say no when his mom asks. But he can lie to her about us.

It's definitely complicated. It's wrong to lie to his mom. But the way his face fell when she went back to wishing he was an accountant... It's like when my mom says, "Are you sure you don't want to join us working here? I created this cookie business for both of you guys."

And wouldn't I worry about losing him if we were dating? I should be working on quelling these feelings, not trying to figure out if they're real. *We can't date.* Every time he hugs another woman, there will be rumors that he's moved on from me—after all, what did he see in me in the first place? I've seen some of the comments about me.

I will have to ignore the whispers behind my back—poor Maddie, she's being cheated on. And even though I know Nick would never cheat—well, today's Nick—what if his mom is right and fame changes someone? But even if he didn't ever cheat, others would think that I was deceiving myself and holding on to some relationship mirage, even if it wasn't fake.

But maybe it would be worth it. Because when Nick and I hang out, he's Nick—not *The* Nick Devlin, rock star.

I sigh. I really need to focus and write this article. But he's still invading my thoughts. It makes sense. He's a rock star—objectively hot. It would be ridiculous if I weren't affected by being this close to him, even if we're just supposed to be friends. Even if I should be used to him.

In incognito mode, I check out Ward's Instagram page. My breath catches. Every two weeks, he has a post with a miniature library scene. I compare the last two photos to see if any differences pop out.

Yes, the sign announcing the book club changes every two weeks. And the location... The location is St Agnes. And two weeks ago, the location was the Mid-Manhattan Library. A shiver goes through me. Those are the names of library branches around New York City. *Is he meeting someone at St. Agnes tomorrow? Is this my break? Is this when they exchange the money? But meeting in person seems risky.*

I check the post for any other clues. The doll is reading a different book each week. A month ago, she was reading *Rescued* by Ellen Gilman. But she's not reading any book this week. The *Caper Crush* bookmark! Are they hiding the money in books? Is that why Pommer said, "Those books add up"? Ward received a book with a bookmark. Did that signal that the money would be in *Caper Crush*?

I've got it! My first big break! I can catch him tomorrow if my theory is right! I jump up and down. *Yes!*

I run down the stairs to tell Nick.

Nick is equally elated, but we both agree we shouldn't discuss my investigation over dinner because of the leak last time. It's hard not to, though. Thankfully, dinner is delicious. I insist on washing the dishes, but Nick helps me. And as I pass the dishes to him to dry, his hand brushes mine. It must be so obvious that I like him. Especially with two women monitoring our every move. At least they will believe that we are dating.

After I wash the dishes with Nick, his mom suggests playing Clue.

The four of us sit around the circular table. Nick hands out extra pieces of paper in addition to the Clue sheet. I take one—I like to note down all the guesses and answers. Nick doesn't take a piece of paper. I'm totally going to win.

We each take turns rolling the dice and making our guesses. There's good-natured ribbing and moaning when someone gets pulled into a room they don't want to be in, but overall, the atmosphere is hushed and intense, everyone shielding their cards and their clue sheet from prying eyes. I've narrowed it down—it's definitely Mrs. White and the candlestick, but I don't have the room yet. And everyone seems to know that the candlestick is the weapon. Nick suddenly says that he's willing to take a guess.

What? *How?*

He guesses the candlestick, White, and the kitchen, takes the cards out of the packet, and he's right.

His mom shakes her head. "He wins every time."

"You've been holding out on me with your detective skills!" I say.

"I can't compare to you," he whispers. "I can't believe you finally have a good clue. We make a solid team."

Nick's mom and Christy murmur that they are ready for bed. Nick's mom suggests we can stay in the living room until we're ready to retire, but she says, "Please be forewarned that noise travels in the house..."

Nick looks mortified, and I feel my cheeks heat.

"I think we'll call it a night," he mutters.

We head up to the bedrooms. This has got to be the earliest Nick has ever gone to bed.

There is only one bed. And it's not even a king-size bed. I'm not even sure it's queen-size.

We both stare at the bed. At least it has a lot of pillows.

"I'll take the floor, obviously." Nick takes off a handful of pillows.

"Don't be silly. I'm sure we can share the bed," I say.

"I'll get more sleep on the floor," he says.

What? He wants to stay away from me that badly?

Nick takes one look at my face and steps closer. My breath catches as I suddenly realize he is saying that he *can't* share the bed because sleep is not what will be on his mind. That heat in his eyes... He *is* attracted to me.

"How can I be sure I'm not violating clause eleven if my hand touches you?" His voice is practically a growl. What that deep timbre is doing to my stomach... He reaches out, stopping a hair's breadth from my arm. I swear I can feel the heat from his hand. He takes a step closer. I back up until my body is flat against the wall. My pulse flickers. Our gazes are locked until his shifts to my lips.

"And if you tease your lip like that, and I'm half-asleep...will I remember to say *thanks much* before I kiss you?

Nick does want to kiss me. And I want to kiss him. I am transfixed by the heat in his perusal. But also, I *don't* want to kiss him, in case I'm a terrible kisser.

He puts one hand next to my head slowly, giving me time to move away. *I can't.*

"I'm a hugger. What if my subconscious, in the middle of the night, completely forgets about all the various terms and my arms reach out to hug you? That's going to happen if we share that bed. Should I ask for permission now? Will that count?"

I swallow.

We stare at each other, and a wave of emotion cascades over me—of longing and desire and fear. So many thoughts rush through my head.

I am falling so hard.

I can't let Nick break my heart.

This is not for real—or even if this chemistry is very much for real (because it has to be), this it not for forever.

Nick takes a deep breath, as if pulling himself together, shakes his head, and pulls away his hand, stepping back and crossing his arms.

It's like the cold wind from outside snuck through any cracks under the windowsill and grabbed me in its icy embrace. I step forward.

"No. I also don't want to kiss you for the first time in my mom's house," Nick says.

For the first time...

And if I'm really a terrible kisser...for the last time.

I step back.

"There's not enough privacy," Nick says. "Why don't I tell my mom that I snore and you have an important meeting tomorrow, so you need your sleep, and then I'll take the couch?"

Nick looks incredibly pleased with himself, nodding as he sits down at the edge of the bed. "Unless you want to be the snorer?"

Chapter Nineteen

Nick

Maddie did not volunteer to be the snorer. I chuckle and receive a glare from a library patron seated nearby.

We woke up early to drive back so we could be at the St. Agnes Library on the Upper West Side when it opened, after a stop at the apartment of Uncle Tony, Maddie's friend's uncle. He works as a costume designer on Broadway. Now we're in disguise, sitting at two computers in the center of St. Agnes Library. Bookcases are on either side of us. At the front by the big windows is the children's section.

We're dressed as two older adults who have seen better days. But then, as Uncle Tony explained, there must be a reason why we're spending the entire day in the library. At first, he was excited that he could use his rag stash (from *Les Misérables*), but then Maddie reminded him that it might scare the children. The library is hosting a pre-Valentine's Day crafting event for the community. In the back, a planting station has been set up, run by Maddie's friend Lily, where children are planting seeds in cups. In the front is a crafting session, where they're making Valentine's Day cards with a lot of construction paper, glitter, and glue. A little girl comes by with a large card filled with button flowers and glitter, and Maddie looks disappointed that she can't participate.

"I'm sure they'll let you make a card," I say to her. We can't see the crafting tables from where we're sitting because our view is blocked by bookshelves, but a number of adults have walked by with handmade missives.

She glances at me and shakes her head. "I should stay in character." Uncle Tony has given her a sort of Mrs. Haversham vibe, with flowing gray curly hair and this floaty white outfit, but she still looks adorable. I'm wearing a worn blazer, wool pants that are a bit loose on me, and this peppered-gray wig, which doesn't look half-bad on me.

"I can't believe I'm finally going to get a break in this case," Maddie whispers to me. "I can't believe he signals to his accomplice via his Instagram posts."

"I'm impressed you figured it out," I whisper back.

Maddie nods and resumes typing.

Iris and Bella are on the lookout upstairs. Maddie showed them photos of the three deputy commissioners and Beatrice so they know what the potential suspects look like. Bella is working on her next novel on her laptop, and Iris also said she could easily work from here as well as from home. Maddie said she didn't believe that since Iris seems to have an elaborate home computer setup, but she appreciated the help.

Meanwhile, we sit here and wait. Maddie is working on an article, and I'm doing the books for January for our band and for the few businesses I freelance for. I also text back and forth with Amira about the logistics for our concert next weekend. I shift in my chair again. I'm not cut out for waiting. What if Ward doesn't show up? *Those clues seemed solid. He's going to show.*

"Can I ask you a question?" I whisper to Maddie.

"Sure," Maddie says.

"Why did you say yesterday that living in a cookie factory was every child's dream 'at first'?"

Maddie's eyes look at me out of a face that seems aged with wisdom. "Because my mom was obsessed with making her cookie business a success, and that was her priority, and because I was a bit chubby in middle school and the kids teased me that it must be because I was eating all my mom's cookies. It was hard, and I didn't want to tell her that they teased me because she was working so hard. I was also proud of her. It was impressive that she made it a success. Especially as a single mom after my dad died. And then she was upset when I didn't want to work for the business. I can understand your frustration with your mom's pressure to have a different career. I'm lucky that my sister is happy to work with my mom and will take over the family business. But that also means that they're super close, and sometimes I feel like I'm on the outside." She pauses. "That's probably more than you wanted to know." She ducks her head.

I touch her arm. "I'm sorry."

She shrugs. "I love being a reporter. Like that high yesterday when a piece of the puzzle finally clicks into place." She faces me. "Your mom. I'm trying to picture her falling for a musician, and I actually can kind of see that."

"You can?" I ask.

"She was dancing in the kitchen while making pancakes before you were awake and before she knew that I'd come down. That's why I went back up and waited until I heard you." Maddie's eyes look at me with concern, and my chest warms with how much she cares. "What happened with your dad?"

"They met at a concert, and you know what happened next. She traveled around with him on tour until I arrived. He didn't want to settle down. He had said he'd take care of everything, but as she explained it, she soon realized he was too addicted to the rush of a performance and to alcohol, later drugs, and he would get antsy staying at home. He couldn't do it, and he began to resent both of us, blaming her for tying him down when he was on the cusp of success. Not that I think he was."

"But she must see that you're different?"

"Maybe that experience happened when she was too young and it was so overwhelming—suddenly being a single mom and trying to create a career in her twenties but also take care of me. But I think your visit helped. You helped verbalize what I've been trying to show her." I shrug. I don't want to dwell on my relationship with my mom. It's complicated.

Maddie nods and thankfully turns back to her writing.

"That Instagram post didn't have a time, did it?" I ask.

"Not that I saw," Maddie says, and she studies it again. I peek over her shoulder, but I also can't see anything indicating a time. The miniature library doesn't have a clock.

We also checked for *Caper Crush* when we first arrived, and it was not on the shelves. That's not a good sign.

At least waiting around gives me time to think about my mom's parting remark: *She's a good one. At least she has a plan. Don't mess it up. Much better than that Christina, who was only using you. I'm still not sure I believe it's for real, given that you slept on the couch, but I hope it is.*

My mom approves? Is living in the Catskills mellowing her? Or maybe it's the frequent visits from Christy's grandchildren. Or maybe it's finally clear that I'm not my dad... I didn't drop out of high school. I majored in music and accounting. I don't do drugs. I've managed to support myself with my side jobs and my music.

Maddie gets up to go to the bathroom, and I pay even closer attention to the entrance. But still, nobody who enters looks like any of our suspects enters the building.

Maddie shuffles back into view but sits on one of the couches that allows her to see both the entrance and the crafting area.

I walk over to the crafting area and hover by one of the bookshelves. The problem is that these are all children's books. I look for the books that Dylan likes and pull one out, pretending to read it as I study the room. The children's section has a carpet with the alphabet on it and birch round tables with matching chairs. Currently, every table is occupied with children and adults making Valentine's Day cards.

A man with sunglasses and an enormously large overcoat enters. He walks into the stack one over from mine and talks to a librarian.

Maddie: *That's Galliano! Terrible disguise.*

Maddie: *Is he an accomplice picking up the money for Ward? Or has he also figured out Ward's Instagram posts and is here to catch him in the act?*

Are we actually going to catch someone picking up the money today? I can see why Maddie loves being a reporter.

Galliano is wandering around the stacks, but he doesn't seem to have a plan.

Maddie hobbles into the stack where Galliano is studying the shelves. Only then Galliano passes her and heads to the back section near the potting stations, Maddie discreetly following.

A man dressed in rags, with a bowler hat hiding his face, enters. He has the same build as Ward, though.

Me: *Ward!!*

I follow him as he walks towards the back. But then he quickly turns around and leaves.

Me: *Leaving.*

I stride out the door to follow him but let a woman with a walker exit first. I survey the street. No Ward. And I'm not sure it was him. He had Ward's build and seemed to walk like him, but it was so quick, and I didn't see his face.

Maddie: *Are you sure?*

Me: *Not positive. Don't see him now.*

Maddie: *I'll stay here. Iris and Bella can look along with you.*

Iris and Bella join me outside, below the arched windows of the library, and we fan out to search this block. There are probably ten shops across the street and five or six on either side of the library.

He's nowhere to be found. And it's freezing. I wish I'd grabbed my coat when I ran out after him. We stored our coats in the library staff room, courtesy of Lily.

Galliano walks down the steps of St. Agnes, empty-handed.

Maddie: *Galliano just left.*

Me: *No trace of Ward.*

The four of us reconvene in one of the nooks by the crafting area inside the library.

Iris says, "Do we think that was Ward?"

"I think so, and maybe he recognized Galliano and got spooked," I say. "Otherwise, why would he leave so soon?"

"And Galliano did not seem to know what to look for. He didn't pick up anything," Maddie says. "I watched the whole time."

"Ward doesn't hide his miniature obsession in the office, so it would make sense that Pommer and Galliano could learn of his Instagram account and figure out the posts," Maddie says. "But how can Ward be sure that nobody else will check out the book and find the cash? It doesn't seem like a foolproof plan."

We stare at each other. It does seem like a risky maneuver.

"Could the book be on reserve?" Maddie asks. "Now that I think about Ward's trips to the library, he often went to the reserve section to pick up a book."

Maddie texts Lily, asking if *Caper Crush* is on reserve.

Lily: *I can check the system in a minute. We keep the reserved books on the bookshelf by the checkout counter, so you can look there. I need to finish up with these last few children.*

Iris and Bella help clean up the crafting area as we wait for Lily to finish. Finally, Lily takes over the front desk and checks the computer.

We all stand on the other side.

"It's not on reserve," Lily says.

"Okay," Maddie says, accepting this far more gracefully than I would have. "Let's all look in the reserve section. This has to be the mechanism."

We each take a shelf in the reserve section.

"*Caper Crush*!" Iris whispers loudly.

A rubber band is wrapped around it with a hold slip indicating the intended recipient. Maddie removes the paper, handing it to Lily, pulls off the rubber band, flips open the book, and an envelope falls out. A thin envelope, and it's sealed shut.

"Wow," Lily breathes.

"Patron coming up!" Bella whispers.

We take the book and the envelope and retreat to the back of the library, Lily muttering after us, "You need to put the book back though."

"I have another white envelope in my bag in the back, so I can replace this envelope," Maddie says.

That bag really does have everything.

She carefully opens the envelope. We all stare at the thousand-dollar bill inside. Wow!

Maddie takes a photo.

She takes an envelope out of her bag, inserts the thousand-dollar bill into it, seals the envelope shut, and puts it back in the book.

Lily is staring at the piece of paper identifying the recipient. "This isn't an official library hold slip, even though it looks similar. They've clearly copied it to make it look like ours so it will fit in, but that's why there was no record of *Caper Crush* being on reserve."

"That makes sense," Maddie says. "They have more control over the book, then, and there's no chance the book will get reshelved.

It's also missing any library markings." Maddie takes a photo of the reserve slip.

We put the hold slip back on the book and then return it to the shelf. We still have the rest of the afternoon to see if Ward shows up to claim the book, unless that was Ward who entered and he's now been scared off.

"Do you have him now?" I ask.

Maddie shakes her head. "This is still not enough. Maybe if *Caper Crush* had been in the Instagram post. The fact that a *Caper Crush* bookmark slipped out of the book gifted by Beatrice is close, but I need something more. And I still don't know if the other deputy commissioners are investigating him or involved in the scheme."

My shoulders sag. I thought we had him.

"But this is a huge step forward. We're so close." She hugs me. "We can celebrate at your concert on Friday! You guys are coming, right?"

Iris and Bella agree to come. Maddie tells them that she and I can keep watch over the book on the reserve shelf to see if Ward returns to pick it up, and they can go home, adding that she's grateful for the time they've spent here.

Maddie and I take up posts across from the reserve bookshelf. Next to us are two teenage girls discussing their boy band crushes and fantasizing about how they could meet a real rock star.

I whisper to Maddie, "You do realize that with these costumes and our connection to Uncle Tony, we can always go out in public. This opens up so much freedom."

She stares at me, her head tilted, as if she's envisioning a future with the two of us in disguise. I can see it, because I'm sure we'll still be friends.

She gives me a devilish smile. "I can't wait to see what costume he comes up with next."

"At some point, we're definitely going to be clothed in those rags," I say.

She chuckles.

I turn back to doing the accounting spreadsheets, and Maddie types on her laptop, nibbling at her lip as she does.

Ward doesn't return, nor do any of the other suspects show up. This is frustrating. But Maddie is pleased with our progress, even though she has to work tomorrow.

"We figured out part of the scheme," she says. "He posts a miniature scene that tells Beatrice where the drop-off is and in which book. She hides the money in the book, and he picks it up."

"Why not get the money in person?"

"Then somebody could catch them in the hand-off," she says. "Plus, he's so obsessed with miniatures, I bet he likes signaling via his mini scenes. But now he might realize that Galliano is onto him, and that's why they've stopped including the specific books in the post. Galliano clearly didn't know the book because Beatrice provided that signal last time by giving Ward a *Caper Crush* bookmark. Ward and Beatrice are now signaling the book by exchanging bookmarks. But they'll need to figure out another way to signal the book because they won't always have an excuse to meet in person."

Lily walks us out the door at closing time. "I'll try to keep an eye on the book and let you know if I see anything. But I can't watch it exclusively."

"Thanks so much," Maddie says, giving her a hug goodbye. "You're coming to Nick's concert on Friday, right?"

Lily smiles and says, "Promise."

Chapter Twenty

Maddie

Nick is up on stage, strumming his guitar, his face focused on feeling the music. Everyone is waving their hands in the air in time with the beat. I'm standing with Iris and Jing right in the center pit. As Nick sings "Only You," he stares at me. He looks like he's singing it to *me*.

Other women in the crowd are turning to see who the focus of his attention is. Now the spotlight is on me, and I can't see Nick.

Iris's lead singer ex-boyfriend used to sing to Iris at concerts, but I never thought this would happen to me.

Of course, it's not actually happening to *me*, but it's getting harder to separate reality from fiction. I can't help smiling and feeling caught up in the excitement. I make a heart above my head. Jing raises both arms and points at me.

The song ends, and the audience erupts into cheers and clapping.

I can't believe I have to go on stage now, but MusEn wants a public appearance. Especially because so far, the fans' reactions have been positive. I'm the "girl next door." Not just literally. That's also the "vibe" I give off.

I make my way through the crowd and up the little side stairs to join Nick on stage.

The lights are hot, and it looks like there are *hundreds* of scream-ing people out there.

This might be my worst nightmare. How does he do this? And come back energized by it?

Nick reaches to hold my hand and pulls me close to him, his arm slipping around my shoulder. He kisses my forehead as we agreed in advance. We thought it would stave off any requests for something more.

We were wrong.

"Kiss, kiss, kiss!" the crowd chants. "On the lips!"

Nick turns to me and says, "Thanks much."

I can't. Not like this. Not in front of a million fans who will dissect it. *What if they say I kiss like a fish?*

I shouldn't have agreed to this.

I don't reply, but I see the moment Nick registers that I'm not saying yes. I must look stricken, because his brow furrows.

He swoops me up into his arms—all in one fluid motion, before I even have time to react—and leans forward into the microphone, "I'm definitely going to kiss her on the lips, but not in front of you guys, you pervy people. We don't want to stop once we start."

A roar of approval goes up as Nick carries me off the stage. And then we're alone in his dressing room.

He puts me down.

"Okay." He grips my arms, his face full of concern. "I've never seen anyone go pale so quickly in my life. Why don't you want to kiss me?"

I owe him an explanation. He totally saved us right there.

I take a deep breath. "My last boyfriend said I kissed like a wet fish."

His eyes widen. "There's no way you kiss like a wet fish, Maddie."

"How do you know?"

"Who even was this guy? I haven't seen you dating anyone since I moved in next to you."

"We dated for about two months last year. I only brought him home once." And then Nick had played his guitar next door, and I'd thought, *What if Nick hears us fooling around?*

"He was probably just pissed you broke up with him. Did you break up with him?"

"No."

Nick runs his hand through his hair in a frustrated motion. "But you've kissed other guys, right?"

"I have, but it's not like I've dated anyone seriously. Maybe it all ends so quickly because I kiss like a wet fish." I can't believe I'm telling all this to Nick. *Can the floor swallow me up now?*

Nick shakes his head. "I can absolutely promise you that you don't kiss like a wet fish. We'll work on this."

"I don't want to kiss you if I kiss like a wet fish." I fold my arms like a petulant five-year-old, but so be it.

A knock sounds on the door.

"Come in," Nick says.

"I wasn't sure if it was safe to come in," Amira says. Hah. Even Amira is beginning to believe our relationship is real.

"We're finishing this discussion tonight back home," Nick says to me.

"They want an encore," Amira says. "Another song. Although I'm sure if you want to sweep Maddie off her feet again, that will create quite a swoon."

Nick ruffles my hair. "I'm off." He winks at me in full sight of Amira. "But I'm looking forward to later."

The door closes behind him and Amira. Outside, the bass is thrumming, like it's responding to my current heartbeat. I close my eyes and sink down onto the couch.

Why did I admit that my last boyfriend said I kissed like a wet fish?

I put my head in my hands. What is there to discuss? I don't want to repeat how I kiss like a wet fish. *And what does Nick think is going to happen later?*

I should escape, but it might not be safe if that psycho fan is outside. I'm stuck.

Is Nick planning to kiss me? My heart flutters, but I need to remember that Nick is not promising anything, and I want to minimize my heartbreak. Plus, do I really want to spend the rest of my career hearing, *"I know who you are. You're Nick Devlin's girlfriend,"* and having people doubt my credentials?

Chapter Twenty-One

Maddie

It's only the two of us back in Nick's apartment. He has refused to let me out of his sight. He's playing mellow mood music. He can't really be planning a kissing tutoring session, can he?

"I need to shower, but you're not allowed to leave," he says sternly.

"There's nothing more to discuss," I say.

"That's true," he says.

I narrow my eyes. "Then I'm leaving."

He shakes his head. "I'll bang on the wall all night if you leave."

"Clause one," I say. "No noise past ten p.m."

"No music past ten p.m." He tsks. "Should have read that a bit more carefully. And you call yourself a reporter?"

I frown. "Seriously? I'm sure I wrote noise. It's sometimes so hard to distinguish."

He clutches his heart. "Ouch."

I check clause one, and indeed, it is music. I was so worried about the physical contact that I didn't pay close enough attention.

"You're staying, right?" Nick is gathering up a change of clothes. At least he's going to emerge dressed.

I don't answer, and he disappears into the bathroom. I could leave. I have my keys and his keys. But I stay and look around.

So...this is Nick's apartment. I've seen it a few times from the doorway or through the window from the fire escape when I'm knocking to tell him to lower the volume, but not at my leisure. A guitar stand, a blue loveseat, a kitchen like mine, posters of bands everywhere, a photo of him and his mom, a photo of him and another man in front of Pickles—probably that mentor guy, not his dad. Nick seems well-balanced for someone who's been through so much.

The rushing water stops. That was the quickest shower ever. This is my last chance to leave. I bite my lip.

Various shuffling noises sound in the bathroom.

I move from the couch to a chair at his dining table—much more formal. I need to take control of this situation.

I am an amazing *kisser. Men melt when I kiss them. They're practically beating down the door to kiss me.* I wet my lips as Nick peeks out the door, no shirt, one sharply defined shoulder.

"Making sure you are still here," he says.

"I'm not leaving," I say as if I'm completely comfortable.

He opens the door wide, T-shirt in hand. I open up his newspaper. There's a slight swish of the T-shirt being pulled on, and then Nick steps out and takes a seat across from me at his tiny table. He is lounging, though, with his legs on either side of me.

"Sarah's article is good," I say. "She totally mocked my *Meet the City Agencies* series idea. 'Everyone will be buying copies to read that.'"

"You're avoiding the topic," Nick says.

"Not at all. I've decided you're right that my ex wanted to throw off my confidence. And you're right. I'm a good kisser."

For a second, Nick's eyes flicker. I've surprised him.

"Great. We can kiss next time, then?" he asks.

No. Ugh. He's so annoying.

"Let's practice," Nick says. "You've insisted that we practice for everything else, and this is probably the most critical piece of the puzzle."

"Way to up the stress level."

"I'm absolutely sure you're a good kisser," Nick says. "Maybe I'm the bad kisser and you'll have to give *me* pointers." He leans across the table at the same time as his foot slowly traces a line up my calf. His gaze is so intense.

He wants to kiss me.

My heart rate jumps. I can do this. He's right. We need to practice. I'm a great kisser. Not like a wet fish at all.

He reaches across for my hand and laces his fingers with mine. I love the feeling of the rough calluses on the tips of his fingers.

"But do we have to try it across this table?" he asks. "Because I'm not going to be able to impress you if I'm trying to kiss you with a table in the way."

I nod. *Nick Devlin and I are going to kiss.*

"You're thinking too much," Nick says. "I can see it in your eyes. You're analyzing this." He pulls me up by the hand. "Couch?" he asks.

I nod. I don't think I *can* speak. Nick's couch is this deep-blue velvet loveseat, but instead of letting me sit down, Nick sits and pulls me into his lap. He smells so good—a combination of Dove soap and spicy aftershave. And he radiates heat.

"Are you comfortable?"

The weird thing is, I *am* actually comfortable. Sort of. This is Nick, my infuriating neighbor, but these past few weeks, he's moved from annoying, attractive neighbor to something...*more.* We used to just hang out when we ran into each other in the neighborhood, like at my favorite dumpling place or at Craic and Laughs, but we were more casual friends. If I'm honest, though, I've always tried to see him perform at Craic and Laughs. But I didn't show up at his other performances because I was afraid he'd realize I found him attractive, and that would ruin our casual vibe.

Now I've shared my hopes with him. I trust him.

And this is one kiss. I can do this.

"Are *you*?" I counter, bringing my attention back to his question. "I'm the one sitting on your lap."

"I'm not comfortable." He puts my hand on his heart. It's beating so fast. "But I like holding you close."

Yes, I can definitely kiss the socks off Nick Devlin.

I tilt my head. "Is this part of our fake dating?"

"Maddie, have some confidence in your effect on me. I can't fake my racing heart." He leans his forehead against mine and looks deep into my eyes. "Tell me you're *not* un-attracted to me."

"Nick, you have to know your effect on women."

"I want to know my effect on you, Maddie," he whispers.

His eyes are filled with something that looks like desire as his peppermint breath lightly brushes over my heated skin. I swallow.

"I want you to kiss me," I whisper back, somehow finding my voice. It comes out deep.

He tucks a piece of my hair behind my ear and then cradles my face. I can feel myself sinking into his warmth and comfort.

Nick tilts his head, my eyes close, and his lips find mine, teasing, exploring, as I give myself over to this moment. Shivers of desire flicker and flitter throughout my body, and I want more. I grab his shirt as he pulls me closer, slanting his head, not stopping. He tastes so good. I shift my hands to run them across his back muscles. He moans and shifts our positions so I'm lying beneath him on the couch in one motion, all while still kissing me.

His hard, lean body rests on mine, but I like the weight. I like the solidity of it.

But then all conscious thought ceases, and I lose myself in the kiss, in Nick making me feel all the feels. This is all that counts—the shivering sensations, the heat, the glowing embers being stoked to a simmering fire, his lean back muscles rippling under my hands.

We finally part to breathe. Nick tenderly sweeps my hair back from my face and then drops a kiss on my nose. "You're a very good kisser, Maddie. I don't want to stop."

"I don't want to stop either," I say.

"I can kiss you again?" he asks.

"Yes," I whisper.

"But just kissing?" He traces the collar of my shirt, leaving hot, shivery embers in his thumb's wake.

My stomach dips. I *want* to say, "More," but I haven't thought it through.

Nick chuckles, this deep laugh that makes me feel aglow. "You're thinking too much. Clearly, I need more practice kissing. You'll practice with me, right, Maddie?"

He kisses me again, and all my thoughts quiet as I focus on exploring these feelings with Nick.

Chapter Twenty-Two

Nick

We're in the studio recording another one of our songs. I'm hyped up. It sounds unbelievable.

"And that's it for this one," the producer says. "You guys can take a break in the lounge."

The lounge has two black leather couches and a fully stocked fridge, filled with name-brand water, seltzer, the latest fruit drinks, hand-pressed juices, and your usual selection of sodas. I hastily drink an entire bottle of water. I nod as my band members excitedly talk about the album.

I can't get kissing Maddie out of my mind. I wrote another song last night after she left, but I haven't shared it yet with the band. It's too raw, too unfiltered. Because what was that? I hated to let Maddie go. I wanted her to sleep over, even if we were just going to be sleeping. Me? *Mr. No Long-Term Commitment, My Career Comes First?*

But when she grabbed my shirt... I felt such a feeling of...elation? Satisfaction? A high. Like I'd conquered a mountain.

But this is Maddie.

She was clearly born to drive me crazy.

And I'm still not the right guy for a woman like Maddie. She needs someone who will be home, not someone who will disappear for months at a time on tour. Even if she pushed back on my mom when she said that I wasn't partner material. Was that part of the charade?

José says, "I have some exciting news. Elena is pregnant!"

My mouth opens wide.

"Congratulations!" Sayo says, as do Amira and Kyla.

"You're having a baby?" I ask.

Amira punches me as I realize that my tone sounded full of disbelief.

"Yes, congratulations," I say, trying to disguise my shock. *Is José about to leave us?*

José is glowing. He shows us an ultrasound photo. But how is José going to go on tour? He keeps talking about Elena's morning sickness and how excited he is, as if this is totally thrilling news and not an announcement that he might be quitting the band.

How serious is Sayo's relationship? Will she quit the band eventually, too? I'm standing on my own little solitary island. But they want this as much as I do. They work just as hard. But maybe that's because they have a ticking clock, because how long can you keep it up? And we've already spent ten years pursuing this dream.

But now we're finally about to make it.

We're called back into the studio to record the next song.

I toss and turn. I haven't seen Maddie since our epic kissing session last night. I'm avoiding her. I'm not proud of myself. But I need to figure out my feelings first. I need to tread carefully. I don't want her to think she's not an amazing kisser and I'm not into her. But if I give my usual excuses for why we can't date, she'll see through them.

I shake my head. I mean, she might think it's her kissing and not me, when it's definitely my career. But Maddie hasn't been calling me, either.

Her no-bullshit brain probably recognizes I'm a bad bargain.

And I can't believe José is starting a family. We're about to go on tour. He can't leave Elena here. But a tour is no place to raise a baby.

Beep, beep.

I turn over again. What is that noise? Is Maddie trying to torture me?

Beep. Beep.

It's that alarm. That sensor alarm that Luca suggested installing. I sit up and grab my phone to turn on the camera.

A figure dressed in dark clothes with a ski mask is climbing up the fire escape.

I blink. Is this for real?

Did Luca hack my camera to play a practical joke on me?

No.

He's on the fire escape above us. And getting on the ladder. With a *hammer.*

My blood runs cold.

Maddie.

I jump out of bed, grab my T-shirt and sweatpants from the nearby chair, my keys, and run next door. I bang on her door and then fumble with my keys. My hands are shaking. I find her key and unlock her door and slap on the lights.

"What the...?" Maddie sits straight up in bed.

"Guy on the fire escape. Need to get out. Now." I pick up Sherlock.

Maddie is out of that bed in a flash and grabs her bag and her laptop as I pick up her sneakers by the door.

"Keys?" I ask, holding tight as Sherlock squirms.

She grabs the keys from the hook, and I grab her sweatshirt next to it.

CRACK!

We both jump. He's hammering the window behind the curtain.

I push Maddie out the door, follow her out, and close the door firmly behind me.

"Where do we go?" she asks.

"I don't know. My place isn't safe."

"Did you call the police?" she asks.

I shake my head. "I came to get you first."

There's a thud. He must be in the apartment. *We need to get out of here.*

Now it sounds like he's hitting something with his hammer. Maddie flinches.

We run down the hallway to the staircase.

"The laundry room?" I ask. "He came from the roof." If he doesn't know the building, he won't know the bookcase leads to a laundry room, and we can bolt the door. Plus, that back door escape route means we wouldn't be trapped down there.

Maddie nods, and we hurry down the stairs. On the first-floor landing, she dials 911. Her fingers tremble. Sherlock is quiet, as if he knows we're in trouble. Maddie tells the police there's an armed intruder in her apartment and whispers our location.

"They'll be here soon," she says.

As we near the bottom floor, I insist on going first to make sure nobody is waiting in the vestibule. I hand Sherlock to Maddie.

The first floor is clear. But then we hear heavy footsteps above us. He's coming down the stairs.

We scoot around the staircase to the bookcase in the back. I pull out Shakespeare's Sonnets from the middle shelf, and the door un-latches. Maddie pulls it open, and we both slip through the opening. I bolt it behind us. *We're safe.* This door is made of metal. We jump down the short cement stairs, and we're in a cavernous, brick-walled basement. A basket of unclaimed clean laundry sits on the dryer, like it's a normal night.

Sherlock meows. Maddie takes him from me and puts him down on top of the washer. He shakes himself out and licks his paw.

We both slump against the washing machine and dryer and take a moment to breathe. My heart is still pounding. That was close. That was fricking close.

"Are you okay?" I ask.

She looks pale. It could be the fluorescent lighting down here. I move the basket of laundry to the center. "Here, sit." I pick her up and stick her on top of the dryer. She protests at first but folds when she feels the solid metal beneath her. She closes her eyes. Finally, I take a moment to really look at her. She's still pale and looks shaky, but she's still beautiful. I can't believe she wears spaghetti strap lingerie to bed. I quickly look away.

She was so calm and collected when I woke her.

"I'm okay," she finally says. "Are you?" She gestures to the clothes I had forgotten I was holding, as I stand here in only my boxers.

"That was scary." That guy could have killed Maddie.

I slip on my shirt and sweatpants and then pull her close to me and hug her. "Maddie." My heart is racing. That was too much.

She squeezes me back. "I'm okay, really."

Sherlock butts in. So *not* a good wingman.

"Sherlock and I are both okay," she says.

"If we hadn't installed that sensor device..."

"Did you see him?"

"I saw him on the monitor." I pull the camera monitor back up on the phone to show her.

Maddie dials the police again to tell them. "How long does that app save the footage?"

"For a week. But we can download it." I do that.

"We should meet the police at the front door so they don't break the door in or anything."

"Right." I hand Maddie the sweatshirt. "Put that on before you meet them."

Maddie looks down at her silky and revealing lingerie and blanches. She quickly covers herself in her sweatshirt.

"Why didn't you say anything before?" she asks.

"That wasn't a priority," I say.

"Right." Maddie nods. "You probably didn't even notice."

Women. I'll never understand them. She looks upset about this—when she just survived some crazy dude breaking into her apartment.

Here I thought I was supposed to be a gentleman. But at least I can lighten the mood.

I tilt her chin up. "I very much noticed, Maddie. And now I regret that all those times you told me I was keeping you up and threatened to come over and throw out my guitar picks, I didn't take you up on the offer." I smile.

She sniffles but looks away, a small smile playing around her lips.

"Maybe you should wear my sweatpants," I say.

"You're going to greet them in boxer shorts?" she asks. "No. What if the press gets a picture of that?"

"I prefer that to their seeing your legs."

"Don't be ridiculous. This is practically miniskirt length," she says. "You wear the sweatpants."

I give her the sneakers, and she laces them up.

Then I text Luca. The guy is in security, and we need that now. No response.

After a brief call with *The Intelligencer* security department, she picks up Sherlock, and we head back to the lobby to meet the police.

"Don't mention my story or my investigation," Maddie says.

"But what if it's related?" I ask.

"I can't reveal my story. That's the protocol," she says. "Our paper's security will also investigate."

We explain to the police what happened and take them up to Maddie's apartment. They say they'll check it first before we can enter. Maddie and I hold back in the hallway while they survey the apartment. But her ransacked studio is visible through the doorway. Maddie shivers. Her monitor is shattered and in pieces on the floor. I put my arm around her and pull her close to me.

"I'll get you a new monitor," I say. "Should we wait in my apartment? Let me get you some sweatpants."

Maddie takes a deep breath and nods. I unlock my door and open it for her to proceed in.

"I can't believe you didn't even grab one of your guitars," she says.

"The guy had a *hammer*. I only thought of *you*."

We stare at each other for a moment, registering what I said. Maddie looks like she's about to ask a question. Her eyes are filled with uncertainty, but also a dawning awareness.

I don't say anything more. What I said is true. I did think only of Maddie.

The crackle of the police radio next door interrupts the silence.

My comforter is in a heap on the floor, where I threw it in my haste to grab clothes and get to Maddie. Sherlock promptly makes his way over there to settle down. I hand Maddie a pair of sweatpants. "Now, can you humor me?"

She takes the sweatpants and retreats into my bathroom. Sherlock meows at the door, and Maddie opens the door a bit and lets him in.

She probably needs a moment to herself, as do I. I collapse into a chair. My phone beeps.

> Luca: *Are you okay? Can't talk right now. In a client meeting.*

> Me: *Yes, but worried about Maddie.*

> Luca: *Send me the video, and I'll run it through my database.*

> Me: *I need to protect Maddie.*

> Luca: *Got it. It seems unsophisticated. More like a warning. She would have woken up when he smashed the window.*

Unsophisticated. That's one way to look at it. She might have woken up, but she might have frozen and not been able to get out in time.

> Me: *Maybe.*

> Luca: *You can stay at my place. I'm out for the month. Work.*

As I start to text back that I'm not leaving Maddie, another bubble appears.

> Luca: *Both of you.*

I take a deep breath, and a framed poster catches my attention. It was my first live performance—in middle school—in an after-school band. I knew then that I loved that feeling of playing, listening to what the other band members were doing, and finding my own way to express what I wanted to say but also to fall in with their rhythm. I'd been obsessed with playing. Boy, had my mom been opposed. The music teacher had taken her aside and said I had a gift. And my mom acknowledged that it was clearly not something I was going to give up.

I really like Maddie. And not just as a friend or as a temporary girlfriend.

That same feeling I had with music back then, that this is right, that this clicks, is what I feel about Maddie.

I put my hand over my heart. I feel like I ran a marathon. We're both okay, but we can't stay here.

Chapter Twenty-Three

Maddie

"I only thought of you."

I splash my face because it feels hot.

Even though I should have been terrified when Nick woke me up, his solid presence was so comforting that I only focused on getting out.

And when he hugged me, it felt right.

I like him so much. I'm done pretending that I don't. He didn't even grab his guitar.

"You're a very good kisser, Maddie. I don't want to stop."

"But just kissing?"

Why am I turning him down and taking it slow? For what reason?

Nick and I could date now. If it doesn't last, I'll survive. I've survived worse. At least I'll have experienced dating Nick—I like him more than any other guy I've ever dated.

If I'm honest with myself, the reason I haven't been dating much the past few years is that whoever I meet won't compare to him. Not in my heart.

"Are you okay in there?" Nick asks on the other side of the door.

I'm more than okay. I'm going to go for it with Nick.

I come out of the bathroom, and Nick takes in that I'm now fully covered.

There's a knock on the door, and the police officer says, "We're done. We fingerprinted the place, so we will take your fingerprints to confirm. You can go back."

My apartment looks like it has been hit by a tornado. My desk drawers are strewn on the floor, with papers littered about.

The officer shows us a photo in an evidence bag. "The suspect left this photo of you two, with Maddie crossed out, so it could be a stalker fan, but…"

"But then why go through my desk?" I ask.

"Exactly," he says. "They were looking for something. Unrelated to Mr. Devlin, is there anything somebody could want from you? Or a reason to target you? You're a reporter with *The Intelligencer*, right? Are you working on a story?"

"I'm always working on a story," I say.

But does this mean that the suspect thinks I've figured something out? What clue do I have that triggered this? Did the suspect recognize us in the library?

I sit down as a wave of exhaustion suddenly overtakes me. I don't want to stay here tonight, in this apartment invaded by some malevolent force.

Nick pulls up a chair next to me and holds my hand.

"Well, it's late now, and obviously you can't stay here with the broken window, but maybe you can come down to the station tomorrow if you want to give us any further information," the officer says.

"Let's go to Luca's apartment. He replied to my text and said we could go over there," Nick says. "I'm not sure my apartment is even safe enough."

The officer starts to leave but then turns back around. "This isn't exactly protocol, but can I have your autograph?"

"Sure." Nick stands.

"No, Ms. Hughes's," he says.

Nick steps back.

"I've always been impressed by your reporting. Your article on that police investigation last year—my colleagues thought you handled that fairly and got the facts right. That's rare, unfortunately. I'm sorry this happened to you. We'll keep an extra eye out around this building until the window is fixed."

"I'm honored." I sign yesterday's copy of *The Intelligencer* right next to my article.

Nick butts me with his shoulder. "It looks like I'll have to get used to having a famous girlfriend."

I'm making the bed in Luca's spare room as Nick puts the pillowcase on my pillow. This room has a queen bed and a luggage rack. Not even a dresser. Luca must subscribe to the philosophy that guests shouldn't get too comfortable. But it did have an amazing shower in the bathroom with jets from all directions. I'd put on my sexiest lingerie. And a sweatshirt because I don't want to be completely obvious.

Sherlock is curled up in his cat bed that I brought from my apartment, along with all essentials. And this time, Nick left with two of his guitars.

"We can stay here," Nick says. "Luca is going on an assignment for a month, and he said the apartment is ours. We can outfit our apartments with proper security in the meantime."

"Let's think about it. I didn't want to sleep there tonight, but I'm sure after a thorough cleaning, I'll be fine. It is my home." Why do I feel like I'm trying to persuade myself too?

Nick puts the pillows on the bed as I spread out the comforter.

"So..." He shifts his feet. "Sleep well. I can turn out the light as I leave."

I gaze at him. "I don't want to sleep alone."

His brow furrows. "Right. I can understand that. I can share the bed with you. We'll sleep."

I take a step closer. "No, actually. I want you. Not just kissing. All of you."

I touch his arm, and he looks down at my hand on his arm. I feel the tremor that goes through his body. His glance meets mine. The look of tenderness in his eyes almost makes me tear up. He puts his hand gently on my waist.

"Are you sure?" he whispers.

"Yes." I brush that curly lock of hair that always falls down on his forehead away from his eyes. Both his hands now encircle my waist.

He pulls me in tightly against his hard body. "Maddie. Do you know how happy that makes me?"

"Not as happy as it makes me," I say with warmth in my voice.

He pushes my hair back from my face and kisses me hard, like he was afraid he was going to lose me—like he wants me to remember only this. And I hold him tightly. I want to block out everything else but Nick's taste and touch.

We walk backwards to the bed without letting go of each other and sink into it. Only when I lie on the bed beneath Nick does he stop kissing me. He leans his forehead against mine.

"Oh, I'm going to make you very happy, Maddie," he says. "But first, we really have to get rid of this sweatshirt. I didn't have a chance earlier to admire your lingerie."

He shifts to his side and unzips my sweatshirt. I watch his tan hand, his capable fingers, pull the zipper down, and my breath comes out in shaky gasps. He pushes the sweatshirt off my shoulders, and I help him pull it off.

"Maddie." His voice is deep and gruff. "You're sure, right? This isn't some reaction you're going to regret in the morning?"

I push him down onto the bed. "No regrets. Unless you keep talking."

He growls and cradles the side of my face with his hand, angling his own head to tenderly kiss me again. My body melts as we show each other what it means to be alive.

No regrets. I still have a huge smile on my face from last night. I must have looked like an insane person when I told my boss, Felicity, that an intruder broke into my apartment last night with a hammer, and yet here I am, buoyant—unable to stop smiling in delight. The police officer whom I met today with *The Intelligencer* security said I was the most cheerful victim he'd seen.

My smile falters, though, as I approach my building and see the boarded-up window of my apartment. The street seems its usual self, except for the policeman on the corner.

I text Nick that I am here. He'd agreed to meet me at my apartment. I need to clean it up and take the rest of my stuff to Luca's. My landlord called to let me know that he'd boarded up the window. But it's best to stay at Luca's for the time being.

I walk up the narrow stairs, the extra suitcase I borrowed from Iris's parents banging against my legs. I angle the suitcase so we both fit around the landing.

Footsteps race up behind me on the stairs, and I flinch. I shrink back against the wall. *What if...?* Nick's face comes into view. With pink tulips.

He bounds up the last steps and hugs me.

"I missed you," he says.

"It's been less than eight hours." I laugh.

"You haven't missed me?" he asks.

I kiss him on the lips. "I missed you."

"What did your boss say?"

"She's worried," I say. "She talked to her contact at the district attorney's office. The paper's security team is also investigating it."

Nick takes the suitcase, and I hold his hand as we walk up the last flight of stairs together.

Outside my apartment, I pause and take a deep breath but quickly open the door. I put the tulips in a vase with water, while Nick pulls on gloves and disinfects my counter and my bathroom. My heart feels full as I watch him doing his best to erase all traces of last night's invasion.

He sweeps up the monitor pieces and bags them to be recycled, while I stack on my desk all the papers that have been thrown around and put back my desk drawers. I pack my clothes in the suitcase. I leave most of my writing books, except for a few I use over and over. On top of the essential supplies, I add the framed photos of my family and my friends and the clipping of my first published article. Nick confirms I'm all right and then disappears into his apartment to pack more of his belongings, although his main priority is bringing the rest of his guitars to Luca's.

I sit on one of the stools by my kitchen counter. What would have happened if I had been home alone and Nick had not woken me up? Would I have been able to get out in time once I heard the hammer banging? *What did the intruder want?*

I sort through the papers that were strewn on the floor: some newspaper clippings of articles I'm particularly proud of, my passport (thankfully, that wasn't taken), and some travel articles or restaurant articles I've clipped. Almost all my documents are electronic, so it's not much. I pack my felting kit for making minis and the cat I bought at the mini show.

Nick comes back in with a candle.

"Are we doing an exorcism now to get rid of the bad energy?" I ask.

"No. We're burning our fake-dating contract," Nick says.

Yes, we're dating! For real! Nick felt invested last night, but I still worried that maybe he'd have second thoughts today.

"Are you sure we shouldn't keep some terms—like the sound-proofing?" I tease him.

"I'm still going to invest in soundproofing, but I don't think I'm going to be keeping you up anymore by playing my music. I've found another means." He grins.

"I'm all for this new approach," I say.

Nick puts his arms around me. I lean back against his chest, feeling comforted and safe. He kisses the top of my head. When he finally releases me, I flip through the folders in my desk drawer.

But I can't find the folder with the contract. I search through the hanging folders again.

My stomach dips.

"It's gone," I say flatly.

Nick goes through the stack as well.

"It's not there," he says. "Could you have put it anywhere else?"

"No," I say. "Did that guy take it?"

We both stare at each other, dismay written all over Nick's face.

"He's got our fake-dating contract," Nick says. "This is bad. What if he releases that to the press?"

"If it's Karigan Fonston, she's going to put it up on her channel," I say.

"Sarah at the paper is going to have a field day with this, isn't she?" he asks.

I nod. Nemesis is totally going to crow that *she knew* Nick would never date me.

"What about your label?" I ask. "Now you have to tell them that you signed this contract to fake date and you're not in a relationship with me."

"I *am* in a relationship with you," Nick says. "But yes. I'm not sure how I should tell them I misled them about this, but I didn't lie to them about YouTuber."

"It's bad for me as a reporter that I lied about being in a relationship." I sink into my couch. "What if this ruins my reputation as a reporter who tells the truth? I didn't think this through." I wanted the chance to date Nick and hoped that our contract would never be revealed.

Nick drops down onto the couch next to me. "And that's not like you. And it's not really like me either. Let's stick to the truth—that we both liked each other, but neither wanted to admit it, so this seemed like a win-win situation where we could explore these emotions safely and then maybe muster up the courage to tell the other one we liked each other."

I stare at Nick. "Is that why you wanted to fake date?"

"Not consciously. I'll admit this wasn't at the conscious level. But I was being honest in that interview when I said I looked forward to talking to you at the end of the day. Sometimes I'd play music so you'd come out and talk to me."

"Are we in kindergarten?"

Nick pulls me into his lap and kisses me on the lips firmly. "Thankfully not. But there must be some way we can preempt this reveal. Maybe you could reach out to the YouTuber and do a story on her? She seems to want publicity. And she probably wouldn't be able to resist crowing that she has this contract if you interviewed her."

"But still, would she have really hired someone to break into my apartment? With a hammer? For what reason? It doesn't make any sense that it's her. The fact that the guy was looking through my desk makes me think it's related to my corruption investigation. He was probably looking for any notes and was told to destroy my computer, but since that wasn't here, he destroyed my monitor."

"What about the picture?" Nick asks.

"To me, that seems like a red herring. The intruder even brought that photo, because it's not like I had clipped that picture out and hung it up," I say. I had saved it on my phone. "If that was the message they wanted to send, they could have mailed that to me since they know my address."

We stare at each other, digesting these points.

"It's between Galliano and Ward, or it could be that they are both corrupt," I say. "We know Ward is getting kickbacks from the property manager because he's signaling to Beatrice via the Instagram posts the library where the hand-off should be made, and she told him which book via the bookmark. We know Demoraux was getting Galliano's daughter booked to play at various clubs as a quid pro quo for closing violations. That benefits Galliano, but it could be that Ward is behind that to throw shade at Galliano. Or Galliano is also corrupt. Galliano was introducing his daughter to the Parks Commissioner, and Ward said how much Galliano is always promoting his daughter."

"I'll reach out to his daughter again to see if I can figure anything more out," Nick says. "But should you reach out to the YouTuber just in case?"

"No," I say. "She's been neutralized, and it doesn't make sense to bring her back into the picture."

"'Neutralized.' Are you hanging out with Luca?"

"We did meet with our security team today."

"You did?" Nick's eyes search mine. "And you weren't going to mention that?"

"I didn't want to worry you."

"It makes me worried that your boss thinks it's serious enough to bring in the security team, but I also feel better that they're taking precautions." Nick tucks my hair behind my ear. "We need to communicate. You need to tell me what's going on."

"I agree. But back to our missing contract. Given that this is a bribery investigation, I bet he's going to offer a bribe—drop the investigation, and he won't reveal the contract."

"So, we still need to 'neutralize' its disclosure."

"But it would be good if he approached me with that bribe. That might reveal some clues. In my limited experience, people want others to know how clever they've been, and I can get them to open up."

"No."

"No?" I ask.

"He hired a guy with a *hammer*. It's not safe."

"You're right. I don't want to meet Hammer Guy again." I sigh. "I need to tell Felicity about the missing contract."

"I need to tell my label the truth—that we were fake dating and now we're really dating. Their PR experts can figure out what to do."

"Okay. But I also need to be in the loop about whatever they are going to do, because this could affect my career." I bite my lip. Will this revelation hurt my career beyond repair?

Nick pulls me close to him and strokes my bottom lip with his thumb. "I've wanted to do that ever since I first noticed that you bite your lip when you're thinking hard. We'll pull through this together, Maddie, I promise you. Don't worry too much." He kisses me hard and pulls me onto his lap. He massages my tight back, and I melt into him, giving myself over to the shivery feelings he is evoking. This is what I want right now.

Chapter Twenty-Four

Nick

I pull the covers up over Maddie's bare shoulder as she sleeps. She looks content. My lips curl up in a satisfied grin.

I should be exhausted too. But my brain is on fire with new lyrics and ideas to try.

Her face is peaceful, with no mischievous glint lighting up in her eyes. I'm tempted to kiss her awake to see it. But she needs her rest. She seems okay after yesterday's break-in, but maybe she's not sharing her fears with me.

Is it one of my crazy fans? Or her investigation?

At least we're safe in Luca's apartment, but she's going to be out *there* investigating this.

I can't protect her. My stomach clenches.

I run my hand through my hair. I haven't given Maddie my usual disclosure that this relationship isn't for the long-term. I wasn't thinking straight last night. I wasn't thinking at all last night.

I'm in deep.

But the last person I want to hurt is Maddie. I need to be upfront that I'll be on the road a lot, and that's no life for a relationship. My chest tightens with pain.

And it's even worse now with social media.

Our Ciel date inspired mostly positive comments, but there were the usual negative ones. *She's trying too hard. She's only dating him for the money.* As if. Maddie hasn't mentioned them, and she tried to reassure me that she wasn't going to check the comments—based on Iris's advice.

Will that really work?

Especially now that I've seen how Maddie reacted to her middle school bully.

I slip out of our room and downstairs to Luca's soundproofed library, where I've stored all my guitars.

The best way for me to work out what I feel is to write it down and create music.

I pick up my guitar and strum the opening notes of the song in my head.

I write the last stanza down.

I *don't* want to tell Maddie that there's an expiration date on this relationship. *I can't.* Let me believe for once that this can work out. If it's going to work out with anyone, it's Maddie.

I rush back to our bedroom.

Unless the culprit is one of my crazy fans. Then it's safer for Maddie if we break up. I crawl into the bed next to her and wrap my arms around her. She snuggles into me, and I breathe in her soft scent. *Let me enjoy this for now.*

Luca's kitchen is stocked. I'm impressed. He must dine in more than I realized. He's cooked the gang some late-night pasta, but I thought that was a one-off. Maddie peppers me with little kisses as she leans into me. I hug her tightly, and her stomach growls.

"Let's feed you," I say.

"He has everything here," Maddie says. "This is better than a breakfast buffet at a fancy hotel. Does he host people here a lot?"

"Maybe clients? He's not dating anyone right now," I say.

I scramble eggs for our breakfast while Maddie burns the toast.

"Should I make more?" She scrapes off the blackened edges. "I'm used to my toaster that barely works."

"No. I like my toast crispy," I say.

"You'll forget it when you have my magical smoothie." She hands me a spoon to try her pink concoction.

I sip the frothy mixture. "Mm. This is really good. I can't believe you've been holding out on me all this time."

"It seems like we were both holding out on each other," she says.

"I definitely didn't think you liked me," I say.

She opens her mouth and then shuts it, as if to reconsider what she was going to say. "I didn't think you'd be interested in *me*."

"Because I'm Nick Devlin?" I ask.

"I was going to say that," she says. "But also because your last girlfriend worked for *Vogue* and looked like she could be a model there. And I work the city beat and can blend in with a crowd."

"You don't blend in with a crowd for me, Maddie," I say. "I've found your face every time you've been at a concert—when the lights aren't blinding me."

She pulls me in for a kiss. "You're just Nick to me—this guy who is creative and passionate about music and other endeavors." She blushes.

I can't wait to make her blush again.

"Hold that thought, or our eggs are going to burn too." I quickly turn off the burner and divide my scrambled eggs between the two plates and set them out on the table. Then I pick her up and stick her on the counter, sliding between her thighs to very much resume that thought.

But eventually we pull away so that we can eat our now-cold eggs and toast.

"I woke up last night, and you'd disappeared. Did you write?" she asks.

"You're good for my songwriting career, but don't worry. It's about the emotion I feel. I want to keep our day-to-day moments as private as possible. I want to hide away with you and protect us from the world."

"It's okay, Nick," she says. "I'll be careful with my investigation, and it's good for us to show the world that we work together."

"Let's hope that they accept our explanation for why we were fake dating," I say.

"This is not a conversation I'm looking forward to," she says. "But I'm excited to come home to you tonight."

Our MusEn producer can't be too mad about our fake dating, right? Isn't it common practice in the music industry?

Nonetheless, the entire band is waiting with me in this conference room lined with framed band posters. They insisted on coming to "have my back." And of course, this affects their big break. *Again*. Why is this such a roller coaster? But I feel a wave of gratitude towards them that we're sticking together.

Our producer breezes through the door and rushes up to me, putting both hands on my face. "We're so relieved you're safe from last night's attack. Are you okay?"

"I'm okay," I say. "My security camera alerted us, but it was scary. And now we've moved into my friend's place, which has more security."

"You're sure it's enough?" she asks.

"As sure as I can be," I say. "But that's not actually why we asked to meet with you."

"Oh?" She sits down. "You all look serious."

"Maddie's apartment was ransacked." I take a big breath—that shattered monitor still shakes me. "One of the things stolen was our dating contract. We were fake dating, but now we're dating for real." I then hand over a printout of my photo of our contract.

She blinks and stares at the piece of paper.

"We thought we should warn you and any PR people," I say. "And also, I wanted to say I'm sorry I wasn't upfront about this arrangement. But now we are truly dating."

"You lied to us?" Ashley asks.

"I didn't lie about my feelings for Maddie," I say. "My feelings for Maddie are recorded in my songs 'Fever Dreams' and 'Peony.' And I dedicated 'Knocking' to her, although that was before we were dating when I was teasing her about always knocking on the wall to tell me to stop making noise."

"But can I even believe those are about Maddie?" Ashley asks. "How do I know you didn't just say that for the interview? Let me get PR in here." She texts someone.

"They are definitely about Maddie," I say.

"I suggested that they fake date because it was clear to all of us that Nick liked Maddie," Amira says. "But he'd never act on it because..." She pauses.

No. Not my childhood dissected in this cold conference room.

"He didn't think she liked him," Sayo says.

I shoot her a grateful glance.

The PR person knocks on the door, and our producer steps out to talk to her.

We all stare at each other. This doesn't bode well.

"I'm sorry again that I suggested it," Amira says.

"I'm not," I say. "I appreciate your matchmaking, and it worked. We're dating. I am happy."

The PR and our producer return, but their faces are serious. Is this really that big of a deal? I was more worried about Maddie having to tell her boss. They sit across from us, and the PR person clears her throat. She takes another look at my printout of the contract from my phone and then turns the paper facedown. "Lying to your fans is not a good look. Especially given your brand image of open and honest and vulnerable. We would never have thought that *you* would fake date."

My chest clenches. *She's right.* I've always tried to be real in my lyrics and to speak my truth.

She continues, "The best thing to do would be to break up. That solves the problem. Then it doesn't matter if you were fake dating. The relationship no longer exists, so how excited can the fans get over this brief interlude where you guys pretended to date? They'll be happy you're single again and that they can imagine you're a possibility for them to date. But in keeping the relationship going, there will always be people who don't believe it's real. Breaking up makes it a nonissue."

My eyes narrow. Breaking up seems like a drastic response, and I don't want to end things with Maddie. My producer must have some ulterior motive. Have they decided that my dating the girl next door is not the image they envision for me?

I like Maddie. But at what cost? How much leverage do I have?

Chapter Twenty-Five

Maddie

Felicity, my editor, agreed to meet me for lunch at a small café not usually frequented by reporters from *The Intelligencer*, although she first suggested we stay in the building because of safety concerns. We're having another meeting later with security, even though we still don't know if my investigation was responsible for the break-in. The café is empty at two p.m., so it's only us in the back corner.

I can tell she's upset about the break-in because she has her red hair up in a tight bun on the top of her head. When she's upset or working intensely, that's when her hair goes into an all-business bun. But wait until she hears that Nick and I were fake dating. My stomach plummets. I really messed up. I'm supposed to stand for truth. I don't want to lose Felicity's respect. When her eyes widen at a good point I've made, I feel such a swell of satisfaction.

On the wall next to us is a framed poster of "Lunch atop a Sky-scraper," with eleven men eating lunch on a girder high above the sky. Eleven men. Just short of one man to be a jury. I'm about to be judged and found wanting.

I could never have done that job. I'm too afraid of heights. Balancing on a beam high above the city streets with the possibility of falling? That's what this feels like. It's as if I'm walking a tightrope between two desires. I want to be with Nick—he makes me so happy—but I'm so fearful of the repercussions of my signing that dating contract.

"Are you sure you're okay?" Felicity asks as she sips her coffee. "Do you need counseling?"

I shake my head. "I'm okay. It was scary, but a lot less scary because I was with Nick."

I take a deep breath. Best to lead with the crux of the story. "But I have to confess something... Nick and I were fake dating originally, but now we're really dating. And whoever broke in stole our fake-dating contract." I show her the terms of the contract.

She studies it. Her face is not revealing any clues.

"I like Nick. I was trying to help him, but I didn't think through all the possible repercussions to my career," I say. It was supposed to stay *private*, but as a journalist, I should know how little privacy there is anymore.

"Right... That's not good." My boss shakes her head. "Why do you think the thief took the contract?"

"As leverage. To bribe me to drop my investigation," I say. "*If* it's related to the investigation. If it's one of Nick's fans, who want to reveal that we're not dating, then that person should disclose it relatively quickly."

"You really think it's tied to your investigation?" she asks. "What about the picture of the two of you, with you crossed out, that was left on the floor?"

I shiver. Seeing a big red X over my face had not been a cheery sight.

"I don't know. But if I'm a fan and I have a choice between breaking into Nick's apartment or his girlfriend's, I'd much rather meet Nick."

"But this wasn't a female fan."

"That's right. This was definitely a man," I say. "And that hammer didn't give him a huge fan vibe."

She's not saying anything about the contract. Is that bad or good?

"And that's all that was stolen?" she asks.

That was more than enough.

"I think so," I say. "I didn't do the most thorough search, but I can't think of anything else that's missing. He didn't take any jewelry, not that I have much."

"You're getting close. Especially if he felt the need to destroy evidence or send a message. Have you backed up your laptop in case it gets stolen?" she asks.

"In multiple places."

"What are your next steps for the investigation?" she asks.

Is the contract a nonissue? Is it good that she's only asking about the investigation?

"I'm monitoring Ward's Instagram, and I'm coordinating with Tasha and her friends to monitor Beatrice and the deputy commissioners," I say. "This Saturday, though, I have to cover the Chinatown parade for an article. But still, that should give me a chance to follow Deputy Commissioner Pommer. He should be there. It's his district, and he was on a float last year."

"As far as the contract, yes, it won't help your career if this gets out," she says. "It's been very public, and it certainly seemed real…"

"Because the feelings were real," I say.

"That is better," she says. "It helps that you are really dating now."

"That does help, right?" I ask.

She nods. "I think so. Whether it affects any promotion, I don't know."

I am making dinner for Nick because that talk with my boss went better than I expected. She was more interested in the investigation. And she wasn't definite that it would hurt my chance to be promoted.

I call my mom to tell her I'm now truly dating Nick and that our contract may be published. I'd told her before that we were fake dating.

"You're really dating Nick now? That's great!" my mom says. "I always liked him. He seems kind. He helped me carry up my grocery bags once."

"He's a good guy," I say.

"I'm relieved to hear it. I always worried that maybe your father's death made you a bit closed off, and that's why you weren't dating."

I don't think so. Maybe it made me a bit more cautious, but I've been dating. Until the fish review.

"Mom," I say. "It's not like you're out there dating."

"I'm so busy with the business..."

"I'm busy with work, too."

"But I also had twenty-five years with your dad. I loved your dad. I want that same experience for you."

"I really like Nick," I say. We change the subject and catch up a bit more, and then I promise to stop by soon.

> Lily: *I checked the book, and it now has a blue envelope! Someone picked up the other envelope! But I never saw it.*

> Me: *Do you have another envelope so we can see what this one contains?*

> Lily: *Bella is on her way over. She's going to buy one and bring it here so we can open the envelope, see what's inside, and replace it.*

> Me: *You guys are the best!!*

As I wash the potatoes, my phone beeps again.

> Lily: *It's the title of a book: Rocky Mountain Heat. I read that! She has good taste in books.*

She sends me a photo of a piece of paper with the title typewritten on it.

> Me: *Thank you! This is great.*

Yes. We're making progress. We know now how they're communicating which book holds the pay-off.

I hum as I put the tray with the beef and potatoes in the oven. I splurged. But also, I'm so happy that Nick likes me. I feel all bubbly inside, like my veins have become twinkly sparking lights.

And when Nick finally comes home and hugs me, it's as if I've been plugged into the socket and filled with a rush of energy. Until I realize that Nick is clinging to me. When I pull back to look at his face, he looks tired.

"What happened? Did the recording not go well?" I ask.

"The recording went really well," he says. "Although I didn't get a chance to work on my latest song that I started composing last night."

"So MusEn was upset about the contract," I say.

"What did your boss say?" he asks.

He's deflecting. It must be bad.

"That it could hurt my career," I say. "But she was more interested in my current investigation."

"Did she have any suggestions on how to get conclusive proof?" he asks.

"No. I told her I recruited Tasha and her friends to follow Beatrice because I will be in Chinatown for the parade this Saturday, and I can follow Pommer then."

"I'm coming with you."

"I'm going in disguise again," I warn him.

"As you should," he says.

He still hasn't told me what his label said.

"Felicity thought it was good that we were actually dating, so it wasn't as bad as I feared." I take his face in my hands. "Tell me. We'll figure it out."

"They suggested we break up because then there would be no issue," he says. "I told them that wasn't an option."

No.

"Okay." I bite my lip. That wasn't the response I expected from MusEn. "And they were okay with not breaking up?"

"They said we could wait and see and 'keep it in our pocket as a possibility.'" Nick makes air quotes. "But I think we can ride it out together."

He kisses me, and I give in to all the longing I feel for him. He enfolds me in his arms, and I feel protected. *We will be okay. There has to be some way we can make this work to our benefit. This is definitely a feel-good story that people should support.*

As he pulls away, he says, "What are you cooking? It smells good."

"It's a roast, so it needs more time," I say.

He peers through the oven door. "I didn't know you could cook like this. Have you been holding out all these years? I feel like I would've smelled this deliciousness in the hallway."

"The last time I cooked a roast was several years ago, during the holidays, so we'll see if it actually turns out okay," I say wryly.

He bumps me with his shoulder. "I have faith in you. Do you want to practice my latest routine with me?"

"I don't think I'm that coordinated." I laugh. "Won't I throw off your timing?"

"It'll be fun," he says.

"Famous last words..."

He turns on the song and shows me. "It's eight counts, so on the eighth count, we start."

I cannot be in sync for the life of me. I feel like I memorize the choreography, but I can't put it all together, and my body is always behind my brain. That is, if my body even decides to cooperate and imitate the way he's moving. Three steps right. Arm up. Arm down. Heart gesture with arms. Kick. Spin. I spin the wrong way and crash into him.

We collapse onto the floor, laughing. We both needed that release.

"You'll get the choreography eventually," he says when he finally catches his breath.

Nick takes a photo of us, all joyful, our heads together.

"I don't have a photo of us," he says. We take a few more.

"How long have you been dancing?" I ask.

"I took dance lessons in high school. Not because I wanted to, but because my mom wanted to support our neighbor, who taught dance class, and she thought it would be good for all my energy. I played soccer, but I didn't want to play basketball during the winter. Too many friends jammed their fingers, and I didn't want to hurt my hand when guitar playing was my priority. And it's not like we could afford to pay for tennis or some low-contact sport."

The timer beeps.

As we sit down for dinner across from each other, the candle in the teacup holder flickering, I feel warm and content.

Hope is blossoming inside me that this can last. It's so easy between us. When he holds my hand, I feel safe and secure and wanted.

But what if his label insists we break up? His dream might be at stake. I need to protect myself and remember that this may not last. He's got a life ahead of him that's very different from mine—and our two careers still don't seem compatible. I can't be the story. I need to be someone who's not noticed, who blends in with the crowd.

I also can't follow him around and attend his concerts. I'm not sure I have enough confidence to listen to all the people doubting our relationship and tearing me down. *She's trying too hard.* I had looked at a few comments. To be honest, mostly they seemed like unhappy people.

But I also could see why they didn't think we would last.

"We're playing a concert on Valentine's Day, so I can't spend that evening with you," Nick says, looking worried.

"That's okay," I say. "It's too expensive to eat out that night anyway, and I like nights like this, eating with you. That's more important to me."

"I bought you an early Valentine's Day gift." He hands me a wrapped box.

"I don't have your gift yet..."

"I didn't expect you have to have one, but I wanted to give you this."

I unwrap the box, and it's a pair of sunglasses. Interesting. Is this meant to signal that we'll still be dating in the summer?

"They're rearview spy glasses," he says. "They have a mirror so you can see behind you."

"That's so cool." I put them on, and they work. I practice with Nick standing behind me. I hug him. I'm so happy with this gift.

We go to bed early, as the past few nights are catching up to us. As Nick tucks me into his warm, hard body and his breathing slows, I want to hope that this is the beginning of our life together.

The next morning, Nick's phone beeps, and he picks it up. His face falls.

"Is the contract public?" I ask.

"No." He shakes his head. "It's nothing."

"It's clearly not nothing," I say. "We said we'd be honest with each other."

"Someone posted something online about you," he says, clicking his phone off. "Remember, Iris said to ignore this and that you shouldn't look at them. Sayo was upset about it and wanted me to know. I'll make a statement that you're my girlfriend and hurtful things said about you hurt me as much as they do you. And I'll alert the police."

The police!?

Let it drop. Iris did say to ignore these things. But his face... It must have been terrible. Why do we need to alert the police?

"Now I'll probably imagine something that is much worse than it is," I say.

He shakes his head. "You have to ignore the haters. Just remember, what matters is what's between us."

He cradles my face in his hands and kisses me gently. The way he looks at me, I can almost believe that's all that matters.

"Still, if you have to alert the police, I should see the comment," I say. "It's also a matter of safety at this point, if the intruder was a crazy fan."

"You're right." Nick wraps his arms around me and shows me the comment.

She needs to disappear.

Cold ice fills my chest, and I shiver. Is this the same person who invaded my apartment?

Nick hugs me tightly. "I'll talk to Luca about a bodyguard."

I let out a choked sound. It was supposed to be a laugh. "I'm not walking around New York City with a bodyguard. I'm not letting them get to me. But I will let the paper's security know. Maybe the police will be able to track down this comment. This might be a clue to who broke into my apartment."

"You don't have to put on a brave front for me," Nick says, pulling back from the hug to look me in the eye.

"I'm not."

Nick raises an eyebrow. Mmm. He looks so cute when he does that.

"Maybe a little. But I'm also mad. Ms. or Mr. Anonymous wants to threaten me from the safety of their keyboard." I also use my keyboard as my way to fight injustice. But I put my byline on my articles. I put my name and my reputation on the line, and I keep to the facts in my writing. "And this really might be a clue that reveals the perpetrator. At least, I hope so."

She should disappear.

I'm *not* going to. I will take extra safety precautions, but I'm not hiding. I tried that for a while in middle school, trying to make myself smaller so that the bullies wouldn't pick on me, so that I wouldn't attract their attention. It doesn't work. It only made me an easier target. I will figure out who is responsible for the bribery and these sham repairs. And I *will* be a part of Nick's life for as long as I can.

Chapter Twenty-Six

Nick

I talk to the label about the threat to Maddie, but they imply that this comes with the territory. Plus, the way our producer Ashley's eyes narrow, it seems she's registering this as some way to persuade me to give up Maddie. The police are far more interested, thankfully, and promise to track it down. The various videos the police have been able to retrieve from around our neighborhood of the night of the break-in into Maddie's apartment never show the guy's face. But after some research, the police don't think this is the same culprit. The label reports and blocks the commenter, but that seems to be all we can do for now.

What if the culprit is one of my crazy fans? I want Maddie, and I want a career making music—but not if Maddie can't walk the streets of New York as a civilian.

I put down my guitar. Writing more lyrics doesn't seem to be the way to figure this out.

José has also been more distracted this week. Elena had some spotting, so now he's worried and says that if he's not watching her, she's doing too much. We're both basically trying to protect our women—without much success.

The label and the police suggested that Maddie and I not have any public dates for the time being. That's fine for now. We're swamped rehearsing for our upcoming performances. Maddie is busy trailing the deputy commissioners and writing her playground article. But I don't want our relationship to *have* to be in the shadows.

I open my laptop to study the Infrastructure Department budget from last year to see if it reveals any clues. The corrupt commissioner should have the highest numbers for repair expenditures, because all the projects in his domain are adding an extra cushion to pay the bribe that is shared between him and Beatrice. But we can already assume that he's not limiting himself to his assigned buildings to spread the suspicion, unless it is Galliano.

The amounts seem to be evenly distributed across the deputy commissioners' assigned housing developments. I give the perp credit for hiding it well.

My mom calls, but when I tell her I'm worried about my fans threatening Maddie, she says, "One more reason *not* to be a rock star."

She's super helpful, as always.

Except then she calls back. "Can't the music label pay for your security? They should pay for security, for both of you."

I say that I will ask again. I feel like this is a small step by her, that it's a tiny acknowledgment that this is my career.

I meet Maddie for dinner back at Luca's place and explain what the police told me.

"Okay. I have to accept that it's a hateful comment directed at me," Maddie says. "It hurts, but I also don't want to hide our relationship. Let's post one of our happy photos on your Instagram account. I may be a writer, but sometimes a picture is worth a thousand words."

I pick the one that is not my favorite and post it, adding a bunch of hearts in the accompanying text. My favorite ones are only for Maddie and me. But even this one photograph clearly shows our happiness.

"At least I can spend this Saturday with you at the Chinese New Year Parade, but I'm about to go on tour, so I'm not going to be here full time. Will you be okay?" I ask. "Will you please only follow someone when you're disguised?"

"Yes. I promise. I even bought my own wig from a company recommended by Uncle Tony. I'll miss you, though. I like coming home to you," Maddie says. "I'm busy with work anyway. It will be good, probably. You're distracting when you're here. When you come home, I don't want to work on my story anymore. I want to relax with you."

I tug her onto my lap on the couch. "Why do you think the contract hasn't been revealed yet?"

"Hopefully, it's related to my story," she says.

I don't want it to be related to either, to be honest. I want it to be a random home invasion that is not related to either of our careers so it has no effect on our future.

"I'm *not* hoping it's related to your story. I'm worried for you," I say.

She sinks into me, her soft curves tempting me. I'm going to make tonight a night she will remember. She can catch up on sleep tomorrow night.

Chapter Twenty-Seven

Maddie

Nick and I stand in the crowd that lines either side of the street where the Chinese New Year parade is proceeding. The rain has stopped for now, but the sky is still gray, and everything is wet. The loud percussion beat announces the approaching drums. In front of us is a float with people dressed in traditional costumes, covered in rain ponchos or under umbrellas, waving to the crowds on either side. A sign on the side of the float proclaims it's the Chinese American Friendly Trading Association. Small children are the closest to the street—right behind the metal police barricades—so that they can see all the action.

I spent the better part of this week interviewing the parade organizers for my article and what it means that it is the Year of the Snake. They suggested that people will need to be more tenacious and resourceful but also intuitive and introspective. And before I slipped into my costume (using the bathroom at Columbus Park), I obtained some great quotes from the people watching the parade. I saw the paper's photographer a few times, and he showed me some fantastic shots that captured the warm feeling of the parade.

The parade is almost over. But that's not the only action we are here to see—although I do love this event. As expected, Pommer is here with his entire family. So glad my hunch paid off.

Ward's Instagram post refers to the Chinatown library. It couldn't be more perfect. It's as if he knew that I needed to be in Chinatown today covering the parade. But another post has the 125th Street library as the location of another book club. Tasha is covering there. No book is featured in either scene.

"Do you think Uncle Tony had way too much fun creating these disguises for us?" Nick asks. "This beard is so itchy. Not to mention these bushy eyebrows."

"A beard is a good way to disguise your face."

"I'm not sure I agree with his concept," Nick says. "Did we really have to be an elderly retired couple from California visiting New York?"

"He does like to age people. It's kind of his signature move. And honestly, with that beard and those eyebrows, it's hard to recognize you," I say. "I'm more worried that I'm somewhat recognizable if you know me. He hasn't always been successful with his disguises."

"I think I'd recognize you, but that's because of your eyes. Put on the sunglasses. I'm completely on board with disguises—just not beards," Nick says.

Nick is so worried about my safety. It's weird having someone other than Iris so concerned about me. I haven't told my mom about any of the threats, and she thankfully thinks reporting is merely talking to people. Then again, I've never done such a high-stakes story before.

The people walking in elaborate dragon costumes are amazing. It's hard to take my eyes off the festivities. Traditional Chinese music plays.

A few raindrops hit my head. Not again. Nick puts his arm around me and pulls me closer as he opens up our tiny umbrella that barely covers both our heads, but at least it does. I snuggle into him. He looks down at me, and his eyes twinkle.

"We should have asked Tony if I could kiss you while wearing this beard," he says. "Or has it completely put you off?"

I tighten my grip on his waist. "No. It's still you underneath. But I can't get distracted. You know I lose all sense of time while kissing you."

"I did *not* know that." Nick leans down and kisses my forehead. "Later."

The rain ceases, and we put away the umbrella. And now the snake is weaving in and out down the street, the dancers holding its body and making it come alive.

Pommer leans to whisper something in his wife's ear. That's so endearing. Except that...he's leaving.

"He's on the move," I say.

"He's leaving his wife with four kids at a parade?" Nick asks. "She must be a superwoman."

Between our disguises and the sheer multitude of people, it doesn't seem like he'll see us following him. It's slow going for all three of us as we duck in and out of people pressing to get closer to the parade. Periodically, a popping sound splits the air as someone releases a popper, and confetti shoots out. Vendors hawk confetti tubes, snake stuffies, and other goods.

Lion dancers are prancing down the street. One seems to take great delight in blocking me from following Nick. He thinks I'm dancing with him, when really, I'm trying to dart around him. And I've totally lost Pommer. *Where is he?*

There he is! Back in my line of view, Pommer turns the corner. Nick and I reunite and run after him.

I stop at the street corner where he turned and peer around the side. There's a loud pop, and I almost jump. Confetti hits my head.

"He's ducking into one of those illegal betting parlors!" I say.

"Do you think he has financial problems?" Nick asks. "That would give him a motive. Especially with four kids in New York City."

"We have to catch him in the act. I can't just assume," I say.

"Let me go in," Nick says. "You might have to take off your sunglasses inside."

"Okay," I say reluctantly. "But text me what's going on. I'll be in that bookstore next door. They have a backyard, and maybe I can see something from there."

"You really know this city so well," Nick says.

"At least this part, having grown up on the Lower East Side," I say but can't quite hide that I'm pleased I impressed him.

"I'll keep you updated," Nick says. He disappears into the illegal gambling den. It's poorly disguised as a baby store called Good Luck. The window has a bassinet and diapers and other things you'd need if you had a baby, although not with that fine layer of dust. What gives it away is that almost everyone entering is elderly and male. Unless it's where the grandparents buy gifts, it's a gambling den.

I enter the bookstore next door and wave hello to the woman behind the counter. "Is the garden open?"

"It is today," she says. "But all the chairs are wet."

I hastily buy a hot chocolate so I can use the café seating and hurry outside.

> Nick: *He's meeting with Inspector Demoraux!*

> Nick: *I took a photo for you.*

> Nick: *Pommer and Demoraux going outside to the back garden.*

The wooden fence between the two backyards is tall and doesn't give any view of the adjoining garden. Thankfully, nobody else is out here with the rain. I creep along the fence and stop when I hear the two men talking. I sit in the nearest chair. I can hear their conversation better than I expected, but I missed the beginning.

Pommer asks, "Is she investigating?"

Who is she?

Demoraux says, "She is."

> Me to Nick: *I can hear them clearly. You don't have to get close.*

Pommer speaks again. "How did she figure out that you were negotiating for slots for Ophelia in exchange for fixing tickets?"

Demoraux says, "I don't know."

He says it as if I must have magical powers.

Pommer asks, "Who does she think is behind it?

Demoraux says, "She doesn't buy that it's Galliano."

"Too obvious?" asks Pommer.

Demoraux says, "I'm not a mind reader."

Glad to see Demoraux is still his usual charming self.

Pommer then asks, "But are you sure you've destroyed any proof that you're connected, right? Because—"

Pommer's involved!

Demoraux cuts him off. "Yeah. I'm careful like that."

Pommer speaks again. "I expect you'll disappear now again."

"I thought I had disappeared after quitting. I'll go off grid this time," Demoraux replies.

> Nick: *He just handed him a thin envelope.*

Is that the final payment? I need that envelope. I need physical proof. How do I obtain that?

> Me: *We need to follow Demoraux and get that envelope.*

> Nick: *Are you crazy? How do we do that?*

I meet Nick outside the fake baby shop, keeping an eye on a disappearing Demoraux. We follow but stay back so he won't pick up that we're trailing him.

"You can distract him," I say. "You can ask him directions as a tourist, and I can try to pickpocket him."

"Do you know how to pickpocket someone, Maddie Hughes?" Nick asks.

"Bella was once writing a scene in a novel that required pickpocketing—don't ask—and so she wanted a friend to pickpocket her to see how it felt. You might not believe it, but there are videos that explain how to be a master pickpocket. We both learned. She wanted to know if she would feel anything if she were the victim."

Nick shakes his head. "The skills you've acquired... Here I was thinking that you were leading a blameless life."

Demoraux is halfway down the block. The parade is over, so the crowd is dispersing. He's picking up his pace, and a group of people, all wearing the same jackets, are suddenly between us. We race after him, weaving between the people setting off poppers, but lose him when he suddenly disappears out of sight.

We walk up and down the block to survey the stores but don't see him anywhere. The street is filled with vendors and people dressed in raincoats and transparent ponchos of all the colors of the rainbow. Tourists crowd the souvenir shops, while others line up outside a restaurant with a row of glowing red paper lanterns hanging from the awning. The streets are littered with wet slips of colorful sheets of paper from the poppers, making a beautiful collage.

"Back to Plan A," I say. "I need to cover the library." The two of us turn and jog over to the library—which is closed for the New Year celebration. It has to be the other library pictured in the posts then. I take out the envelope I've pre-prepared, with a slip of paper with the typewritten title of a romance book inside. Beatrice seems to be a romance reader. I show Nick, frustrated that I was so ready to exchange the envelope. He gives me a hug.

I call Tasha, who picks up immediately.

"Nobody has visited this library," she says. "My son is having a good time, though. He likes all the books they've read in the reading circle."

"I'll come up and relieve you," I say to Tasha.

Nick looks conflicted. "I have to leave." He's playing in Hoboken tonight, and tomorrow they're the first act in Jersey City. "Please be careful."

"I will," I say.

He gives me a look like he has his doubts but hugs me goodbye and jogs off to return to his apartment while I take the subway up to meet Tasha.

As I enter the library uptown in Harlem, Tasha's son is sitting in a circle listening to the librarian read *The Family Book*, and Tasha is holding the baby. I walk up to Tasha, who gives me the cold shoulder. I realize I look like some elderly tourist from California. I forgot to tell her I was in disguise. I text her. She looks up, shocked.

"Wow, I didn't recognize you at all. That costume is so good," Tasha says, peering closely at me, and then rocks her baby. "She just woke up."

The baby looks like she's about to cry. Tasha distracts her with a puppet.

"Thank you so much for staking out the library. I feel bad that you're doing this with the kids."

"We're all pretty fed up with these crappy repairs. The wind whistles right through my windows, and I caulked them again, but this is something maintenance should be doing. She had a cold last week, and I worry it's because the apartment is too cold at night because all the heat is escaping," Tasha says. "And to be honest, this has been a relaxing day for me. My son made a red lantern during the craft activities earlier for Chinese New Year. Now he's happily listening to the stories."

"Still, thank you," I say. We make a plan for how to catch Beatrice in the act if she ever shows up. Distraction will be the name of the game. Tasha reassures me that she's perfected this as a mom. I pull the extra envelope out of my bag in case I am able to pickpocket the current envelope. I'm hoping that with this replacement envelope, they won't immediately notice the switch.

"But how can we give this envelope back to her to replace the one I took, so that she doesn't immediately suspect anything?" I ask. "I know how to pickpocket, but not how to put a different envelope back in her pocket."

"Let's give this envelope to my son to hold. I will pretend that my three-year-old son has just pulled the original envelope out of her back pocket and then I'll hand this replacement envelope back to her. She often has candy in her back pocket or her bag for the kids, so it's not actually unusual that sometimes the kids inspect her pockets to see if she has any candy. She just treats it as a game, usually. One thing I will say for Beatrice is that she does love children," Tasha says. "It makes it a lot harder to actively dislike her."

She tells her son that they are going to play a game. "You have to hide this envelope under your shirt, and then when I ask you where the envelope is, you pull it out, okay?"

"Okay," he says.

"Remember when your daddy showed you those magic tricks?" Tasha asks. "This is like one of those magic tricks. We're going to pretend you took the envelope from Beatrice, but really, you had it under your shirt. Like when Daddy hid that card in his sleeve. Do you understand?"

He looks puzzled, but he says that he can hide the envelope and then give it to his mom when she asks for it.

"There's Beatrice!" I move quickly away from Tasha and disappear down an aisle. I put in my earplugs and pick up Tasha's call.

"She's going into the romance aisle. It's two aisles down," Tasha says.

I wait in the aisle with the books on reserve. Beatrice enters the aisle. Yes!

> Tasha: *I'm in the aisle next to you.*

I busy myself with looking at a romance. I put on the rearview spy glasses that Nick gave me. I can see Beatrice. These work so well.

Beatrice pulls a thick envelope out of her handbag and sticks it into the book while removing a thin envelope out of the book.

I text Tasha.

> Me: *Now.*

Before she puts that envelope in her purse.

Tasha enters the aisle with the baby and her son. Beatrice hastily shoves the envelope in her back pocket.

"Beatrice," Tasha says. "The windows need to be caulked. You promised you'd send someone last week, and you still haven't sent anyone."

Tasha's daughter makes a small cry.

"Oh, your daughter is adorable," Beatrice says. "Did she just wake up?"

"Yes," Tasha says. "Do you want to hold her? You have such a good touch with kids."

"I'd love to hold her," Beatrice says. "I have six grandchildren, you know." Beatrice takes the baby, and the baby starts crying and squirming.

The letter is sticking out. I pull it out and walk away to the aisle next door, where I can hear everything.

As I walk away, Tasha says to her son, "Where did the envelope go? Can you give it to me?" She then says to Beatrice, "He probably thought you had candy in your pocket, and he took this out of your pocket. I'm sorry about that."

"What?" asks her son. "I hid it under my shirt."

"Yes, good job," Tasha says.

"I didn't even realize. I was so focused on calming the baby." Beatrice turns to Tasha's son. "Next time I will bring candy, but I don't think you're allowed to eat in the library."

"We can go home for lunch now," Tasha says to her son. "You're probably hungry."

I retreat to a corner of the library, where hopefully Beatrice can't see me.

Tasha: *Beatrice left.*

She soon joins me and hands me the thick envelope. "I can't believe that worked, and we got it."

"I know. You were brilliant!" I say.

"*You* were brilliant," Tasha says. "I didn't see her even register your touch."

I open up the thin envelope.

It's a handwritten letter.

REPAIRS NEED TO INCREASE. I'LL GIVE YOU A 30% CUT. BE CAREFUL. VULTURES CIRCLING.

"This is it! This is the evidence I needed." I want to do a dance of joy. "I have a sample of Commissioner Ward's handwriting and a sample of Commissioner Pommer's handwriting." I pull up the photos on my phone of my mailing list and the books signed by the deputy commissioners. We compare the scripts.

COMMISSIONER WARD
`Commissioner Pommer`

Commissioner Galliano

It's Ward!! We have the proof that it's Commissioner Ward.

"It's Ward, then. It's the same handwriting," I say.

"Exactly the same," says Tasha.

We stare at each other.

"We did it. We solved this," I say.

"We make a great team," Tasha says.

We open up the thick envelope, and it's filled with two thousand dollars. I take a photo and put the money in a new envelope. We replace the envelope in the book.

"What happens now?" Tasha asks. "You'll stay to see if Ward comes by to pick up the envelope?"

"Yes. I'll write my article while I wait. It might take me a few days, but then I'll hand it in to my boss. She'll have revisions and questions. I'll text you when it's going to be published. Thank you so much!"

"Thank you," she says. "I can't believe we actually figured it out."

"It's a feeling like no other, right?" I ask.

It's such a shot of adrenaline when I find the missing pieces and solve an investigation. And then there's the thrill of writing it and sharing it with readers. I can't wait to tell Jing tonight at her New Year's party. This article will be a joy to write. I pull my laptop out of my bag and start typing.

Chapter Twenty-Eight

Nick

> Maddie: *Huge news. Call me after your concert tonight. I'll wait up.*

> Me: *Are you okay? Did they find the intruder?*

> Maddie: *I'm great. Not yet. We'll talk later.*

I put my phone down, take another swig of water, and get back out on stage. The band is rehearsing in Jersey City doing a run-through. Ashley suddenly arrives and asks if she can talk to me. Is this related to Maddie's text? Ashley pulls me aside.

"We don't understand why this contract hasn't been revealed yet," she says. "It's making the big guys nervous. They want you to break up."

"I'm not breaking up with Maddie," I say. "This isn't negotiable."

"Plus, they've found Lucy Colgan to be a romantic interest."

"What? Who's that?" I ask.

"She's an up-and-coming actress. Her movie is doing well in theaters right now, and so you could both win with the publicity."

There's the ulterior motive. I knew it. "They're okay with me fake dating this woman? How's that different? That's not going to win me points, if I break up with Maddie—the girl next door—and fake date some film star. I thought my brand was being open and honest and down-to-earth."

"You're the one who asked for security. That's also not very down-to-earth. You're on the road to making it big. The label thinks that we can let go of the 'down-to-earth' image. Plus, there wouldn't be a written fake-dating contract. And the publicity would get you in the spotlight. It would drive up sales. Dating Maddie doesn't drive up sales."

"It will be obvious that I'm fake dating her. Or people will think I'm a player. Is that really the image management wants? Because that's not me." *I am not my dad.* "And that's pretty clear in my music too." My themes are about finding "the one" or being the one betrayed.

"That's what I told them," Ashley says. "I wanted to make sure we were on the same page."

"By freaking me out first?" I ask. Testing me. Everything is a test. I knew that it would be like this, but it's still more depressing than I thought it would be to find that out.

I don't trust that Ashley and I are on the same page. We're on the same page as long as I can make an argument defending my position, but she would be happier if I had agreed to date Lucy Colgan.

"Did you see the latest attacks on Maddie? They're clearly some trolls, but I thought you should know. Is she still not looking at them?" Ashley asks with a side glance.

"That's what she says," I say slowly. I have to give Ashley credit. This is a much more persuasive argument if she wants to convince me to break up with Maddie.

I scroll through the comments and the videos posted. One has Maddie without makeup on the subway. A chill goes through me. Someone is trailing her. Is this related to the apartment attack?

Was Maddie's investigation not the reason for the break-in?

Is she truly not safe dating me?

We finish our practice session, and Amira relays the dates of our upcoming short tour. We're back in New York to record another single, and then we're driving up to Maine, stopping at Providence, Burlington, and Boston on the way. Then we'll be back in the recording studio, and then we'll hit a few festivals on the East Coast in May and June.

"Are you okay leaving Elena when she's pregnant?" I ask José.

"Yes, she seems to be fine. The doctor said sometimes spotting happens, and she has to take it a little easier. She promised me that she will. She's excited I'm finally touring. Apparently, I'm driving her crazy with my protectiveness. Her mom lives nearby, and she's not due for months. We tried to plan it so that she's due when we're working on the next batch of singles for release, if MusEn keeps to this waterfall strategy of our working on singles and releasing a single every few months. We're lucky she got pregnant so soon."

I nod.

"Your face," José says. "Did you think I'd leave the band? After how hard we've worked for years? Now that we're about to make it?"

I shake my head. I'm an idiot. José wasn't going to leave the band.

Maybe it *is* doable. José seems confident that it is.

"Elena already bought a 'my daddy is a rock star' onesie," José says. "My family is backing me up."

I don't have family backing up my rock star career.

Maddie calls me that night and shares her news.

"That's brilliant!" I say. "I'm impressed both with how you and Tasha distracted her and with your pickpocketing skills. And now you have proof."

"I still don't know if the other deputy commissioners are involved, but Felicity says we can run the story with what we have. We have definite proof that it's Deputy Commissioner Ward. But that conversation between Pommer and Demoraux was suspicious. Pommer knows something."

Chapter Twenty-Nine

Maddie

Putting down my carryall bag next to an empty table, I breathe in deeply the café smells of freshly baked croissants and hazelnut coffee being ground. I'm no closer to figuring out if Pommer or Galliano are also involved, although I don't think Galliano is involved, based on his library visit. As I wait for my coffee order, I check my phone.

Nick Devlin and Lucy Colgan an Item? screams a headline.

My heart stops. I click off my phone. It must be fabricated. It is *The Squirrel*. Nick wouldn't cheat.

But will this last? He's magnetic on stage; women must be throwing themselves at him. Won't he change? His mom asked me if I was worried about success going to his head. He seems grounded. Still, I feel I need to prepare mentally and emotionally to be left alone, picking up the pieces of my shattered heart. But how? It's like when my dad was ill, and I thought I was prepared for his death. But nothing can prepare you for that hole when your family suddenly shifts from a family of four to a family of three. I'm envisioning a future with Nick, but I need to stay in the present and enjoy this for now.

My phone rings. It's Nick. I pick up, eager to hear voice after so many days away.

"This is so early for you," I say teasingly. No rumors can infringe on what we have.

"*The Squirrel* released some photos of me with Lucy Colgan. I met her last night after our concert, and we hugged hello, all perfectly friendly, nothing more," he says in a rush. "She went in for the hug. I couldn't help but reciprocate, but some paparazzi managed to make it look incriminating. Luckily, I moved just in time, so when she tried to kiss me on the lips, she kissed my cheek. I wanted to warn you."

It makes my heart melt that he is so concerned about my feelings. My eyes tear up. "It's okay," I say. "I know this comes with dating you."

"I wish it didn't," he says. "I talked to this other guy on tour. He said it dies down when you show you're committed to your girlfriend. And I *am* committed to you. I miss you."

"I miss you too." So. Much. I miss talking to him every night and snuggling with him.

"How's the writing?" he asks.

"It's going well so far," I say. "How are the concerts going? I saw your latest single is climbing the charts on Spotify."

"It's amazing. The crowds are getting bigger and bigger. Word of mouth is spreading," he says. "Still, I'm looking forward to seeing you Sunday. But I have another reason I called."

"Another reason?"

"I met Ophelia for breakfast this morning. She applied to this musician-in-residence program that I'd recommended to her at our concert at the playground, and so she was here. She was grateful to me, and I said something like, it's so hard to get these opportunities. And she said, yes, that she'd been offered a slot to play at the Chubby

Cat, without her even asking, and that had seemed too good to be true. She turned it down because it sounded like some quid pro quo and her dad's a government official, so she has to be careful. Her dad and his best friend—Pommer, apparently—were investigating."

"That's interesting. Do you think she was trying to feed you that information?"

"I don't know," he says. "From what you said about his remarks at the interview, Pommer obviously knows we're dating. But I honestly got the feeling that she was grateful and telling the truth."

"It makes sense that they would work together, especially with the possibility of one commissioner being fired," I say. "But it's not conclusive. I'll ask someone at the Chubby Cat if she ever played there."

Nick has to go, and the barista calls out my name for my coffee order. The photos on *The Squirrel's* website do look incriminating, but I also can see how it could have been a friendly hug. I'm not looking forward to running into Nemesis later. She's not going to be able to resist making a remark about this. Still, my lips curl up in a delighted smile, remembering what Nick had said. *"I am committed to you."*

I send him a gif that says, *I like you.*

I grab a table in the back. Paranoia may be my new friend, so I'm wearing a wig. I switched into it by ducking into our offices on the way here. I warned Bella. We're meeting to discuss writing and bounce ideas back and forth. I'm still not sure how to frame my article, and I love brainstorming Bella's plots.

As I sip my coffee, I check Ward's Instagram page. No more libraries? His last post is a miniature New York City alleyway scene. Are they planning to meet in an alleyway? My miniature rat that I had made recently would be perfect for that scene. Where is my rat, actually? I haven't seen it since...the break-in. I pull out my box of needle crafting tools that I carry with me in case I'm on stakeout and I have extra time. My rat isn't in the box. *Was Ward the Hammer Man?* And he couldn't resist the rat?

They signaled the new book the last time via a note back. But what about the library? I never searched to see if Beatrice has any type of account. "Beatrice the Grandma" has a bookstagram account on Instagram where she talks about what she's reading. She's reviewing a book—with a library as the background. *Is that how they are now signaling to each other the library location and the book?*

I bet it is.

Bella comes into the café and looks around. Her glance passes over me twice. This wig is better than I even thought. But the third time, she tilts her head and then comes over.

"I didn't recognize you," she whispers.

"Good," I say.

I show her the latest posts by Beatrice and Ward and explain how I think they're now signaling the drop-off location.

My phone rings, and I click yes, thinking it's Nick calling to respond to the GIF.

"Is this Maddie Hughes?" says a voice. It's not someone I recognize. Great. Someone wants to sell me something.

"I'm afraid you have the wrong number," I say.

"Do I?" the voice says. It's a squeaky, high-pitched AI voice. "I know that you met Demoraux and you're working on a story about corruption in the Infrastructure Department. I have more information than Demoraux. I can tell you which deputy commissioner was responsible for paying Demoraux."

My eyes widen, and I put the phone on speaker so Bella can hear it as well. The voice is jarring compared to the message.

"I also have your fake-dating contract," he says.

The contract!

"I'm sorry, but I don't think meeting you would be safe for me," I say. Nick would be so proud of me. Even if it does sound like I'm talking to a three-foot-tall cartoon character that I can definitely take.

"I thought you would risk all for a story," he says.

Chills go through my body. I once said that. Did he google me? Is he tracking me? I survey the coffee shop, but Bella and I are the only customers here this morning.

I don't reply. I don't know what to say. Turns out I'm not willing to risk it all? I can't say the truth: *Not when I don't have to, because I know Ward is taking corrupt payments from Beatrice.*

"Kill the story, or I'll publish your fake-dating contract," says the squeaky voice.

"What will that get you?" I ask.

"People won't believe your article. They'll know you're a liar."

I'm not a liar. I'm a journalist.

"Because I signed a contract to date Nick for a few months? I doubt it." My voice sounds stronger. Sure. More certain than I feel. "Why haven't you published it already?"

"To exchange the fake-dating contract for your article," the voice says. "We can't have the Infrastructure Department tarnished with a story about corruption."

But I need this story even more now if the fake-dating contract is about to be published.

"Is it a deal?" asks the squeaky voice.

"I need to think it over," I say.

The line goes dead. There's silence at the other end.

Bella and I stare at each other.

"I bet that was Ward," I say. "He must have figured out that we intercepted that letter."

"You should tell the police about this call."

"I need to talk to our paper security first, because this is definitely connected to my investigation," I say. "I need to get my article out before the fake-dating contract is published and to meet with Ward to ask him if he has any comment on the story. It's ready to go, except for whether he has a comment. And I still don't know if the others are involved. But if I talk to him, maybe I can get him to reveal that."

"You're going to meet him in person?" Bella asks.

"Yes," I say. "I have to let him know that I'm working on an article and ask him if he has any comments in response. If we publish without giving him a chance to comment, we have legal liability. And I need to talk to Nick because I promised him that I would be careful. But Ward might reveal if Pommer and Galliano are in on it and who Hammer Man is. I want him behind bars."

That afternoon, as I curl up on my couch, Sherlock purring next to me, I replay the conversation over in my head. He has the contract. There's nothing I can offer him that will stop him from revealing it. I will publish this story. That means our fake-dating contract will be public.

It's going to be horrible. I can see the comments now: *I knew he wasn't really interested.* And they're not going to believe us now when we say we're dating. But if we break up now, MusEn is right that it will be less of an event. How can fans get too excited over the revelation that Nick fake dated me if we have broken up? It's already over. Why would they bother attacking me?

And of even more importance is my career as a reporter. The trolls are going to have a field day with the fact that I am supposed to tell the truth. We should break up now and preempt the attack. I *should* do it for my career. I've worked so hard, and this story should be the ticket to the promotion. I feel sick to my stomach. But I like Nick so much. More than like. *I love Nick*. I will never love anyone like I love Nick.

I *can't* break it off with him. Not when he's doing his best for us.

I need to meet Ward and get this article published.

I call Nick.

He picks up the phone. "I'll be back tomorrow morning. I can't wait to see you."

I explain about the call I received and that I'm going to meet Ward, hopefully at his office, so I can get his comment on the story.

"Do you have to meet with him?" Nick asks, his voice laced with concern.

"Yes." I explain why.

"But isn't he already going to publish the dating contract?"

"I think he will wait to see if I take the deal he is offering," I say. "I'm going to call him right now and suggest a meeting. He'll want to keep that dating contract in his back pocket until he meets with me and figures out exactly what I know."

"Don't set up a meeting until I'm back and can be your backup. Just in case. Let me also check if Luca is back."

"Okay," I say. We talk for a few minutes longer about how the tour is going, and hearing his voice on the other end of the line makes me feel like it will work out. He makes me laugh, and as I imitate Squeaky Voice for him, it suddenly feels less threatening.

I call my boss, Felicity, and we confirm the plan. She has the article ready to go, but it will be held for any final information from this interview.

The next morning, I call Deputy Commissioner Ward's office number, and he picks up.

"Hi, this is Maddie Hughes from *The Intelligencer*. I'm writing a story about the Infrastructure Department and would like to discuss it with you today. We're planning to publish this evening. Would you be free to meet at your office today as soon as possible?"

There's silence on the other end. Good. I've taken him by surprise. I don't want to give him too much time to prepare.

"Just me? What about Commissioner Johnson?" he asks.

"I think you will be particularly interested in what I have to say, but I should discuss it with him too. I want to talk to you in person first."

"Yes, today, noon. Here. That sounds like a good idea. I'm sure I can help you out and give you some insights you may be lacking."

"Excellent. I'll see you soon."

Chapter Thirty

Maddie

This is already *not* going according to plan. Ward changed the time to five p.m. and the meeting place to Doyers Street, a street known as the Bloody Angle in history because of the gang warfare centered around its blind angle. But I'm determined to get this article published in tomorrow's paper. I can't back down now. We're meeting at a Chinese restaurant. It has to be safe.

The restaurant light is dim when I enter. Nick's voice in my earpiece says, "I can barely see anything, but my eyes are adjusting. I'm here for you." I'm wearing a little camera on my jacket so Nick can see what is going on, and the recorder pen is turned on.

A gold cat, Maneki Neko, is waving its paw at the checkout counter, which somehow makes me feel better. I'm hoping it brings me luck. Red curtains shroud the windows.

Ward is at a table already, and he gestures for me to join him. I order myself a green tea.

"Thanks so much for agreeing to this change of venue. I think I can be more honest outside the office," Ward says. "You must admit that your call was quite short notice."

"I appreciate you taking the time to talk to me," I say. My voice sounds young and high-pitched. Great. Now I'm the one who sounds like a three-foot-tall cartoon character.

"I think we've been investigating the same thing, so it makes sense we pool our resources," he says. "But let's keep this discussion off the record."

"I'm writing an article about corruption in the Infrastructure Department. It's my understanding that certain property managers ask for a kickback in order to assign a repair contract."

Ward nods. "Off the record, I discovered that as well. It apparently started innocently enough. One contractor offered a bribe to a property manager to get the job, and the property manager couldn't resist the extra cash and thought it would just be this one time, but the money was too tempting. We've been doing an internal investigation into that. I have a sting operation running right now, so I'm going to have to ask you to hold off on writing any articles until we can catch the guilty mastermind behind this."

A sting operation? Could it be? No way. Not with the handwriting proof and my missing rat.

"Is that how you figured out this was happening?" I ask. "You were doing an internal investigation, and the property manager explained it in that way?"

"Yes, exactly. I can understand how hard it is to resist that extra money, of course," he says. "I've discussed this with Johnson, and we think Galliano and Pommier have teamed up to do this to get extra money. Galliano needs money to support his daughter's career. He paid off an inspector who's been threatening bars with fines unless they let his daughter play. You know that."

"Do you have proof?"

"Demoraux came clean to us. You have the proof. You have a list of the bars where the tickets were issued...and then quickly resolved." He chuckles. "Ophelia was offered spots at all of those places."

Except that Ophelia never played at any of those bars. I confirmed that.

"Think about how little money Galliano makes as a deputy commissioner on a government salary and how much money he spent on her education. He's also paid for publicity for her band. And it's even worse for Pommer. Four children. What was he thinking?"

He drinks his tea.

"Pommer has huge debts," he says. "He thought he was going to inherit money from his dad, but it turns out his dad was swindled out of his earnings by some fraudster. Pommer is in trouble, and he doesn't want to tell his wife. Those two might be in this together. They're close. I followed Pommer last Saturday, and he met with Demoraux."

"So this started with one property manager, but then once the deputy commissioner discovered this, instead of reporting it, he decided to take a cut?" I ask.

"That's what we think happened, but our internal investigation is ongoing."

"The property manager puts the deputy commissioner's cut in a book in a library, and that book is picked up at the library by the deputy commissioner, right?"

He tilts his head. "You've got it. And Galliano was at the Harlem Library last Saturday, ready to pick up the money, right?"

Yes, except Galliano seemed to have no idea what to pick up. Ward must have seen Galliano at the Harlem Library last Saturday. Nick was right that Ward came in and left. Wait. *This is proof that Ward knows we were at the library too.*

It's time to stop playing cat and mouse and see if he has a comment.

"And yet, you seem to be signaling via your Instagram posts which library and book," I say.

His eyes narrow. "Purely coincidental. I like to do posts featuring different libraries. I don't think I feature any particular book."

"No. But Beatrice gave you a book with a *Caper Crush* bookmark, and we found one thousand dollars in cash in that book."

He blanches but quickly recovers. "That's the proof you have?"

"No, not all. I also have the handwritten letter you sent, asking for more. And proof that it is your handwriting."

He leans in. "That was part of the sting operation."

"Is that your on-the-record comment? Is Johnson going to confirm that you were doing a sting?"

Red-hot anger flares across his face. "No comment. You publish that article, and I'll sue your paper. You'll never work in this town as a reporter again." He storms out.

"It's totally him," Nick says in my earpiece. "Should I join you?"

"No. Hang back by the blind corner. He was very angry."

"Then I should join you."

"Not yet. I need you as backup. Ward was angry enough to do something stupid."

And I'm keen enough for this promotion to *also* do something stupid and let myself walk into his trap. But I have Nick as backup, and he will call the police if he thinks it's unsafe. That was our compromise.

I text my boss what Ward said off the record and that Ward has no official, on-the-record comment. And that I think the other deputy commissioners are not involved.

I pay for both our teas (thanks, Ward) and exit. It's dark already at five p.m. There has to be a reason he chose Doyers Street.

It turns out that knowing there's a blind corner does give off a sense of danger. Red. Flag. My heart is beating so fast. I stop. Retreat. I have proof that it's Ward. This is a stupid move. I'm not an action hero.

A rat scurries across the narrow pathway towards the dumpster, and I jump.

Take deep breaths.

I turn the corner. The streetlight is out.

And there Ward is, waiting for me.

He comes forward. I shift slightly so that the streetlight shines on his face. Eyes give away so much—and my jujitsu teacher often said to focus on the eyes, which can telegraph an opponent's next move.

"This is your last chance. I won't publish your dating contract if you kill the story," he says.

I step back. "Did you do it because you need money for your miniature projects?"

"Projects? They're works of art." He puffs out his chest. "I'm an artist."

"They are," I say. Maybe that will help defuse the situation.

"Did Pommer tell you about the *Caper Crush* bookmark? Those two ganged up on me and have been trailing me nonstop. It's like having Inspector Clouseau on my tail. Idiots. Galliano should have worn a proper disguise like your boyfriend did."

Pommer and Galliano are not in on it.

"You recognized us?" I ask.

"I recognized your boyfriend. He didn't hide the way he walks. Were you there too? What a crowd I had waiting for me at St. Agnes. Pommer and Galliano have no proof, or they would have told Commissioner Johnson, but you…"

"Did you pay Demoraux to offer bribes to the bar owners to make Galliano look guilty?"

"You have no proof linking me to Demoraux," he says.

"Except that you just told me about the scheme. How did you know about it if you were not involved?"

He sputters.

"You won't gain anything from publishing the contract."

"But I will. I want you to hurt too. If you're going to bring me down, you're coming with me. Make sure you put in your article how much Johnson values his corruption-free reputation." A raspy laugh emerges from Ward. "He should never have been promoted over me. I worked my way up. I know the Infrastructure Department. He was flitting from department to department, the commissioner position his for the asking because of his connections. I thought I didn't have connections, but once I discovered that property managers were taking cuts of repair contracts, it turned out I could be the connection for construction jobs and with a lucrative payout. Right under Johnson's watch." He laughs and takes a step closer.

I scoot back.

"Your colleague cornered me the other day. Seemed to be trying to figure out why you'd be interviewing us. Who was she again? The daughter of the editor of *The Big Apple*? Very connected. You understand, right?"

"I do understand," I say.

"And you'll change the article?"

"No."

He is in my face now. "Do you think I won't hurt you because you're a woman?"

"No." I take a step back and grip the pepper spray tighter in my pocket.

"You were supposed to be scared off when I destroyed your apartment," he says.

Ward is Hammer Man!

"Do we have a deal? I won't release this fake-dating contract, and you don't run the story."

"That story is being printed as we speak," I say.

"You witch!" He reaches to grab me.

I whip out the pepper spray.

"Aarrgh!" He screams and covers his eyes.

The pepper spray works.

I grab his arms, pull him off-balance, sweep his foot out from under him, and flip him. I sit on him. I have a moment while he's still shocked, but then he struggles to push me off.

"Nick!" I yell. Can't. Hold. Him. Down. Much. Longer.

But Nick is right there next to me, immobilizing Ward.

"I told you not to mess with her," Nick says, tightening Ward's arms behind his back.

A siren sounds, followed by running footsteps. The street is lit up with flashlights. It's the officer who wanted my autograph.

"I called him as soon as I saw Ward stop here," Nick huffs out.

The police take over, and it's a blur as we go to the police station. I call Felicity to tell her that Ward confirmed that the other deputy commissioners are not involved. The article is focused on Ward, but I'm relieved to know that I don't have to write a follow-up article adding the others. We give our statements to the police, and then we're released, although they may follow up with more questions. But at least Ward is spending the night in jail.

Suddenly it's Nick and me, alone at my apartment, sitting at my kitchen table. I sag against him. All the adrenaline has left me. He hugs me.

"You were brilliant with that flip."

"You saw it?" I ask, leaning into him.

"I ran to you as soon as he cursed at you." He pulls the Sherlock hat out of his coat pocket, puts it on my head, and then kisses my forehead. "My own Sherlock Holmes."

"I wish I'd been able to convince him not to reveal our contract," I say.

"He has to find a paper willing to publish it. And he won't be able to reach out to anyone tonight since he's in jail," Nick says. "If he was honestly offering you a deal."

We both look at each other. Integrity is clearly not Ward's strong suit.

"I forgot to tell Felicity earlier, but I'm worried she is going to say we should break up—that this could distract from my big story."

"I don't want this to distract from your front-page news," Nick says. "I'll let my team know and ask them if there is any way that they can protect us, without our breaking up."

We go to bed, but our lovemaking feels like we're both trying to prolong it, to memorize each other's bodies, as if this might be our last time. What we're not admitting out loud is what we're revealing as we cling to each other, desperate to hold on to what we have.

Chapter Thirty-One

Nick

Sleep eludes me. My heart was in my throat, watching Maddie face off with Ward. My pulse is still racing. I slip out of Maddie's bed and disappear into the bathroom. Maybe our fake-dating contract won't be published. I click on *The Squirrel*. It's there. The contract is public.

And the troll comments are horrible:

Fan5001: *I knew the girl next door couldn't keep him.*

I can't engage, but I wish I could write back that the girl next door has me for life—if she will keep me.

Fan2245: *I told you it was fake.*

It's never been more real.

Fan3345: *There's no way he'd be dating her. She dresses like she lives at the gym.*

She dresses like she has things to do. I am dating her. And I like the way she dresses.

Fan2022: *Why are they trying to say it's real?*

Because it is.

Fan450: *No wonder they didn't kiss at the concert.*

Fan43045: *Wow. He even put in a no kissing clause – that's how much he's not attracted to her.*

Cybergirl: *Maybe she put in the no kissing clause.*

Exactly. I'm willing to spend the rest of my life kissing her.

Cybergirl is on our side, though, and keeps writing that everyone knows that fake dating leads to love.

Cybergirl: *Why would he fake date her if he didn't like her? It's not like he would have trouble finding people to date.*

Fan3345: *He could date me for real anytime. And now he's free!*

Cybergirl: *He's not free. They're dating. For real.*

It's also in *The Intelligencer*, her own paper. I come out of the bathroom and watch Maddie sleeping, and I worry. Why should she put up with this? It's hurting her career. Her story breaking the details of the corruption at the Infrastructure Department is on page one, and then on page six, there's our fake-dating contract. Why does it have to be the same paper?

I email our PR contact at MusEn to put out a statement that we are dating and that we only entered into the dating contract because neither of us wanted to admit we had real feelings for the other. Once we spent all that time in close proximity faking a relationship, we admitted that we liked each other, and we are now dating for real.

People love a happily ever after, right?

Chapter Thirty-Two

Maddie

Nick wakes me up with coffee and *The Intelligencer* on a tray. I pick up the paper, and there it is: my article. My byline. Front page. I clutch the paper to my chest. I did it. I broke a major story. I sniff in the smell of paper and ink.

Nick hugs me. "You did it! We need to buy more copies. I only bought ten."

"Ten copies!"

"Not enough, right?" he asks.

"That seems like enough," I say. "I think it's only my family and me."

"And me," Nick says. "One of those copies is for me. I'm framing it."

"Me too. Let's go to the deli on the corner. I need to send one to my mom."

"But the fake-dating contract is on page six."

"Are you serious? Ward released it way before we even met, if he was able to get it into today's paper. Such a scumbag."

My phone is beeping with congratulatory texts from my friends. My mom calls.

"Front page, Maddie! This is amazing!" she says. "I'm so happy for you."

"I'm really happy," I say. "This is my dream. Front page. I broke a major story about corruption, and now these families should have better housing conditions."

"I know! You did good. There's nothing like seeing your dream succeed," my mom says. "That's certainly what I felt with my company, and I'm glad you've found your dream. Sometimes I worry that your sister just adopted my dream without really confirming that this is what she wanted."

"I thought you were upset that I didn't want to join the family business."

"Well, yes and no," my mom says. "If this were your dream, that would have been great. I wanted you to pursue your dream of being a reporter but for you to know that you had this backup plan and a safety net. I felt that when your dad died, my security blanket disappeared overnight. I mean that in the best possible way. I leaned on your dad for strength and for warmth, and I felt lost without him."

"I wish I could give you a hug right now," I say.

"Well, come home soon, and bring that young man of yours too, although right now, I'm getting a sticky embrace from your niece. Wait!" my mom yelps. "Did you just put a lollipop in my hair?" she asks, her voice muffled. To me, she says, "I have to go."

I turn to Nick and tell him about my conversation with my mom. "I bet it was even worse for your mom, with a baby and no partner."

He nods. "I know. But I don't know how to break through her current mindset."

"Has she met the band?"

"No. She refuses to come see me play, and I didn't want her to meet the band in case she was rude or dismissive. You've heard her."

"I don't think she'd be rude to their faces," I say. "And if she met the band, she'd understand that you're all committed artists, not in it solely for fame or some kick."

"Maybe," Nick says.

My phone rings again. It's Felicity. "Congratulations! But be careful on the way to work because angry fans are milling about the front entrance. Take a cab and come in the back way."

"I'm not coming in the back way," I say. "But I'll take a cab."

"We'll go together," Nick says. "We need to be seen together."

In the cab, I can't stop staring at the front page. It's my first time with a cover story. It's my name in print right there. I run my finger over my name. *Madeline Hughes.* Nick is holding his own copy. Our cab driver is having a conversation in Bengali.

"I love the way you wrote this part about confirming the handwriting," Nick says. "That was so well done."

The cab slows down as we reach City Hall. Our cab driver turns to us to say his friend, who just dropped someone off in this area, said there's some sort of protest outside *The Intelligencer.*

We pay and exit, both pulling our black baseball hats a bit farther down.

"It can't be about us, right?" I ask, but as we turn the corner, it's clear that it is.

About twenty fans are holding signs that state. *Did they lie to us?* outside *The Intelligencer* building.

"I'm so sorry," Nick says.

"At least you have twenty fans," I say.

He looks at his phone and growls. "It's the Cara-wannabe woman. She's the one organizing. She's already uploaded a video saying she knew our relationship was fake."

Suddenly, going in the back entrance seems like the better way to handle this.

"I don't think it's good if they get a picture of you with those placards," I say. "And I prefer the focus to be on my front-page story rather than our relationship. Let me just go in the back way."

Nick says, "If that's what you want."

I kiss him on the lips. "Yes. This will blow over if we show that we're committed to each other, but we shouldn't engage with it unnecessarily. Don't worry about me."

"All right. I'll see you tonight. Go celebrate your victory," he says. "I'll go to the studio and work on our next song. I came up with some more ideas."

"Inspired by real-life events?"

"Real-life feelings. And you." He seems reluctant to let me go, squeezing my hand, but he does. His phone rings again.

"It's my mom," he says.

"You better take that," I say.

"I think she will believe that my feelings were real," he says. After one quick kiss, he answers his phone and waves goodbye.

I sneak into the building through the back entrance.

"Way to go, Hughes!" One of the senior news editors high-fives me. "That was some sharp investigative work. Very impressed."

More congratulations greet me as I make my way to my desk in the newsroom, but I also feel like conversations stop as I pass by certain people. Am I being paranoid?

Nemesis turns to me as I sit down. "I knew you weren't dating for real."

"Except that we *are* dating for real," I say.

"Delivery for Maddie Hughes." Jing drops off a vase with a dozen red roses and a card that says *LOVE NICK* in large letters. "I brought them up from the front desk. So sweet of Nick."

I meet Jing's concerned glance. I have the best friends. And this is so Nick—looking out for me, even when I told him I was okay.

Felicity comes by. "Maddie, let's talk in my office."

I'm not sure if this is good or not.

"I'm worried that this fake-dating contract revelation is overshadowing your huge story," she says.

"It will die down because we *are* dating," I say more confidently than I feel.

Her phone beeps, and she reads the text. "The district attorney is holding a press conference to announce that they're investigating these allegations. They'd like a copy of the letter with Ward's handwriting."

"This is good, right?"

"Very good," Felicity says.

I return to my desk and focus on writing my next article. But security messages me that I should take the back exit because more fans have gathered outside the building with signs that label me a liar and ask *The Intelligencer* how they could have hired a reporter who lied when our motto is "Truth Above All."

This is so much worse than I imagined.

But then I am summoned to Shane's, the managing editor's, office. Based on the tone of the email, it's not going to be about my article.

I want to be called in for my reporting—for a promotion—and instead I'm being called in for my relationship. My shoulders slump as I re-read the command.

I should never have agreed to fake date. I was such an idiot. No matter how much I liked him, I knew that I didn't want to be the story. I knew that being a rock star's girlfriend is incompatible with being an investigative reporter. And if I didn't truly realize that when I signed the contract—if I hoped we could date—this is a cold reminder of reality.

I walk into his office. The walls are covered with framed articles. His expression is stern, his hands steepled.

"Did you sign a dating contract and then appear in the press as a happily dating couple?" Shane asks. No preliminaries.

"Yes, but we weren't faking our relationship. The photos captured us hanging out together, and we like each other, so that came through. We are dating now," I say. "Nick's label issued a statement already, and he said that I was his new love when the articles about 'Nick's New Love' were published." All those articles were published after we were ambushed outside the midtown restaurant.

I'm being defensive, and he doesn't look convinced.

"As you can no doubt surmise, Nick Devlin's fans calling you a liar and questioning our hiring is not helpful."

"I'm sorry. I exercised poor judgment. Not in dating Nick," I say. "But I should have asked him out at that moment when we discussed it." That moment in the hallway when I thought he was asking me to date for real, I should have asked him. I should have known my worth and said, *Let's date for real.*

Shane looks like he doesn't know what to do with that response. I don't think that's the takeaway he expected.

"I shouldn't have fake dated him, because being a reporter is about telling the truth, and that's normally my motto."

He appears mollified with that response.

Hayden enters, clearly delighted with my downfall. He suggests I be put on probation, but the phone keeps ringing for the managing editor with congratulations about my big scoop. Another editor pops her head in to say it's the most-clicked article and seems to be especially hot because I previously ran that *Meet the City Agencies* series. People are shocked that the miniaturist is corrupt.

"We'll discuss internally what the repercussions will be. Without this article, we would have dismissed you." Shane waves me out.

Those words hit me physically.

If I hadn't signed that contract, I'd be basking in the glow of success while seated next to him, taking those calls. But instead, I've been dismissed from his office—and possibly from this job.

Should I stay to make the case for myself? Isn't my article enough to show I'm a good reporter, that they should promote me? This is my personal life and should have no impact on my career. Hayden shuts the door as I hesitate outside on the threshold.

I'm not going to beg in front of Hayden. Shane is smart. He'll make the right decision. And if not, I'll find a paper that knows my worth.

Chapter Thirty-Three

Nick

MusEn is back to "Maddie and I should break up" to get rid of this problem. Five suits are sitting across the table from me in some sort of power play. It doesn't impress me. It makes me feel better that they seemed to think that they needed *five* of them to persuade me. I've dealt with adversity before and come through it. This will blow over. It's YouTube woman getting her petty revenge. Try performing in a New York City subway station and making five dollars after three hours. Try looking in a biker bar for a father who doesn't want you. Maddie is the one for me, and I'm not giving her up.

"I'm not breaking up with Maddie," I say. "She's my girlfriend."

"It's either her or your record contract. The label will exercise the morality clause."

"I thought any publicity was good publicity," I say.

"You're just starting, and this type of publicity—that you lied to your fans—is not good publicity. The label tried the 'I always liked her' story, but it doesn't seem to be swaying fans, so they'd prefer you break up. Be apologetic and say you've realized it's best for both of your careers. The fans are out in full force at *The Intelligencer.* It can't be good for her career, especially with signs calling her a 'report-liar.'"

I gulp. Signs are calling her a report-liar?

On her big day.

These aren't my fans, though. How could my fans want love to fail? And be so vindictive towards someone I love?

I love.

I love Maddie.

And dating me is destroying her career.

"Give me twenty-four hours to see if I can change the narrative," I say.

I leave the studio and make my way to *The Intelligencer* to wade into a group of fans. There are *a lot* of "Report-liar" signs. I really hope Maddie doesn't see these, but I'm sure she's already aware of it.

"Hello," I say to one group of women holding up a bunch of these signs. I want to tell them that I don't want them as fans if they can hold up such cruel signs, but that's not going to help.

Their eyes widen in shock as they realize it's me. I can feel the energy that pulses through the crowd as they realize I'm here, and they press forward. I stand with my feet planted.

"Nick Devlin?" one asks in disbelief.

"In the flesh," I say. "Here to ask you to forgive me but also to ask you to let me date Maddie in peace. She really makes me happy."

"But you lied to us about dating."

"I didn't lie about my feelings for her," I say. "Those only got stronger the more time we spent together. Why are you so upset about the fake-dating contract when now we're dating for real?"

"How can I trust you? How can I believe in the words that you write?" a female fan asks me.

"If my words resonate with you, it's because of your own lived experience, so that's your truth," I say.

They lower their signs.

"Can I get a photo?" asks one.

"Can I get your autograph?" asks another as she hands me the poster to sign. Seriously.

"I'm not going to sign that." I sign postcards about our last single that I keep in my pocket and hand those out. The crowd presses against me. My breathing quickens. I'm suddenly light-headed. I should have brought security. But I picture Maddie's face and her huge bag—which she hasn't been carrying lately. Is she reading the comments? Did she see the remark about her bag?

I talk to more fans, making the same argument over and over—*please let me date Maddie*. Gradually, most disperse. I don't recognize any of these fans as the ones who have followed me for years at bars and clubs around New York City, which makes me feel a lot better about my first fans. I haven't seen the Cara-wannabe woman yet, and I don't want to.

Some "fans" are not going to budge. "You lied to us. You took us for fools. We knew she wasn't your type."

"But she is my type," I say. "She's my girlfriend."

"How can we believe anything you say now? And she's supposed to be a reporter who tells the truth? Give me a break."

Amira texts that YouTube woman put up another video about the protest, and it's clearly from this morning, given the light.

Heavy drops land on my shoulder. The sky darkens, and the rain pours down. The remaining protestors try to use their soggy signs to shield themselves from the elements. And that finally cools their outrage. The last ones leave. I wait for Maddie, texting her that I'm in the coffee shop nearby and that the protestors are gone.

It's getting colder, the raindrops turning to soft flurries.

And there she is.

But it's not the happy Maddie I hoped to see. Her shoulders curve as she sticks her hands deep in her pockets. It's a very different Maddie from the one I dropped off this morning, who was so excited about her first-page story.

And no big bag.

When did her big bag disappear? Was it after that troll comment?

She pushes open the door to the café. The chime above the door tinkles. And I see the moment she plasters a smile on her face to greet me.

A chill runs through me.

This is the first time I've felt like we're fake dating.

I cross the room to her and envelop her in a big hug, burying my face in her neck. I don't want to see that charade of a Maddie smile. "I'm so sorry. I'm sorry I ruined your big day with my fans."

She hugs me back, and it feels like she's clinging to me for comfort.

I lead her to a small table at the window. The snow is starting to stick now, blanketing the cars and the lampposts, making everything look clean and bright, including my outlook. I'm sure our love can transform this contract into a positive story.

She unwraps her scarf and takes off her coat but then shivers and pulls her coat back on. It's cold by the window.

"What can I get you to drink?" I ask.

She tilts her head at the window. "Looks like a hot chocolate kind of day."

There's my Maddie. She's not down and out.

I place my order for two hot chocolates at the counter. A display cabinet with enticing chocolate muffins beckons, but Maddie doesn't look like she has much of an appetite. As I return to the table with the mugs, Maddie is staring out the window, a pensive look on her face. I hand her one.

"What happened today?" I ask.

"I was called into the managing editor's office, and it wasn't because of my article." Maddie gives me a weak smile. "But I would have been fired if I hadn't uncovered corruption in the Infrastructure Department, so that was good."

"You would have been fired?"

This is so much worse than I imagined. I knew I shouldn't date. Dating a musician is not easy.

"It's still up in the air whether they will keep a 'report-liar' on staff." She has both her hands circled around the mug as if drawing warmth from it. "What about your label? Do they still want you to break up with me?"

"They put out my statement that I was always in love with you, and I negotiated for them to give me twenty-four hours to change the narrative. I managed to persuade most of the protestors to leave."

"Change the narrative, or…?"

"They threatened to invoke my morality clause if I don't break up with you."

Maddie winces. "Nick." She says my name with so much sorrow.

"But I don't think the protestors will be out tomorrow. It will blow over, Maddie," I say.

"They're not going to be out tomorrow because a Nor'easter is hitting us."

A waiter stops by our table. "We're closing up soon so the staff can get home before the storm really hits."

We nod, and he goes over to another table to tell the couple there.

"They've also scheduled a bunch of concerts across the country to separate us," I say once he's gone.

She nods. She looks out the window, away from me. She is pulling away.

I'll be on tour, and she'll be here alone, facing whatever new rumors swirl up. I can't protect her.

She was going to be fired. *Fired.*

I almost cost Maddie her career.

And she was only trying to help me realize my dream.

"Maddie, I'm so sorry. I think..." I can't say it. I can't break up with Maddie.

"When are you leaving?"

"Tomorrow," I say. "They just texted me the schedule."

She nods but doesn't say anything. The silence is killing me.

"Maybe you should write a tell-all that you dated me to write an exposé," I say.

"I'm not going to lie to my audience," Maddie says. "I've learned my lesson. Plus, we promised to be nice to each other if we break up."

There it is. It's out in the open now. But she doesn't look any happier about it than me.

We finish our hot chocolates in silence and bundle up to go back outside in the frigid air.

As we push open the door, the wind practically shuts it back in our faces. I push it harder. The wind and door are metaphors for our lives right now. We can push through these headwinds.

I pull Maddie close to me as we hunch over to shield our faces from the biting wind. We make it to the subway entrance. Everyone looks cold and wet on the platform. My phone beeps.

It's a text from my producer.

> Ashley: *They insist you break up. They're offering the Governor's Ball in June and the following gigs for you. But only if you break up.*

"Your face went white," Maddie says. "What does the text say?"

I turn my phone off. "Nothing. My face was already white from the cold."

"Let's break up," Maddie says.

My heart falls to my feet.

"Did you see the text?" I ask.

"Yes. It looks like the text from my boss." She shows me the text:

> Felicity: *I know you're in love, but this is your career. Look at the investigation you just did. Think of how many people you helped by rooting out that corruption. Dating Nick Devlin is not helping your career. Will it last?*

"I want you to have the career that you deserve. You're a great reporter, Maddie."

"And I want you to have the career you deserve. You make a lot of people happy, Nick."

But *I* won't be happy. *Not without you.*

Chapter Thirty-Four

Maddie

I shut my apartment door behind me and sink down to the floor. My insides have turned to a soggy puddle, and my spine that kept me upright has crumpled, but I did it. I'm not standing in the way of his career. I was being honest when I told his mom that the last thing I wanted was for Nick to *not* succeed at being a musician. He's so passionate about it, and if he sacrificed his career for me, giving up the Governor's Ball and other venues, and never got the chance again, would he become bitter? Would he resent me?

Will it last?

That is the question. My feelings won't change. I love Nick.

But he's about to go on tour. He could meet a female musician who riffs with him on creating lyrics, who can accompany him on tours. He'd never cheat, but wouldn't he regret being tied to me? Happiness can be so fragile. Especially when I can't go on tour with him. Can't fly out to see him. We'd be away from each other for months at a time. And if a story came up when he was back, that would have to be my priority. The news is 24/7.

This won't be the last time fans try to cancel our relationship.

And I can return to being an incognito reporter.

Still, it was incredibly awkward to pick up Sherlock together from Luca's place and then come back home and separate at the doors to our apartments. But maybe it was good that we were forced to be together so that we can establish that we can be friends—sort of. Next time, it will be easier. Especially since now he's leaving tomorrow, and I won't even see him. And it was good to hear his bandmates happy about the tour schedule when Nick called to tell them the news that the band was leaving tomorrow and will be playing at the Governor's Ball in June in New York City.

Even if Sayo and Kyla kept asking if this meant that we had broken up.

"We've broken up for now," Nick says.

I chime in, "We'll still be friends. You guys are going to be traveling for a month now, anyway."

When we hang up with the band, Nick says, "I hate that false cheerfulness in your voice."

I stare at him, drinking him in. "I am happy for you. I would feel terrible if you guys didn't go on tour. And it will be a lot easier with you gone."

"I want it to be hard."

I lean my head back against my door, still thinking of our conversation.

I take a deep breath. Everything aches like I've come down with the flu. I feel like I've been walking for ages in the cold, chilled to the bone.

Sherlock meows.

I let him out of his cat bag. He wanders around, sniffing. Does he smell the chlorine from when Nick tried to sanitize the whole place? Is it still the same? It all feels completely different.

Nick, sitting at my kitchen table, teasing me, tempting me with dumplings. Nick sleeping in my bed, gazing at me with those eyes of his that really saw me, with that face full of love and desire and laughter.

Nick is going to get his wish. It's going to be hard. Tears pour down my face.

Nick's playing again, and I can hear the melancholy sounds through my wall.

It's going to be impossible. Maybe I should move. Bella is looking for a roommate now that Lily is moving in with Rupert.

I lean my head back against the door.

The Sherlock Holmes hat is still on the table from last night. Nick put that hat on my head and kissed me on the nose. The top knot has come undone. I thought we were that knot—that we could make it. That we made sense, looping in and out, complementing each other, coming together to make a whole. But look at how easily we came apart. One pull at a loose end. The two flaps are drooping. I should wear it like that, with the flaps covering my ears so I can't hear about any new woman he dates. So I can't hear what they say about me—and especially when they say, *"I told you it wasn't serious."*

I really believed it was serious. I wipe away another tear. Sherlock sniffs my face and curls up next to me. I bury my face in his fur.

A discordant note pierces through the wall.

I need to write. That's the way I'll get over Nick. That's the way I process my emotions. I'll write a tell-all, but a truthful one. One that tells how I feel, how much I love him, how he cared for me, how it felt to be attacked by trolls, criticizing everything about me, even my bag, and how important it is to be kind.

The Intelligencer may not publish it, but I'm not going down without a fight. Why should they make me choose between the person I love and the career I love? Why are they giving in to faceless demands, when this is my private life? If I want to fake date someone, I should be allowed to fake date someone. I've been an exemplary employee. No, I'm a rock star employee. I reported on a scheme that was funneling taxpayer money into a corrupt official's pockets and leaving families without working repairs.

And maybe I can get Nick back. I don't want to give up on our relationship yet.

I explain how I first found Nick annoying, if very attractive, but I appreciated how hard he worked. How he was always playing music and thinking of lyrics. How he would play at all hours of the night. But also how sweet he was. How he volunteered for my friend's community park festival. How he took care of me when I twisted my ankle. How I agreed to date him because I liked him and thought this might be my only chance—oh yes, fans, I can see why you didn't understand what Nick saw in me, because I had my own doubts—that even fake dating Nick was better than not dating him at all. But it felt real when we were together—so real that I'd forget and have to remind myself that it was fake. Until we both admitted that it was real and that we liked each other. And then how happy we made each other. How Nick was a great partner in crime as I was investigating the big story. How many men would be okay with someone who wants to spend her time following around suspects while dressed as an older couple? Or who insists on meeting a suspect in a blind corner? I told Nick he couldn't punch the perp. He could be my backup only if he promised not to hurt his hand or himself because of his upcoming tour. But when we dressed up as an older couple, I thought that Nick was the man I was going to grow old with. I end with the final paragraph:

We both worked so hard on our careers. With ultimatums on all sides, I didn't want to stand in the way of his success, and he didn't want to stand in the way of mine. But Nick made me believe that a rock star could love me. So, for all those "girls next door" and women who don't think a rock star will love them, I hope you find your very own rock star—the type of guy who supports your career and puts it before his own happiness. I know what real love is now. I will always love Nick.

I wipe yet another tear away and save my document. I email it to myself as a backup and then close down my computer. I'll read it over in the morning and decide whether to send it to Felicity.

No sound comes from the apartment next door. There's an emptiness in the air and in me. It's as if he's already gone.

The next morning, the office feels subdued, like the night after a late party, and I feel drained. Yesterday, the excitement about my front-page article kept me going, but now the cold hard truth that I've lost Nick and possibly my job is staring at me in the silent looks I get from my colleagues. Except for Nemesis.

"I have to say that I was following you guys because I couldn't believe you were dating, but I really did think you were dating," Sarah says. "Especially that Strangelove bar. Why did you guys go there for drinks? I took one look inside and decided I'd wait outside for you."

"I was meeting the inspector there," I say.

Sarah's face falls. "If only I'd known. I could've followed him instead of you guys."

Sharing my love letter to Nick feels like the wrong move in the fluorescent lighting of the halls. I don't want to watch my memories shredded or mocked.

Nick was also interviewed on a morning show, and he looked okay. When he said we'd broken up, I'd cried again, disappearing into the office bathroom. My eyes are red and puffy.

An email with the title "Probation" appears in my inbox. I broke a story about City Hall corruption, and I'm on probation because I signed a dating contract?

Apparently so.

My whole body folds. I have no energy to fight now that I've lost Nick. I want to go home and curl up in my bed and cry.

Chapter Thirty-Five

Nick

This ballroom has so many mirrors that it reminds me of one of those fun houses, where the mirrors present various distorted images back to you. As I glance at my reflection, I don't look like myself. I look haggard and thin. I miss Maddie. The late nights and the demanding choreography are also taking their toll, especially because I have no appetite.

They want a bad boy. I'm giving them that. But not a sexy bad boy.

I slump in the armchair that looks like it came off the *Bridgerton* set and unbutton the top buttons of my shirt as directed by the photographer. His staff is busy setting up their equipment and figuring out the right angle for the lighting. Lucy Colgan arrives next, wearing a red dress that looks like she was poured into it and high heels. She walks in like she owns the room, air-kissing with the photographer.

She stops short when she sees me.

"What are you wearing?" Colgan asks.

"You don't like my striped pajamas?"

"You look like a felon. This is supposed to be a date," Lucy says.

I pull out my phone and read the text. "It says 'Photo opportunity with Lucy Colgan.' Nowhere does it say that this is a date. I'm not dating anyone."

"You knew this was supposed to be romantic." She stomps her foot.

"You know I'm still in love with my ex-girlfriend. You also knew I was in a relationship when you tried to kiss me last time."

"Okay, get a little closer," the photographer says.

"What is that smell?" She gags.

I stifle a chuckle. I was taking no chances this time. "I didn't shower after last night's performance. And I just ran six miles on the treadmill in the gym in these clothes." And then to make sure she didn't try to kiss me again, I saved all of my bandmates' sweaty T-shirts from after last night's performance and borrowed some sweat-soaked gym rat's shirt and rubbed them on me right before I showed up here. I smell awful. I'm only bearing it because I don't want any pictures of the two of us remotely close to each other. People were clearing away from me as I passed through the hallway to get here.

"Ugh. You really smell," she says. "And not in a good way."

"Alright, put your arm around her," the photographer says to me.

"Don't," she says. "Don't you dare. What if I were to smell like you?" She scoots away. Far away.

I put out my arms, as if to give her a hug, and almost gag at the smell from my underarms. Whew. Rank.

"You need to be next to him. I can't take you halfway across the room," the photographer says.

"No. Forget it. He looks like crap. No one is going to believe this." She storms out.

"I hope you got the shot of us on separate sides of the room," I say. "I think that tells its own story."

"MusEn is not going to be happy," the photographer says.

"Maybe not, but MusEn is happy right now with how we're climbing the charts." It was true. Two of our singles were in the top ten. And I was giving every performance my all.

I was not meeting fans, though. But that was not a clause in my contract. If they wanted to add that, I had some changes too. We were at a stalemate. But I was not going to be canceled that easily. We'd kept most of our catalogue when we'd negotiated our contract, only agreeing to do a specified number of songs on an album for MusEn. Our backlist was picking up steam on Spotify and other services too.

Some fans had also come out in favor of my dating Maddie, saying I had looked happy with her and that I should be allowed to date who I want.

Tonight, I'm playing "Breaking My Heart." It's not in our rotation, and MusEn doesn't know, but I don't care. It's the song I wrote in the apartment, listening to Maddie cry next door. I wanted to hug her so badly and tell her not to cry—that I would change the narrative. Maddie is the only one for me.

But first, I need a shower. I put on my sunglasses, a bulky sweatshirt, and a droopy hat and leave. As I enter the elevator, all the other occupants flee.

Maybe I should ask YouTube woman if she wants to meet. I guarantee that would be the last time she would want to be near me, I think as I chuckle.

Chapter Thirty-Six

Maddie

My cell phone buzzes, and it's an unknown number. I ignore it. If it's not a spam call, it might be an angry fan. Although at this point, I'm almost tempted to pick up and chew them out. I miss Nick, even though it's only been a week. Honestly, every day does feel like it's endless. I'm just surviving, trying to get through the hours until I can return to my bed and sleep my heartache away. Maybe it was the wrong decision. But Nick's singles keep climbing the charts, and his songs are getting more and more playtime. It saved his career, and that makes me happy.

The blinking cursor taunts me as I think about how to describe where to get the best hot chocolate after ice skating—another one of the thrilling articles Hayden has assigned me while I'm on probation. My office desk phone rings, and I pick it up.

An unknown voice says, "Will you hold for Twyla Jackson?"

"Yes!" I say, shocked.

After a moment, her well known voice fills my ear. "Hi, Maddie." She continues before I can speak. "I wanted to interview you—about the story you broke about the corruption at the Infrastructure Department."

"You do?" I felt like I was box office poison. Yet, Twyla Jackson wants to interview me?

"You're getting a raw deal," Twyla says. "You broke a major story about corruption in city government, and you're on probation? Because you signed a contract to date someone for three months, with mutual consent to any physical contact, and you fell in love? Ridiculous."

When she puts it like that, it *is* ridiculous.

"How did you know I was on probation?" I ask.

"I'm a news reporter," Twyla says. "Can you come on *Spill the Tea* tomorrow morning? Reading your article was like being immersed in a detective story. It was compelling writing. It will be fun to discuss."

"Should I bring Tasha too?" I ask.

"I knew I liked you," Twyla says. "I like the way you want to share the credit. Yes, please do." A voice murmurs in the background. "I have to go, but my staff will be in touch. And have fun telling *The Intelligencer* that you're interviewing with me. We'll be sure to highlight that it was their story first. But that should make them think twice about keeping you on probationary status."

I wish Felicity were here, but she retired the week after I was put on probation. She said she disagreed with the decision, and she'd been planning to retire anyway because of her health, but it was so much more satisfying to do so in protest of the probation decision. She only regretted that it left me with Hayden. She recommended I take a vacation until this blows over, but I refuse to waste my time off on this.

I ask the general counsel for permission, as per the paper's policy on communications with the press, and he emails me back an enthusiastic yes. Tasha also responds to my text that she would love to be on the morning show with me—she can't believe she will get to meet Twyla Jackson!

Hayden's office is down the hall. I knock on his door, and he beckons me to enter but then proceeds to make me wait as he says he has to finish typing this email—and apparently another email.

"Yes?" he asks.

"Twyla Jackson invited me on her morning show tomorrow to discuss my investigation, so I'll be out tomorrow."

"Twyla Jackson? *Spill the Tea with Twyla*?"

Twyla was right that it does feel good to see him look shocked. But then his eyes light up, and he gives me an assignment, due tomorrow. Something that would take me all night to research.

"I'm not going to be able to do that story," I say.

"You're not?" he asks.

The door opens, and Shane walks in. "Congratulations on the Twyla Jackson interview. She chewed me out about the probation, and she's right. You're off probation. You should go home so you're ready for tomorrow. Hayden, you must be thrilled at the publicity."

"Thrilled," I repeat.

"Thrilled," Hayden says with a grimace.

I pack my laptop back into my carryall bag, but as I exit the office through our revolving doors, I run into Pommer.

"Thank you for your in-depth reporting," he says, stopping me in the street. "I'm sorry I ever doubted your skills. Galliano and I could not figure it all out. We knew there was some connection to the library from Ward's miniature posts, and we finally tracked down Demoraux, who told us he'd met with you, but we couldn't get him to reveal anything about Ward."

"What was in the envelope you gave Demoraux?"

"A written proposal that if he came clean about Ward's activities, we'd work with any prosecutor to seek a reduced sentence," Pommer says. "But he was very certain that he could disappear. Talked about his ability to live off the grid when we first met. I guess he made some enemies in that small town that he went to, and that's why they reported him to the police."

Demoraux had been arrested late last night, but I hadn't had a chance to dig into the details yet.

He shakes my hand. "Thanks again. And thank you for those articles on the new playground design. We're hoping that will help with additional funding."

"I hope so." My chest feels a bit lighter. My articles are making a difference.

As I let myself into my apartment, Sherlock winds himself about my legs as if I've been gone for days. My phone beeps, but I'm too tired to look at it. I know it's not a story for me. I should go to sleep early because I have to wake up at four a.m. to be on the show with Twyla Jackson. If it *is* Hayden giving me an assignment for another day, he can forget it.

My phone rings. The only one who calls me is my mom, so I pick it up.

"Is this Madeline Hughes?" a deep male voice asks.

"Yes," I say hesitantly. What crazy person has gotten ahold of my number now?

"This is Tristan Saunder from *The Carrier Pigeon*."

The managing editor of *The Carrier Pigeon*? Nick's friend?

"I'd like to offer you a job at *The Carrier Pigeon*. As you may know, we've been a finance-focused paper with a Washington bureau focused on political decisions at the federal level, but we're expanding our market in New York and planning to take on *The Intelligencer* and *The Squirrel*. Given the story you broke, you're the type of reporter we need."

Exactly. And then my imposter syndrome kicks in.

"Did Nick put you up to this?" I ask.

"No." He laughs. "I'm not running a charity. Nick didn't even ask me for help with that YouTube star. I interviewed that older couple on my own initiative to prove Nick wasn't her boyfriend. Nick has been suspiciously reluctant to introduce us, not that I've been in town much. But hopefully you can come by my office tomorrow, and we can discuss the position. I'm hoping you'll accept. Nick did say he'd bet your network against mine any day, so I'm looking forward to meeting you."

We set a time to meet after the Twyla Jackson interview. A potential job at *The Carrier Pigeon* and an interview on network TV… *I'm not going to be able to sleep tonight.*

Tasha and I are sitting across from Twyla on the set of *Spill the Tea with Twyla*. This is a total "pinch me" moment. Her skill at interviewing is really something to emulate. I feel like I'm talking to a friend. Twyla wanted me to discuss it as I discovered each clue so viewers could feel the thrill of the investigation.

Tasha explains how she alerted me to the possible corruption when she found out I was a reporter. I explain each clue as we found it, and the audience gasps when Tasha and I re-enact with Twyla how I pickpocketed the envelope from Beatrice and the photo of the message flashes on the screen.

I also explain that we've since found out that Ward paid Demoraux to frame Galliano.

I'm still on a high after my interview with Twyla. When I leave the studio, people want my autograph. I'm *not* behind the scenes anymore. And I think I'm okay with that.

The Carrier Pigeon offices are close to *The Intelligencer* offices and right near City Hall. As I walk into Tristan's office, I do a double take. He's attractive—not as attractive as Nick, obviously, but he definitely commands the room. I'd researched him to prepare for the interview, reading his most recent articles, but when I tried to find out anything personal, I had to wade through so many articles about who he was dating or not dating and how magnetic he was that I didn't find much, other than he's a good reporter himself. I should have been prepared for his presence, but I didn't expect the articles to be right.

"Please take a seat," he says after I hand him my resume.

The office is modern and has an airy feel with the huge windows, but the minimalism and lack of any personal touches also make it feel as if this is a recent or even temporary arrangement.

He waves at some boxes in the corner. "Our main office is over by Wall Street. But if we want to cover City Hall, we also need an office here. We're expanding to cover local politics now, as I mentioned. I was impressed by your investigation and the story you wrote. It was clear and persuasive. But I also need to have people I can absolutely trust."

He thinks I'm trustworthy, even after all the report-liar signs?

"Here's the position description. You would be responsible for building our team here as a senior reporter–city politics." He explains that I will report to a well-respected reporter in Washington, D.C. for *The Carrier Pigeon*.

He must see the question in my eyes.

"She wants to move back to New York City for a few years." He hands me a position description with a salary that is more than what I'd make even if I were promoted at *The Intelligencer*.

He asks me to meet her in the next room. That is a real interview, and she asks me some tough questions, but we also click. She escorts me back to Tristan's office and says, "It was a pleasure meeting you, and I look forward to working with you, so I hope you accept."

"The sooner you can start, the better," Tristan says. He radiates a confidence that I will accept the offer.

My phone beeps. The Manhattan District Attorney's office is indicting Deputy Commissioner Ward. I explain to Tristan why I have to go but that I'll get back to him tonight. I need some time to think it over. It should be an easy decision, but I'd grown up as a reporter at *The Intelligencer*, and even though I'd felt betrayed lately, I still had this feeling of loyalty. I'd always envisioned myself as an *Intelligencer* reporter. And what if this venture didn't get off the ground? *The Intelligencer* is established, although Tristan seems sure that he will succeed. Plus, it makes sense to wait and not accept immediately to convey that I have options.

After I cover the indictment and write up an article for tomorrow's paper, Jing comes by my desk.

"The interview with Twyla was great. And you looked healthier than you've been looking."

That's a polite way of saying I look much better with my hair washed.

"Amazing how they can cover dark shadows with makeup," I say.

"How are you doing?" she asks. "My mom made you some dumplings. We could eat them in the park outside. It's not that cold out today."

"Sounds great," I say.

We walk over to the park and sit on a bench to eat her mom's delicious dumplings. The chicken broth inside feels like it's replenishing my strength. I tell Jing all about the offer to work for *The Carrier Pigeon* and that I plan to accept it. She agrees that I should.

"You can't report to Hayden," she says. "He has no loyalty to you."

"I know. I've realized that one of the most important things in a job is having a boss who cares about you, at least in terms of your career development," I say.

"I wish they were hiring for their business section," she says. "But those positions are practically impossible to get."

As we savor the dumplings, I say, "I wish Nick and I hadn't broken up. I made a mistake in questioning our relationship. I should have trusted in us."

"Well, you can still get back together," she says. "If you resign, you can give two weeks' notice and take your vacation time and fly out to wherever he is performing."

"Tristan said he wants me to start as soon as possible. But that would work because I have to give two weeks' notice," I say. "What if Nick has moved on?"

"Did you hear Nick's latest song?" Jing asks. "I need to be upfront and tell you that I messaged Amira and Sayo and told them you were miserable, and they said Nick is miserable too. They're worried about him because he's not eating. They sent me this."

It's a video of Nick performing "Breaking My Heart." The lyrics are about how helpless he felt hearing me cry, how he wanted to hold me and protect me, and instead he'd hurt me. How he can't eat.

He heard me cry. That ridiculous, paper-thin wall. And here I thought I'd managed to convince him that I'd get over him.

I cry again. I've become such a blubbering mess since we broke up.

"The video isn't over," Jing says. "Look."

The camera then pans to the audience with fans holding up signs: *Go Get Your Girl!* and *We miss Maddie.*

The video ends with Amira's face filling the frame, saying, "He's miserable without you. Please take him back."

I want to.

But first, I need to accept this job offer. I call Tristan to accept.

"You won't regret it," he says.

"I wrote something about Nick and me. It's not an article for the city desk, but maybe you'd still be interested in it once I come on board. It was about how I felt about Nick."

"I'm interested," Tristan says. "Especially if it's an exclusive on your side of the story."

After we hang up, I send him my love letter to Nick.

Then, I draft an email to Hayden, announcing my resignation and that I'm taking my vacation time for the next two weeks.

"You don't want to tell him in person?" Jing asks, peering over my shoulder as we craft the text of my resignation.

"No," I say. "I have no desire to see him again—ever."

The late-afternoon air feels practically balmy.

"I think this calls for some champagne," Jing says. "And then you need to look at flights. He's playing in California this weekend."

I'm going to fly out to Nick tomorrow and tell him that I want to get back together. That we need to tie our knot tighter this time. Maybe even a double knot.

I walk into my apartment, slightly tipsy from all the celebratory champagne and drinks with Jing and Iris at Craic and Laughs. I thanked Iris for being Cybergirl and for defending me. She said it was cathartic. I tilt my ear towards our shared wall. I swear I hear Nick playing in the apartment next door.

As I feed Sherlock, I say, "Do you hear that music? Do I miss him so much now that I'm starting to hear his music everywhere? It was playing in the bar, so it's stuck in my head, right?" Every time Nick's song came on in the mix in the bar, a huge cheer went up. *That's our guy!"*

Sherlock meows.

I shake my head. Maybe it's another neighbor playing his music. But it really sounds so much like him. My phone beeps.

Nick: *I miss you.*

Me: *I miss YOU.*

Nick: *I wish I was with you on the fire escape.*

Me: *It's much warmer in California.*

I hope I can book a red eye to California.

Nick: *Keeping track of where I am?*

Yes, because I'm planning to surprise you. If MusEn invokes the morality clause and drops him, another label will pick him up. He's proven himself now.

Me: *Craic and Laughs was playing your songs tonight on repeat. A local celebrity. They want your autograph on a poster when you return so they can frame it.*

Nick: *Are you hanging out at Craic and Laughs without me? No one better be hitting on you.*

Me: *Says the man who is mobbed by women every time he leaves a concert.*

Nick: *There's a gift for you on the fire escape.*

He had to tell me on a night when I'm tipsy. I put Sherlock in the bathroom, which he doesn't appreciate, put on my sneakers, and open the window.

It's Nick!

"Nick!" I clamber out over my windowsill onto the fire escape. He pulls me into his arms. I melt against him. *Nick.* I've missed him so much. I hug him tightly. His body, so tense when I first embraced him, relaxes.

"It's too public out here. Should we go back into your apartment?" he asks.

"Yes, plus Sherlock was not happy to be in the bathroom."

We climb back through the window. Nick hands me his guitar before he climbs in behind me.

I let Sherlock out of the bathroom; he looks all huffy until he sees Nick, and then he hurries over to him and winds around his legs. Nick reaches for me and holds both my hands.

"You smell of champagne," he says. "Here I thought you missed me."

"I did miss you—so much. But you're now speaking to a *Carrier Pigeon* city desk senior reporter! I resigned from *The Intelligencer* today and accepted an offer to be a senior reporter."

"What? Tristan's paper? Congratulations!"

"That's why we were drinking champagne." I nod very seriously. "I do miss you."

Nick kisses me quickly on the lips. It's so natural that I don't register it for a moment. But then I stare at him.

"I love you, Maddie, and I want to get back together. I was going to fly you out to California and sing my latest song about how much I love you, but I wanted to tell you privately in person. So much of our lives will be public that I want this moment to be for the two of us."

"I thought 'Breaking My Heart' was your public declaration."

"It is. I'm still in trouble for playing that without clearing it first, but since the YouTube clips are going viral, they'll forgive me. I've basically written an album about our breakup. And I've renegotiated some parts of our contract. But this, this is 'My Woman: The Only One,'" he says. "You're the only one for me, Maddie."

He slips his guitar on and sits on my bed, patting the spot next to him. I sit there as Nick sings to me, his graceful hands sure as they pluck the chords. My heart is beating so fast.

The lyrics are raw.

I found the one,
but for so many reasons (all of which I regret),
I didn't blurt out how I feel. And now I sit here alone,
thinking of her smile and how it lights up my soul.

But there's no Band-Aid that's going to cure my broken heart.
There's only one for me.
Maybe someday I'll be whole again.
She's my woman.

Thinking of how she nibbles her lips when she's thinking hard
and how that makes me want to kiss her and distract her.
Thinking of how she carries supplies and surprises in her bag.
Prepared for anything.

But there's no Band-Aid that's going to cure my broken heart.

There's only one for me.

Maybe someday I'll be whole again.

She's my woman.

My eyes tear. I kiss him again when he finishes. "I love you. You're the only one for me too. I've missed you so much."

"I'm so happy *The Carrier Pigeon* recognized your worth and hired you," he says.

"I also wrote an article where I tell everybody how much I love you and miss you. I sent it to Tristan to see if he will publish it."

"You wrote that in an article?"

"It helps me to write out my feelings, and I wanted to fight for us."

I open my draft on my phone and show it to Nick, and he reads it, his eyes watering.

"I'm framing this," he says.

I hug him again because I missed him so much.

"Your Valentine's Day gift also arrived after we'd broken up." I give him a personalized wood box with four wooden guitar picks. *I love you, Nick. Love, Maddie* is engraved on the first one. And then the next three have *I pick you forever. M & N* engraved on them.

"I love it," he says. "And I pick you, Maddie Hughes."

Chapter Thirty-Seven

Nick

The crowd roars as I sing the last lines of "My Woman: The Only One," and the spotlight centers on Maddie walking out onto the stage. Her gaze never wavers from mine as I serenade her. I love her so much, and I want the world to know it. When she reaches me, I hold her hand and take a bow with her. The whole band joins us up front, and we all take a bow. It's our second encore.

"Kiss, kiss!" yells the crowd.

"Thanks much," Maddie says to me, and she pulls my head down for a kiss. The roar of the crowd fades into the background as I savor the promise of this life with Maddie. I pick her up, not breaking our kiss, and head backstage. I missed her so much.

I only put her down once we arrive in the green room. But I don't let her go.

She kisses me again and says, "I love you."

"I love you," I say.

"And you were okay with the public version?" I ask. "I know you don't want to be the story."

Maddie cradles my cheeks. "I'm happy to be the story if that happily ever after includes you. I also realized that being a journalist is not necessarily behind the scenes. Twyla is not behind the scenes, and I'm getting used to that."

This woman. I will never get enough of her. I kiss her tenderly again. When we remember that we don't have all night, she adds, "I like all the versions, but the private concert made me cry because I wasn't sure if we'd be able to get back together and I was so happy."

A knock sounds on the door. "Can we come in?"

"Come in," I yell.

"We thought we were going to be out here forever," José says.

"We didn't hear you," I tell him.

"So we gathered," he says wryly.

I hug the band in our post-concert ritual.

The Beacon. I can't believe we played here. Another band had to reschedule because their lead singer needed knee surgery, and I was able to include it as part of our contract re-negotiation. I choke up, telling my bandmates how much I love them.

José pats my shoulder. "I thought I was getting emotional with the prospect of having a baby. But we're family. All of us. We will always have each other's backs. We've been through too much to-gether."

As Maddie's friends also join us in the green room, my found family is growing. Maddie has two weeks off and is joining me on the tour.

Another knock sounds at the door, and Amira brings in my mom. I invited her to this concert at Maddie's suggestion that maybe if she saw me playing and met the band, she'd change her mind. My mom looks a bit shell-shocked by it all, to be honest. Elena, with her belly, hugs her first.

"Nick's mama, we're so happy to meet you," she says. "You've done such a good job with Nick. I want all of your tips. José and I are having a baby, and even though José may be on the road, I am lining up all the aunties and uncles."

Maddie and I introduce my mom to everyone. I can literally see my mom relaxing and realizing while meeting my bandmates and Maddie's friends that we have a strong community and discipline—this is not the route to a life of dissipation.

I offer my mom a bottle of water, and she smiles at me.

"You have such a wholesome group of friends," she says. "This is nothing like your dad's band."

We may be wholesome, but that doesn't mean that I'm not counting the minutes until I get Maddie alone and in my bed tonight.

"Can I have a band T-shirt?" she asks, pointing at my Orchard Folly T-shirt.

"Yes, definitely," I say, shocked.

"I should advertise my son's band," she says.

I pull her in for a tight hug.

We all leave via the back exit of The Beacon, and I hug my mom good night again as she leaves to return to her hotel room around the corner.

"Shall we go home now?" Maddie whispers as she holds my hand.

"I have a short scavenger hunt for you," I say. "Because I missed celebrating Valentine's Day with you, and you like puzzles."

The band members climb into the van, but I steer Maddie to a black sedan behind it. Inside, on the seat, is a box. She slides in and opens it. Inside is a piece of paper: *What to feed Maddie when she's sad. Go to that place.*

She glances at me. "Dumplings or M&M's?"

I shrug. I'm not telling. Maddie gives the driver the address of the dumpling place.

She snuggles into me as we drive there. "You didn't have to do this. Honestly. You already gave me a great Valentine's Day gift. And I'm just so happy to be with you."

"I wanted to," I say.

We enter the dumpling place, and the woman behind the counter smiles broadly when she sees us and nods excitedly at me. She hands Maddie a plate of dumplings. The dumplings are arranged in the shape of an "I." She also gives her an envelope.

I'm starving after the performance, so I order another plate, and we sit by the window and eat them. It's funny to think of all the times I picked up dumplings for Maddie here when I wanted to curry favor for playing too late, as well as the chance meetings where we'd run into each other here and eat together as casual friends. I was an idiot not to realize sooner how much I liked her.

Maddie opens the envelope. Inside is a photo of graffiti.

"Strangelove!" Maddie says. "That was not on my bingo card for tonight."

"It was very memorable," I say.

She kisses me quickly. "You were so cute and protective that night. Let's go."

The sedan takes us to Strangelove, with Maddie curled into me. I kiss the top of her head and breathe in her peony scent. We step out of the car at the bar.

"Do you notice what's different?" I ask.

"LOVE is spray-painted in red across the door," she says. "How did you know they did that?"

"I did it. I promised I'd come back and add STRANGE tomorrow," I say. "The owner liked the idea of Strangelove graffitied on the door."

"I bet," Maddie says.

We go inside. It's crowded tonight, but somehow it feels a lot more welcoming, especially because the bartender immediately plays "Fevered Dreams." Several men ask me for autographs. Others are grooving to the music. Maddie looks around but then heads straight to the bartender and asks him if he knows where I hid the clue. The bartender hands Maddie an envelope, giving me a big wink.

Maddie takes out a photo of an orchard.

"Home," Maddie says.

Home. My home is Maddie.

We give the driver the deli address on Allen Street. It's still best to be cautious.

The sedan lets us off at the deli, and once the car pulls away, I suggest we walk around the block to the front entrance of our apartments on Orchard Street.

We hold hands, Maddie pulling my hand into the warmth of her pocket and chiding me for forgetting gloves again.

"I brought my gloves," I say, "but I prefer holding your hand."

She kisses me, distracting us from the mission, until we're finally recalled to our surroundings by some catcalls.

We turn the corner.

She immediately looks up at the fire escape to find our connected apartments. Three gold balloons spelling "YOU" are tied to the metal slats.

"I love you too, Nick," Maddie says.

We jog up the stairs to my apartment, and I sit her on the couch. I hand her the last box. When she opens it up, a floor plan falls out.

"What is this?" Maddie asks.

"I asked the landlord if he would let us combine our apartments so we could have one larger one. Here's how I sketched it out, although I'm open to your ideas. It seems it would be relatively easy to put a door in the wall between our apartments where there are no structural supports. I'll also soundproof my bedroom so I can practice in there."

"Nick, this is amazing!"

"You're okay with moving in together? My feelings are not going to change. I know you're the one for me. I can't imagine my life without you. I want the world to know what you mean to me."

Maddie hugs me tight. "Yes! You're the only one for me. Once I met you, I think nobody else compared, at least in terms of the attraction that I felt. And then as I got to know *you* even better, my feelings for you grew because you're such a good guy. I feel so lucky to have found you."

I feel such love and joy. Maddie is my forever family. And I can't wait for her to hear my latest song in California this weekend.

Chapter Thirty-Eight

Nick

Maddie and I fly to California the next morning. The California air is balmy as they set up for my concert tonight. My new producer is way more on board with our relationship, so much so that Maddie is part of one of our songs tonight.

I grip the microphone for our final song, a new one I wrote a called "MRSN: Mr. Right Says No." This is the first time Maddie will hear the full version. I look to the side and acknowledge the thumbs-up that Maddie is in the stage elevator decorated as a fire escape.

The lights come up. I sing about how I'd lost faith in romance. I'm joined on the stage by a whole troupe of backup dancers dressed as reporters, plumbers, and librarians. Books are being thrown back and forth in a complicated synchronized performance. Uncle Tony was responsible for the costumes, but we asked him not to reveal all his tricks because we still want disguises for when we go out. Behind me, a video plays of various couples holding hands, including our friends.

Maddie is slowly lowered into my view. Very Romeo and Juliet. Bubbles float over the stage and the audience. I can't take my eyes off her. I sing about how we met. Her knocking on the wall complaining becomes the percussion beat of this new song.

I sing the lyrics:

Romance was not for me.

I was too blind to see

I'd lost faith in love

I said no to all the above

I say no, no risks,

keep it all for the show

A contract was purposefully defined

No emotions allowed, love tightly confined

Until I met my neighbor next door

Who crept into my cold heart ever more

Her knocking on the wall

There was no meeting too small

It became the beating of my heart

And the inspiration for my art

I say no risks,

keep it all for the show

A contract was purposefully defined

No emotions allowed, love tightly confined

But as life with her

became an adventure

creating a love I could envision
beyond the contract's provisions

I say No risks,
keep it all for the show
A contract was purposefully defined
No emotions allowed, love tightly confined

Until it became a choice between us and our dreams
Because of various schemes
She said no more
I closed the door
Ice filled my heart
It was best to be apart
I can't see my way through this,
But what I would do for a kiss

So I say yes
A life purposefully defined,
Emotions allowed, a love entwined
I say yes to life, to its risks, and to love
I say yes to all the above.

Kyla and the rest of the band sing, "Say yes," as the crowd joins in. Maddie's stage elevator is on the ground, and I step in.

Maddie, her eyes glistening with tears, says yes and embraces me. I hug her back tightly, and then we turn to face the crowd as the stage elevator lifts us back up together.

"I say yes to life, to its risks and to love, I say yes to all the above." I sing the last lines of the song, holding "above" as the final note. The lights dim, and the crowd erupts in applause. Maddie kisses me until we're recalled to our surroundings once again as the lights come back up for an encore, and the stage elevator is back on the stage. I sweep Maddie up once more—I don't think I'll ever get tired of that—and whisk her out to much cheering but return to perform our encore, "Together Forever."

Chapter Thirty-Nine

Epilogue – Maddie: Six Months Later

Nick and I climb into the rowboat in Central Park as he takes the oars. It's hot today, but it feels cooler on the lake. Some ducks lazily paddle by us.

We wave at the other boaters as they wave at us. Some paparazzi are taking pictures of us from Bow Bridge, but for the most part, New Yorkers leave us alone, and we have much more privacy than I expected. And it's not always Nick's fans who ask us for autographs. I have my own fans. As Nick points out, my interview on *Spill the Tea with Twyla* was viewed by millions. I'm constantly invited to talk at New York City public schools now about journalism, and I want to do as much as I can to foster the next generation.

I lean back in the boat and enjoy watching Nick row, his muscles rippling.

"If you keep looking at me like that, I'm not going to be responsible for the boat tipping over," Nick growls.

"Are you promising me a Mr. Darcy moment in a wet white shirt?" I ask. "Very tempting."

He shakes his head. His phone beeps, and holding both oars in one hand, he pulls it out, glances at the message, and hands it to me.

"It's your upcoming schedule," I say. "Here. I'll row, and you can look at it."

"The paparazzi will love that," I say. "Read it aloud to me."

I do. Meanwhile, we pass by another boat where "MRSN" is playing on their waterproof speaker system. We give a thumbs-up.

"I'm glad they're accommodating the fact that José had a baby. That schedule sounds good," he says.

"I'll let Tristan know. I'm excited to continue writing this new series." I pitched a series to Tristan where I periodically travel to other cities (where Nick is playing) and interview city officials about what's working and not working there, so we can compare their initiatives with what New York City is doing. It's been a huge hit, and some of the ideas are even being implemented in proposed legislation. Tristan is all dark glares and cut cheekbones in the newsroom, but he has a soft heart underneath. I tried setting him and Bella up, but I don't think it worked. But I really appreciate that this allows me to spend more time with Nick and still write substantive articles that benefit New York City.

He throws over the anchor. "Come here. I miss you."

I make my way to him as the boat rocks until I reach him and am enveloped in his strong embrace. We look up at the blue sky above, green trees and pink flowers to the side. No clouds today, but even if there were, I know that we're going to make it through the good and the hard times.

"Do you have an umbrella in your bag?" he asks.

"Of course, but it's not raining," I say, pulling an umbrella out of my ever-prepared bag.

He opens it and pulls me under it so we're in our private space, shielded from any prying eyes, me cradled in his arms.

"I love you." He kisses me. I kiss him back with everything I have. The more time we spend together, the more I cherish the facts of our life, sharing our deepest feelings and fears, supporting each other's dreams, and all the little day-to-day moments like this, where we take the time to revel in each other.

FREE NEWSLETTER EXCLUSIVE BONUS EXCERPT!
Find out what Maddie thought during Chapter 37! And what Sherlock thinks of Maddie and Nick!
For a bonus Chapter 37 from Maddie's POV, sign up for my newsletter at https://books.kathystrobos.com/MRSNmore and receive that exclusive newsletter subscriber benefit!

Chapter Forty

About the Author

Kathy Strobos is a writer living in New York City with her husband and two children, amid a growing collection of books, toys, and dollhouses. Born and raised in Manhattan, she loves writing about New York City and the accomplished heroines who live and fall in love there, amidst its vibrant energy and the aroma of homemade chocolate chip cookies. Her books have been translated into multiple languages.

Also by Kathy Strobos
A SCAVENGER HUNT FOR HEARTS
PARTNER PURSUIT
IS THIS FOR REAL?
CAPER CRUSH
My BOOK BOYFRIEND
LOVE IS AN ART
MY SECRET SNOWFLAKE
MY ROCK STAR NEIGHBOR

Chapter Forty-One

Acknowledgements and Playlist

Thank you, as always, to my readers. It makes me so happy to know that my books bring joy and comfort to readers around the world. I cherish all the positive reviews, and I've really enjoyed meeting you at various events. If you would like me to attend a book club by zoom, please let me know.

Thank you also to my ARC team, my newsletter subscribers, the librarians, book bloggers, bookstagrammers, and booktokkers who recommend my books and help me find my audience. You make it possible for me to follow my dream of being an author.

Thank you also to the bloggers of Rachel's Random Resources for such heartwarming blog tours.

Thank you to Ellen Gilman and to Giulia Skye, my critique partners. Thank you to Ellen for reading it multiple times and pointing out where I needed more clarity and for being so encouraging. Thank you to Giulia for being such a great sounding board and suggesting ways to improve my novel. I treasure all our talks about indie publishing and having friends who understand both the highs and the lows.

Thank you to Jane Litherland and Alicia Dean for beta reading it. I really appreciated all your insights and feedback and how positive you were about *My Rock Star Neighbor*. Thank you to Jane Litherland as well for her eagle-eyed proofreading.

Thank you to Jupiter Flynn for answering my questions about being a musician. Thank you to Tucker H. and Monica D. for answering my questions about being a newspaper reporter. All faults are my own. I realize I have a lot to learn about being a journalist (and probably even more to learn about being a musician, although I really loved writing lyrics).

Thanks to Ana Morgan for creating the tag line in Linnea Sinclair's class on blurbs and taglines. What a relief to have that created for me! Thank you to Giulia Skye for suggesting Iris's dad's bar be called Craic and Laughs. Thank you to Pearl Vivies for MRSN as the name of a song (or the band). Thank you to Lori F. for the name of the song "Mr. Right Says No." Thank you to Kristine Bottone who chose the name of Sherlock for Maddie's cat. Thank you to Stefan M. for MusE for the name of the music entertainment company, which I then switched to MusEn because there's a rock band in the UK called MusE. Thank you to Ketsia Elie for allowing me to share her "That means *I love you* in cat language" comment.

Thank you so much to Lauren Ruggles of Bookquoth Editing, who did an amazing manuscript critique, which really pinpointed where my manuscript needed more work, as well as what she liked about it. Thank you to Jenny Rarden of Stormy Edits for her infinite patience and for doing both a copy read and a proofread in record time and with such attention to detail and to my story.

Thank you also to my cover designer, Lucy Murphy, of Cover Ever After. I love my covers.

Thank you to all my friends who cheer me on. Your support means so much to me.

And finally, thank you to my family, whose encouragement means the world to me—and who kindly tolerate all the times I vanish to write my next novel.

And here's the playlist I often listened to while writing *My Rock Star Neighbor*:

My Rock Star Neighbor Playlist

Not Another Rockstar

Sk8er Boi

Mr. 10pm Bedtime

Pink Pony Club

The Best You've Had

Fire For You

Only You

The Man

I Knew You Were Trouble

Shake It Off

Bizarre Love Triangle

You Call Me Your Moon

Flowers

Naked in Manhattan

My Kink is Karma

Don't Go

Just Can't Get Enough

Enola Gay

With or Without You

Oh l'amour

www.ingramcontent.com/pod-product-compliance
Lightning Source LLC
Chambersburg PA
CBHW021211310726
48971CB00006B/1523